A DETECTIVE CHIEF INSPEC

KISSING A KILLER

NEW YORK TIMES #1 BESTSELLER **TONY LEE** WRITING AS
JACK GATLAND

Hooded Man
MEDIA
INSPIRATION • PRODUCTION • PUBLICATION

PRAISE FOR JACK GATLAND

'This is one of those books that will keep you up past your bedtime, as each chapter lures you into reading just one more.'

'This book was excellent! A great plot which kept you guessing until the end.'

'Couldn't put it down, fast paced with twists and turns.'

'The story was captivating, good plot, twists you never saw and really likeable characters. Can't wait for the next one!'

'I got sucked into this book from the very first page, thoroughly enjoyed it, can't wait for the next one.'

'Totally addictive. Thoroughly recommend.'

'Moves at a fast pace and carries you along with it.'

'Just couldn't put this book down, from the first page to the last one it kept you wondering what would happen next.'

Before LETTER FROM THE DEAD...
There was

LIQUIDATE
THE PROFITS

Learn the story of what *really* happened to DI Declan Walsh,
while at Mile End!

An EXCLUSIVE PREQUEL, completely free to anyone who
joins the Declan Walsh Reader's Club!

Join at bit.ly/jackgatlandVIP

Also by Jack Gatland

DI DECLAN WALSH BOOKS

LETTER FROM THE DEAD

MURDER OF ANGELS

HUNTER HUNTED

WHISPER FOR THE REAPER

TO HUNT A MAGPIE

A RITUAL FOR THE DYING

KILLING THE MUSIC

A DINNER TO DIE FOR

BEHIND THE WIRE

HEAVY IS THE CROWN

STALKING THE RIPPER

A QUIVER OF SORROWS

MURDER BY MISTLETOE

BENEATH THE BODIES

KILL YOUR DARLINGS

KISSING A KILLER

PRETEND TO BE DEAD

HARVEST FOR THE REAPER

CROOKED WAS HIS CANE

A POCKET FULL OF POSIES

TOM MARLOWE BOOKS

SLEEPING SOLDIERS

TARGET LOCKED

COVERT ACTION

COUNTER ATTACK

STEALTH STRIKE

BROAD SWORD

ROGUE SIGNAL

ELLIE RECKLESS BOOKS

PAINT THE DEAD

STEAL THE GOLD

HUNT THE PREY

FIND THE LADY

BURN THE DEBT

DAMIAN LUCAS BOOKS

THE LIONHEART CURSE

STANDALONE BOOKS

THE BOARDROOM

For Mum, who inspired me to write.

For Tracy, who inspires me to write.

CONTENTS

Prologue	1
1. Settling In	18
2. Artist's Impression	26
3. Protesters	40
4. First Briefing	49
5. Secrets And Meetings	58
6. Paint Marks	67
7. Visitors	75
8. Back Rooms	86
9. Found Footage	95
10. Brotherly Love	105
11. Post-Race Trauma	116
12. A Mixed Crowd	127
13. Professional Rivalries	135
14. Zero Hours	143
15. Parliamentary Matters	150
16. Changing The Deal	160
17. Slumber Party	168
18. De-Briefing	178
19. Remember The War	189
20. Unreliable Witnesses	200
21. Missing Persons	211
22. Bird Noises	224
23. Leaning Closer	234
24. The Truth	244
25. Catching Up	256
26. Zeroing In	267
27. Visiting Lecturer	277
28. Gun Fright	287
Epilogue	295

Acknowledgements   309
About the Author   311

PROLOGUE

F<small>ROM</small> <small>THE</small> <small>MOMENT</small> <small>SHE</small> <small>ARRIVED</small> <small>AT</small> <small>THE</small> <small>ART</small> <small>GALLERY</small>, Veronica Benson knew the night was going to end badly.

She hadn't meant to clean her husband's home office. He usually stopped her from doing such things, but he hadn't been home for a while, working day and night in the gallery, disappearing now and then to potter around Europe with his brother, the pair of them picking up new art pieces. If she was being honest, the room was a mess. While Miles, her husband was creative and chaotic preferring piles of paperwork and unfinished sketches spread randomly around the corners of an office, Veronica was more organised. In fact, her happy place was when she was tidying something up; and recently, especially with the upcoming exhibition, she had needed to use it to calm herself.

Amusingly, his office at the gallery was almost minimalist. It was just a shame he hadn't progressed to his home desk yet.

So far, she had cleaned every other room in the Stratford

house, so it was only a matter of time before she reached his office. He called it "the studio," although you couldn't really call it a studio anymore, as Miles hadn't drawn or painted anything in ages. The easel still sat in the corner, with a half-finished painting on canvas resting on it that hadn't seen a touch of paint in almost three years.

It was sad, really. Miles had loved to paint when they met, but as the gallery had taken off, his interest in art had been rapidly replaced by an interest in money.

Lots of money.

She tried to file the artwork – the loose, rough sketches, some of which were even sketched on beer mats and napkins by artist friends while having dinner with them – into some kind of structure, but it was to no avail. His filing system was chaotic, and she had almost considered fixing that as well while she was there, but she understood that was a step too far. Miles's filing system, although utterly incomprehensible to the average person, was understood by Miles, which was partly impressive, but partly concerning, considering the chaotic nature of her husband. So, instead, Veronica had settled for bringing in some polish and a duster, and moving things around into a tidier pile of, well, God knows what.

It was around then that she'd accidentally knocked the painting off the easel.

It had been an accident; she hadn't meant to go near that area of the office, but once she started cleaning, she'd fallen into a kind of meditation and didn't stop. And, while moving the easel out of the way so she could vacuum the floor behind it, the sheet of canvas fell to the floor, landing on its front.

But it wasn't the front that had gained her attention; it was the *back* of the canvas.

It was stretched over a wooden frame, but within this was another piece of card cut to the same size and wedged within. It was a thick card, enough to stick a pin through without affecting the canvas on the other side, and there were several cuttings and notes that'd been pinned to the board – items that had concerned Veronica.

She'd placed it back, left the office half-cleaned and sat in the conservatory for a good hour, trying to work out what to say to her husband.

She saw him as she entered their boutique gallery in Chancery Lane. By now, though, she'd already wondered whether she had overreacted, that it was more "art project" than "reason to be concerned," and wasn't that important after all.

The gallery was already half-full when she arrived. Miles had told her he'd organise the event, and the caterers and planners had done many of their launches in the past, so she had no fears of turning up to find some kind of chaotic bonfire, in the "you let Dougal do a funeral" style of her favourite comedy, *Father Ted.* But she did have a slight hint of jealousy, one aimed at the fact she hadn't been allowed to come in and help arrange the paintings, because as she walked through the opening room of the exhibition, she felt the story being told here wasn't quite right and knew she could have done it better.

But, again, this was Miles's thing. This entire exhibition was his baby, and every exhibition Miles had created had always brought him money.

Them money.

The exhibition was for a new artist at the gallery, one who had been around the European art scene for many years, but was almost unknown in the UK. Lukas Weber had been a darling of the Austrian art world for the last decade, and during their travels through Europe, Miles – and Andrew, his brother, as you can't ever forget bloody Andrew – claimed to have discovered him. "Discovered" was a bit of an overstatement, Veronica believed, for although Lukas was pretty much unknown outside of Austria and a few academic circles, he was still a well-known artist in that country.

But Lukas hadn't minded. Lukas was in his fifties now, had been sketching and painting for a good couple of decades now and had probably made the equivalent of the average person on Universal Credit during that time, while his agents and a variety of gallery owners in Austria had sold his work at grossly inflated Austrian prices, and probably bought themselves a couple of McLarens from the profits.

But with their help, life was about to change for him.

Veronica had scanned the rooms as she walked through. Lukas wasn't around, but that wasn't surprising, as Lukas was known to be quite shy. In fact, Lukas had specifically asked not to even be announced so that he could walk around the gallery, watching the people as they examined his work, hearing their critiques without them realising the artist himself was standing behind them. Short, balding, with small circular-framed glasses and a black polo-neck sweater in the style of Steve Jobs, Lukas looked the part; although when you spoke to him, you realised quickly he wasn't what you'd expect from an artist.

Miles, however, was the complete opposite. Standing now in the second of the five gallery exhibit rooms, paintings displayed on either side of him, he sipped his champagne and occasionally explained to three young women about Lukas's art style as they fawned over him. That was understandable; Miles, even in his forties, was a catch. Perfectly styled brown hair and a tailored suit, his shirt open a button too far and exposing his chest a little too much, he looked like George Clooney before he grew the beard and his hair greyed.

'As I stand before these captivating masterpieces,' he was spouting, the girls hanging on every word, 'I feel that the interplay of ethereal brushstrokes transcends the confines of the canvas, evoking a profound dialogue between the artist's visionary expression and the viewer's sensory perception.'

'Oh, absolutely,' one girl replied, enthralled.

Miles smiled, continuing.

'The juxtaposition of vibrant hues against subtle under-tones creates a visual symphony, urging us to contemplate the intangible nuances of existence,' he explained, waving the champagne flute as he spoke, 'and the fluidity of our own perceptions. These profound works challenge the boundaries of conventional artistic discourse, inviting us to immerse ourselves in a realm where the tangible and the intangible converge, leaving an indelible imprint upon our consciousness.'

Veronica wanted to laugh at this. She knew damn well the paintings Miles was talking about had nothing to do with any nuances, and had most likely been drawn by Lukas while on some kind of ketamine binge. But if it sold the paintings, then she didn't care. Lukas would be happy, and the commission they would make would cover anything else.

Miles saw her across the gallery, and his face lit up. He smiled and made his apologies to the women, who glared across the room at Veronica as he hurried over to her.

'Don't leave your fan club for me,' she said, nodding back at them.

'Brunette's dad is a racing billionaire,' he shrugged in

reply. 'And daddy's little princess there wants something for her dining room, but it "has to be over a million, as we don't buy paintings under a million," apparently.'

'Do we have any paintings over a million?'

'We will by the end of the night,' Miles winked. 'I'll find out which one she likes the most and add a couple of zeroes to the highest bid.'

He waved the champagne flute around.

'Look at this,' he said. 'Half the people we didn't think would turn up actually came for Lukas.'

Veronica nodded. She tried to force a smile, but what she had seen in his office was still on her mind.

'What about Lukas? Has he arrived yet?'

'Somewhere,' Miles looked around, still smiling, sipping on his champagne as he grinned. 'Actually, if I'm being truthful, I haven't a clue if he's still here or not. The bugger's like a ghost. Half of the paintings already have tickets on, though; we've got bidding wars on at least five. We're definitely into six figures, if not moving towards seven. I think by the end of the night, if we haven't finalised bids on at least eighty percent of this, I'll be stunned.'

Veronica nodded in agreement, as if impressed by this. But if she had been honest, she hadn't even really listened to the words he was saying to her, images of the back of the canvas still fresh in her memories.

'When you get a moment, we need to talk,' she said.

'Oh, that doesn't sound good,' Miles patted her on the shoulder. 'Have you been spending too much money again? That's fine. We can work it out.'

'No, we need to talk,' Veronica cut him off irritably.

'What's the problem?' he asked.

'There's no problem,' Veronica forced a smile, and she'd learned over the years to make her eyes match it. 'I'm just worried about all of this. All this auction nonsense, it just pisses people off. We should set a price and stick to it.'

Miles visibly relaxed at the comment, and Veronica wondered whether this was because he'd realised it wasn't about the strange cuttings on the back of the canvas.

'Don't you worry yourself,' he replied. 'We've got this done, and anyone who's pissed is only angry because they didn't bid high enough.'

He watched the room for a moment.

'And once Lukas gets what he wants, we can do a new collection. He's got a load of people he knows back home who have never been seen over here. Andrew reckons we can become the exclusive agents for them.'

Veronica decided not to mention the canvas today; after all, she didn't want Miles to be off his game as he tried to sell these items. As concerned as she was by what she had found, she was still aware this was probably going to be their biggest payday in about four years.

'I wish Lukas would come out from where he's bloody hiding, though,' Miles was irritated as he spoke now. 'I saw him no more than half an hour ago. He walked around and complained about the positioning of a couple of paintings. I pointed out they'd already been bid on. He harrumphed and then walked out of the room.'

'And you don't know where he is?'

'Knowing Lukas, he probably went for a walk. I was just really hoping he'd be here soon because we're going to make the speech, and it would really be nice to have the artist whose paintings we're selling stand beside me as I did it.'

'And Lukas doesn't want to make a speech?' Veronica asked.

Miles laughed at this.

'You've met the man,' he said. 'Do you honestly think that Lukas would want to speak, let alone speak in another language? His English isn't great at best, and if he talks in German, we'll all be goose-stepping around, shouting *Heil Hitler*—'

At this, Veronica slapped Miles hard.

It wasn't seen, but the noise made a couple of nearby people look around as Miles, his cheek reddening, backed away.

'I'm sorry,' he said. 'I didn't mean it. It was a joke.'

'That wasn't a joke,' Veronica hissed. 'You do not talk about *that* here.'

Miles nodded.

'I'm sorry,' he repeated. 'It was ... it was a silly thing to say.'

'Damn right it was silly,' Veronica replied. 'There's a lot of people in Germany who have fathers and grandfathers who were in the war. There's nothing they can do about it. You *never* mention his family's past. You *never* talk about things like that unless you want the people here to take the money back away from you. Nobody wants paintings from someone connected to the Nazis.'

'I think you're wrong,' Miles replied sullenly. 'Gabriel Bauer's here. He's already put bids on several of them.'

'Bauer's an Argentine,' Veronica hissed. 'Probably the bastard son of someone who escaped over there. He's the exception, and I'm not sure I'm happy about him being here.'

'He's spent money, Ronnie. Lots. Andrew—'

'I'm still not comfortable with him, and I'm sick of listening to you go on about Andrew's sodding get-rich-quick schemes. Did I see Marcel when I entered? He's not been around for a while. Have you made up ...'

But Miles wasn't listening now, and was already looking around the room again as Veronica trailed off, giving up trying to have a conversation with him.

'Do you think I should do the speech now?' he asked instead.

'Do what you want,' Veronica shrugged. 'You always do.'

Miles grinned.

'Wish me luck,' he said as he turned to walk away... and as he did so, Veronica finally burst, unable to hold herself back anymore.

'Oh, by the way, I tidied your home office,' she said. 'It was a mess, and you had food from, what, three weeks ago in there?'

She saw his back stiffen as he heard this.

'You were in my office?' he asked.

'It was just a spring clean, you know, making sure things were sorted. You'd left the window open, too.'

'Okay. Uh, you didn't move anything, did you?'

'Oh, no, it was just a polish and a dust,' Veronica replied, already regretting saying something. 'Don't worry about it. Go do your speech.'

Miles looked as if he wanted to reply, and Veronica knew she needed to change the subject fast.

'It really is a shame Andrew isn't here.'

'Andrew's stuck in Eastern Europe, you know that,' Miles replied.

'But I assumed he'd cut the trip short for this one,'

Veronica pressed on, knowing Andrew was a topic Miles had much to say about. 'I mean, isn't this the one he found? His golden goose, as he said?'

Miles grimaced at the term.

'Every artist he finds he claims as his golden goose, but he conveniently ignores the fact that half of them are the ones that I found,' he shrugged. 'He's back from Romania or somewhere like that tomorrow. What's the old saying? "Am I my brother's keeper" and all that?'

Veronica had relaxed as all thoughts of his office had left her husband's mind, but she was a little concerned at his attitude here. Miles was usually more protective of Andrew than annoyed at him; Andrew was the younger of the two brothers, but at the same time, was the man more likely to find the next Picasso or Monet in a garage sale. He liked nothing more than rummaging through old buildings, barns, and houses and had an almost Sherlockian ability to deduce the greatest profit from a collection of battered old antiques.

He had even been on one of those TV shows once when he was a teenager; the ones where you have a team that goes with an antiques expert to a car boot sale, buys something, and then tries to make some money from it. Not only had he argued with the experts about a painting he'd found in a sale, but he ignored their advice, bought it, and sold it at the auction for five times the amount they'd claimed it was worth.

Funnily enough, the television station hadn't played that episode, probably because it made them, and their expert, look stupid.

'Look, I don't need Andrew,' Miles said, grabbing a fresh glass of champagne from a passing server. 'I'll do it myself. I always do, and I always will.'

He stage-winked.

'I have a plan for raising the bids, too.'

'You don't need to—'

'Wish me luck. Speak soon.'

Walking to the centre of the room, the largest of the five in the gallery, Miles gently tapped his champagne glass with his ring on the edge, making a *chinking* noise to attract the attention of the surrounding guests.

'If I can gain your attention for a moment,' he exclaimed, with a smile; Miles had never been a shrinking violet and was quite happy to speak to a full crowd of strangers and hangers-on. After all, he was the one paying for the champagne they were drinking. 'Please gather in from the other rooms and thank you all for coming to the Benson Gallery. My name is Miles Benson, and I'm sure many of you know, I am a simple gallery owner.'

There was a smattering of laughter at this, mainly from people knowing Miles would never consider telling people he was a simple owner of anything.

Miles's ego was too big for that.

'Today, we celebrate the unveiling of a new artist,' he continued. 'I know that many of you have seen Lukas Weber's work before. He's been on the independent European scene for quite a while, and I'd be remiss if I didn't acknowledge the many awards he's won in his native land of Austria, which have made him a standout artist in that country. But today, for the first time, we here in the UK get to see his artwork, and I think I speak for all of us when I say how amazing that artwork is.'

There was a smattering of applause and murmurs of agreement.

'Unfortunately, my brother Andrew isn't here to speak as well,' Miles continued.

'Unfortunately?' someone shouted out mockingly, and everyone who had ever met Andrew Benson laughed at the joke.

Miles accepted it, holding a hand up to quieten the audience back down.

'Unfortunately, Andrew is already out looking for the next big thing, having found the *previous* big thing,' he replied. 'And our artist himself isn't a fan of public speaking, so we've let him stay anonymous for the day. If you do meet him and he gives away who he is, don't spoil the secret for the others. In fact, he could stand amongst you right now. Who knows?'

His line gave the desired effect, and the audience glanced around, their minds already racing whether the person standing beside them was the mysterious Weber.

'As you're aware, we're already almost fully booked today,' Miles continued. 'Many of the paintings here have already been bid on, and there's only another hour before we lock all bids on the silent auction. So, if you *are* interested in any of the pieces that do not yet have a bid on, I would suggest you look as quickly as possible. Also, if you have bid on one, keep checking, in case someone else outbids you.'

There was another smattering of noise as his exclusive clientele realised that time was running out; or at least, Veronica hoped they thought that. Chances were they were probably discussing among themselves whether they would even bother buying some of this art.

'Anyway, this was mainly a chance to say hello, thank you for coming, and remind you we take all forms of payments, including credit card, crypto and first-born children,' Miles finished up, and there was another laugh at this. Miles was about to return to Veronica when a young woman who'd moved to the front raised her hand.

She was university-aged, her hair black and shoulder-length, with a fringe at the front. She wore a floral dress, and Veronica was convinced she'd seen her before, possibly earlier in the evening when she'd arrived.

'We're not ... it's not a press conference,' Miles smiled. 'We're not taking questions.'

'No, I just wanted to know whether the people here knew about Lukas Weber's history,' the woman said loudly.

Miles kept a smile on his face.

'Today is a day to celebrate art,' he said. 'I think—'

'No, I get that,' the woman replied. 'I just wanted to know if the audience here knew of the *Nazi* connections of Lukas Weber.'

There was a muttering following the statement.

'If you throw a stone in Germany and Austria, unfortunately, you'll hit something that had a connection to the Nazis,' Miles replied, hoping to quell it quickly. 'They permeated the world, and it's unfortunate that those poor countries must live with a stigma from young people who will not let this pass.'

'But not everyone had a grandfather working for the Secret Military Police,' the woman added, and with this, the crowd muttered again.

Sighing theatrically, Miles looked at the crowd.

'It's not my place to talk about the history of people. Some of the greatest entertainers, some of the greatest minds in the world have, unfortunately, family connections to a terrible time for all of us. In the same way that if we were to go back a few generations, I'm sure many of you here would have family secrets you would rather keep hidden from the time of the British Empire, or the East India Trading Company.'

He was speaking, keeping their attention, while Veronica saw his two security guards gently grab the woman and move her out before she realised what was happening, and her faint protestations were barely heard leaving the room.

Miles held up his hand.

'I am so sorry,' he said. 'Our youth is very passionate about art, and that's a good thing, within reason. If you need to know more about Lukas Weber before you make your purchase, I understand, and I hope you understand we can't wait for you to decide; if someone bids on the painting you wanted while you consider your conscience, we can't reverse that. Today is about the art, not the artist. It's one reason why Weber doesn't like to be seen, and if you can't find that his work speaks to you in some unconscious way, then thank you for attending and we hope to see you again.'

Veronica frowned. Usually something like this would throw him, but Miles was still self-assured and calm - and, with the rumour now spreading through the audience that Lukas Weber could have connections to the Nazi party, Veronica was quite frankly appalled that many of the buyers were now considering upping their bid.

Could Miles have expected this? Planned for it, even? The bugger had said he had a plan. Was it this?

Still talking, Miles was about to wrap up with another joke to salvage what had happened when a scream echoed across the room.

Oh God, Veronica thought. *What's happened now?*

From the side door, one of the drinks servers, a silver platter of champagne no longer in her hand, staggered out, her hand over her mouth in horror.

'He's dead!' she cried out. 'He's dead!'

At this, the crowd standing around Miles no longer cared about the man giving the speech.

'Who's dead?' someone said.

'What's dead?' someone else asked, not even knowing who the victim was.

'The artist, the Austrian, the one here,' the server said. 'He's dead.'

This time, Miles looked genuinely shocked. *Whatever this was, it hadn't been planned.* Nodding to Miles, Veronica walked swiftly towards the woman.

'Show me quickly what you're talking about,' she whispered. 'And stop being so hysterical! The guests here don't need to see this.'

Nodding and shaking, the server did as Veronica asked, leading her, and the following Miles through the doors and into the back rooms where most of the stock was kept. It had also been a makeshift kitchen area for the caterers this evening; there wasn't a need for ovens and fridges, as the caterers brought everything themselves, but they still needed a place to prepare the platters.

To the side was another door, which Veronica knew led to a small stockroom where most of the stationery and marketing supplies were kept. Opening the door, she paused as she stared down at the body on the floor.

It was a man with short, dark hair, shaven, round-framed glasses on his face, and a polo-neck sweater in the same style that Steve Jobs would wear. But the polo neck collar around his neck had been cut away, revealing the neck itself, and on the neck, there was a lipstick kiss; beside it, what looked to be some kind of black mark.

Leaning closer, Veronica took her fingers and placed

them on the side of Lukas Weber's neck. If she was being honest, she didn't know why she did this, she just knew that they did this on TV shows and claimed they could tell if there was a heartbeat or not by doing it. But once she had done this, she realised there was no heartbeat. The drinks server hadn't been lying.

Lukas Weber was dead.

Looking closer at the mark on the neck, she realised it was a fresh tattoo. The blood was still red, and there were little droplets of blood from where the needle had recently punctured.

It almost looked like the lipstick kiss had been signed.

Miles walked up beside her as he stared down at the body.

'Oh, bugger. He's really dead?'

Veronica nodded as Miles paced.

'Don't take any money,' he said. 'If anybody tries to buy the paintings tonight, stop them. The bidding stops right now. Don't take any deposits, even if they're forced into your hands.'

Veronica frowned. 'But the launch—'

Miles pulled her to her feet, turning her so she could stare directly at him.

'The artist who painted those images out there is now dead,' he said. 'These paintings have now tripled in value, and those vultures will try to tear them from the walls right now to ensure we don't price gouge them later - and we will gouge them, believe me. It's the only play we have left here.'

Veronica nodded; it was almost as if she'd expected this kind of response. She looked down at the lipstick kiss, the tattoo "signing" beside it, and said nothing as she left the room and called the police, as Miles looked back at the dead body in front of him.

Miles was quiet now, and Veronica knew why. He was probably feeling bad that his first thought hadn't been to call the police, but to make sure that they didn't lose money on the deal.

But then, they had a dead artist.

And when that happened, it was always about the money.

1

SETTLING IN

DECLAN WALSH WASN'T SURE IF HE WAS ENJOYING THE NEW JOB or not.

The office was pleasant; he'd been jealous of Monroe for many months now, for having his own quiet place where he could contemplate the cases he was on rather than sitting in the bullpen outside. But now he was actually in the glass-walled office, sitting behind Monroe's own desk, he found it was actually quite lonely as he stared out of the window *at* the bullpen, watching Anjli and De'Geer chatting happily to each other.

It had been two months since he'd unexpectedly been promoted to Detective Chief Inspector, and although everybody had stated it was a welcome promotion and they had expected nothing less, Declan still felt like an impostor, working in a role that was too big for him to fill.

And the shoes *were* big to fill. Detective Chief Inspector Alexander Monroe, now Detective *Superintendent* Alexander Monroe sat in the other office, the one recently vacated by

Detective Superintendent Bullman, who in turn had been promoted and was now working mostly from Guildhall.

Monroe was used to working in an office, so he hadn't really found it much of a change. However, Monroe also enjoyed going out into the field when cases came up and now, in a slightly higher role within the organisation, he found himself often desk-bound, talking to superiors and filling out reports.

Declan knew this had irritated Monroe; the Scot had been quite vocal about it on multiple occasions. Watching this, Declan was quite happy he hadn't reached that point yet.

And to be perfectly honest, he probably didn't want to.

Declan sat down at the desk, finished some reports, watched out the window and did his best to ignore what was going on outside the office. But eventually, after twenty minutes of watching his friends enjoying themselves, obviously engrossed in some conversation from which he was excluded, Declan decided he wanted to know what was going on. So, he rose from his chair and walked to the door.

There was a flashback that hit him as he did this; one of the many scenes when Declan would look up as Monroe leaned out of his office to state something, or wander out to chat with people. Now he realised it wasn't Monroe keeping them in the loop, it was Monroe being just as bored as he was right now.

'Everything okay?' he asked, leaning out of the door.

Detective Inspector Anjli Kapoor looked up from her desk and grinned.

'Billy was just telling us how he's decided to update all our systems,' she replied.

Detective Sergeant Billy Fitzwarren blushed as he looked away.

'I was just saying that the system's a little antiquated,' he replied. 'There's a lot of red tape and bureaucracies and I think we can do better.'

'Didn't you argue with Guildhall last time and personally put the system in back then?' Declan asked, remembering that it was only about a year and a half earlier that Billy had undertaken the challenge. 'And didn't you say the same thing then, too?'

Billy nodded, looking back at him.

'Well, yes,' he said. 'But, in my defence, this is way, *way* slower than it should be.'

'So, what you're saying is the problems with the network are problems with *your* installation?' Declan continued, knowing that he was annoying the computer expert sitting at his bank of monitors.

'Well, no,' Billy replied argumentatively. 'I mean, yes, but no, because technology has increased and the speeds we can now bring in are way more than this.'

He stopped, watching Declan, realising he was being ribbed.

'I just think we can do better,' he said before turning sulkily back to his computer.

Declan glanced at De'Geer.

'Shouldn't you be checking bodies or something?' he asked, checking his watch.

'End of the day. I'm about to go back to Maidenhead,' De'Geer explained. 'I was just checking whether Detective Inspector Kapoor wanted to come back with me.'

Declan nodded. Although he was currently in a relationship with Anjli and they lived together in Hurley, they often took separate cars – mainly because nine times out of ten these days, when a case was on, they were going home at wildly separate times. It had been a while since Anjli had bought a motorcycle on Morten De'Geer's suggestion, and recently in the summer months, now the roads were safer to learn on she had started riding it into work in the mornings, leaving her official car in the Temple Inn car park.

'Are you going to be like Hell's Angels and ride down the motorway together?' Declan smiled, looking over at Anjli's face, which was now completely set in stone.

'Exactly,' she replied, as if this was the most obvious answer ever. Declan didn't know if she was joking, or whether this was a serious answer, so he nodded wisely, as if understanding the concept, and wondered whether leaving his office had been a bad idea. Luckily, before he could reply, his awkwardness was interrupted by Monroe, who came out of his own office scratching his white goatee beard.

'Nobody's going anywhere, laddie,' he said to Declan before looking back at the others. 'We've got a case. A death at an art gallery in Chancery Lane. We've been asked to have a look.'

Declan went to grab his jacket.

'Right then—'

'I'm sorry, Detective *Chief* Inspector, but this is a case for the Detective Inspector,' Monroe nodded at Anjli. 'She should be the one going.'

'Oh, of course,' Declan flustered. 'Anjli – *Detective Inspector* Kapoor – you should go and check.'

He stopped as Monroe started laughing.

'Oh, for God's sake, get your jacket and go with her,' Monroe said. 'How many times have you seen me go to a case? I'll catch you when you get back, and I'll send you the information while you're on your way.'

'Is the doc there?' De'Geer asked, already walking for the door.

'She is, and she said for you to bring her tools,' Monroe replied. 'And I don't want to know what horror show that entails.'

De'Geer nodded and left, while Declan's imagination ran riot on what the "tools" could be.

'You ready?' Anjli prodded him, returning him from his daydream.

'Don't you mean "are you ready, Guv?"' Declan replied, pulling his jacket on.

'Yeah, that's never going to happen,' Anjli grinned as she walked to the door. 'Come on, race you.'

THE GALLERY WAS EASIER TO WALK TO THAN DRIVE, BEING effectively on the opposite side of Fleet Street to Temple Inn, and so Declan and Anjli made their way along Chancery Lane, enjoying the warm May evening.

'Are you okay?' Anjli asked, watching Declan carefully as they walked along in almost silence. Declan had been staring off into the distance, deep in thought.

'Why shouldn't I be?' he replied, looking both ways before crossing the road, pausing at a shop specialising in barrister clothing, glancing into the window; more checking his reflection than shopping, wincing a little at the new grey hairs before continuing on.

'I don't know,' Anjli replied. 'It's just I get the impression that you're not enjoying the job.'

'I didn't want the job,' Declan said. 'I was happy being a DI. But it was the only way I could stay in the business.'

'I get that,' Anjli nodded. 'But - and hear me out here, in the same way you said to me and Billy that we deserved a promotion ... well, you kind of deserved a promotion too, and I think you keep forgetting that.'

Declan shrugged.

'To be honest, I think I'm not the one having the actual problems,' he sighed. 'I mean, at least I can still go outside and solve crimes.'

'The boss can still come out if he wants,' Anjli argued. 'Bullman did it all the time.'

'Bullman did it occasionally. Monroe wants to be on every case. You could see he was literally champing at the bit to come out tonight.'

'Then why didn't he?'

Declan chuckled.

'Because Doctor Marcos has banned him from crime scenes that she's at, because she says he needs to finish his paperwork first,' he explained. 'She says he's got "Captain Kirk" syndrome.'

'What the hell is "Captain Kirk" syndrome?'

'So, I don't really know much about this. But in *Star Trek*, the TV show – or the movies, or whichever one it was – Captain Kirk had his ship, and he'd fly around and have adventures, and if I remember from when I watched it, he'd have his shirt torn off lots, and stuff like that.'

'Wow, you seem to remember a different show to me,' Anjli grinned.

'But when they made the movies, they made him an Admiral,' Declan continued, ignoring her. 'The problem was, in the plot, they couldn't find a reason an Admiral who didn't use a ship would now fly the Enterprise.'

'I don't think you fly spaceships,' Anjli gently suggested.

'I don't think spaceships are real,' Declan replied. 'So, I think I can use whatever grammar I want to.'

He checked direction, crossed a street, and continued on.

'Either way, he piloted – or he *commanded* the Enterprise while being an Admiral, and then every film involved him being an Admiral flying the ship – sorry, *commanding* the ship. Is it a ship? Can I call it a ship?'

Anjli nodded, understanding this.

'I get where you're going,' she replied. 'They often found plot reasons to make him sit in the Captain's seat because they had to explain reasons why he'd be in the room.'

She chuckled.

'I never really saw Monroe as a Captain Kirk figure,' she said.

'No?'

'Nah, I see him as more of a Blackbeard the pirate, or *White*beard the pirate kind of thing. You know, the grumpy old hell raiser, more Hell's Angel than starship Captain?'

'Well, you'd know more about that than I would,' Declan grinned. 'What with your new Hell's Angel mates.'

'It's just a cycle club,' Anjli groaned. 'Morten put me onto them. They're very nice. There's a couple of Indian women who ride bikes. It's not just a guy with beards thing.'

'Maybe you like guys with beards? Maybe I should grow my beard out again?' Declan mocked.

'Oh, God, no,' Anjli shook her head vigorously. 'Don't grow your beard out again. I've seen photos. Jess showed me.'

'I liked my beard,' Declan mumbled sulkily.

'I'm sure you did,' Anjli smiled. 'It's just a shame nobody else did, and the white's way more visible now.'

They paused at the doors to a gallery. If they hadn't known what the name of the gallery was, they would still have known this was the location required from the various police vehicles already outside and the line of "do not cross" tape bordering the pavement.

PC Esme Cooper was standing by the cordon waiting for them. Barely regulation height, her checked cap gave her a couple more inches over her short, black hair.

'Guv, other Guv,' she said, nodding to them both in turn. 'Has bigger Guv filled you in yet?'

'He said he'd call us with information,' Anjli looked back up the road, as if expecting a motorcycle courier to appear. 'Guess he forgot.'

'He's on the phone with Doctor Marcos,' Cooper nodded back into the gallery. 'I could update you with what I've been told if you want, then she can fill in the details when she finishes.'

Declan nodded at this, and Cooper raised up the tape, allowing them under.

'Let's go see some art,' Declan said as he entered the gallery.

2

ARTIST'S IMPRESSION

TAKING THE LEAD, COOPER TOOK ANJLI AND DECLAN THROUGH the main door into the gallery itself.

'The Benson Gallery is owned by Veronica and Miles Benson, with his brother Andrew as some kind of silent partner,' she explained as they walked through the first of several half-empty rooms of paintings, the only people within dressed in a mixture of police uniforms and forensic PPE disposable overalls. 'They've been here for eight, maybe ten years. They try to find new artists, and then they do exhibitions to promote them, make them household names and then find the next one to—'

'Rip off?' Anjli suggested, interrupting Cooper.

'*Enhance*, I think, was the term they used,' Cooper grinned.

Anjli glanced around the room, noting the "BID MADE" signs on several of the paintings.

'How many of these paintings were sold?'

'I'm not sure,' Cooper replied. 'I'm gaining what I know on the fly here, until someone radios me something solid. I don't think any were technically sold though, it was some kind of auction, which stopped, when ... well ...'

She shuddered.

'I arrived shortly before you did, and Doctor Marcos is currently telling the Guv what's going on by phone.'

Declan looked around. There were half-drunk bottles of champagne on tables, with half-finished glasses next to them.

'This really finished quickly, didn't it?' he asked.

'Well, once the speech ended, apparently the body was found by one of the serving staff, and everything kind of fell apart.'

'So, what can you tell me about the victim?' Declan continued as they walked into the second room.

Cooper pulled out her notebook, flipping to a page and reading.

'Lukas Weber, mid-fifties, we believe.'

'Believe?'

'We're still waiting for a confirmed age from his passport, which is at his hotel. Austrian citizen, he was the artist behind the exhibition,' Cooper explained. 'According to the people who met him, he's a bit of an introvert, not usually seen at such events and a lot of the witnesses we've already spoken to said they didn't expect to see him here.'

'Cause of death?'

'Doctor Marcos is still checking that,' Cooper replied. 'Apparently, he was discovered during a speech. There was a scream and one of the serving staff – a Stacey Nichols – found him in a back room, lying on the floor, dead.'

Declan nodded. 'Do we know if there were any suspects?'

'Not as such,' Cooper replied. 'Although there was a slight issue during the speech, according to the statements. A woman stood up and confronted the gallery owner about Lukas Weber's history.'

'What do you mean by history?' Declan furrowed his eyebrows as he looked back at the officer.

'Well, apparently she made a song and dance that Lukas Weber's grandfather was a prominent German soldier during the war,' Cooper explained.

'He was a Nazi?'

'Well, that's the term that was used, but we try not to use it that much these days,' Cooper replied. 'Apparently Billy's investigated it, and says his grandfather was a conscript when Austria was taken over. But he did quite well during it, was promoted to a high rank - Ober-Einsatzführer - but there were rumours he was involved in a lot of confiscation of Jewish assets.'

'Nazi,' Declan repeated, his eyes narrowing.

'When they held the war trials, he was found to be following orders while working for the GFP, which stood for "Geheime Feldpolizei," or "secret military police", and that he was seconded to something called the ERR, but there was no tangible evidence he did anything outside the trial's remits. He was released, where he moved back to his small Austrian town and lived there, I suppose,' Cooper read her notes. 'And Lukas Weber was unfortunately connected to all this by blood.'

'I think we've all got grandparents who we're embarrassed about their past,' Declan nodded. 'I definitely had a granddad I'd rather *not* have had. But surely that's unfair to blame Lukas for that.'

'All I know is that a woman at the party made a comment about people not knowing about Lukas's connections to the Nazis, Guv. It could have been done purely to get the potential buyers to decide not to buy the art – or, maybe to get them to spend more on it.'

'Rival gallery, perhaps?' Anjli suggested. 'Or a protestor?'

'Either way, we need to work out whether this outburst was against the gallery, or against Lukas,' Declan pursed his lips as he considered this. 'The protester?'

'Security held her after, even though she claimed she was needed elsewhere,' Cooper replied. 'She's still here if you want to chat.'

Declan nodded as he looked around the room once more.

'Are the gallery owners still here?'

'Yes, in the back room, and some guests have hung around as well. Although I think that's because they're hoping they can keep their bids now that this has happened.'

'Keep their bids?'

Anjli looked at Declan with a smile.

'You really don't understand much about art, do you?' she said. 'The guy's dead. These paintings have doubled in price overnight.'

Declan, in response, shook his head.

'Sometimes humans really disappoint me,' he said.

Now, in the third gallery room, they were walking towards a door to the side that led to a series of back rooms but paused as a woman in a custom grey PPE suit emerged, pulling the hood off, her dark-brown, curly hair now released into the wild.

This done, Doctor Rosanna Marcos pulled off her face-mask and nodded at the trio of officers.

'Monroe updated you?' she said.

'Not yet, actually,' Declan replied. 'Cooper has given us an idea, though.'

'Good,' Doctor Marcos grinned. 'To be honest, you've probably got more information than he has by now, anyway.'

'Do we have a cause of death yet?' Anjli asked.

'We think it's head trauma,' Doctor Marcos shook her head. 'There's no visible wound that we can see, although we've yet to examine the body properly. What is weird, though, is the neck.'

'How do you mean?'

'Well, Lukas Weber apparently has a branding, a media style he uses,' Doctor Marcos replied. 'He wears a black polo neck at all events, like Steve Jobs used to, and a pair of round-framed glasses.'

'Okay,' Declan continued. 'How is this relevant?'

'Well, if you let me finish, I'll continue,' Doctor Marcos said, her eyes tight. 'You see, the polo neck isn't the same as a sweater. A polo neck is called a polo neck because it has a little piece of fabric that goes up the neck and folds down.'

'I understand what a polo neck is,' Declan replied, watching Doctor Marcos carefully. Usually she was far more relaxed, but today she seemed on edge, easy to snap back, and he couldn't work out why.

'Well, this polo neck didn't have that,' Doctor Marcos looked back through the door into the room, where Declan assumed the body was. 'Someone's taken a pair of scissors or a sharp knife and cut it away from the neck.'

'Are we sure it might be the murderer?' Declan asked. 'I mean, the guy's an artist. Perhaps he did it himself, and it was part of his own look?'

'No, he was seen early in the evening with the polo neck intact,' Doctor Marcos shook her head. 'We think the murderer deliberately did this to leave a message.'

'What sort of message?'

Doctor Marcos pulled her phone out, opening an app to show an image, and passed it across for Declan, Anjli, and Cooper to look at.

It was a close-up of Lukas Weber's neck. On it was a lipstick kiss, and what looked to be a tattoo to the side.

'What's this?' Declan asked, confused.

'We're not sure,' Doctor Marcos replied. 'And before you say it's obviously a lipstick kiss, we think there's something more going on.'

She zoomed in on the image.

'You can't really see it here, we'll have better pictures later. But this here? That's a brushstroke.'

'Brushstroke?' Anjli asked, puzzled. 'As in a painting?'

'Yes,' Doctor Marcos confirmed. 'This isn't a case of someone kneeling over the body and kissing his throat, they literally crouched over it for quite a while, painting the image of a kiss onto his neck. Expertly, I have to say, as well. Then, we believe they've tattooed a little signature beside it.'

'They signed their work,' Anjli whistled at this. 'To sit in a room with a dead body, drawing on it while next door a party's in full swing ...'

'We'll know more once the body's back,' Doctor Marcos was pulling off her gloves at this point and unzipping the PPE suit. 'Currently, there's nothing more we can say. We know he was at the party. We know he was in pleasant form, apparently, according to the owners, although he didn't really want to speak to anyone. Then he was found, dead, with this weird tattoo on the neck.'

'You said head trauma?' Declan asked.

'Did I? Oh, yes,' Doctor Marcos returned to the present. 'There's a bruise at the base of his skull. We think he fell backwards, slammed his head against a table edge.'

'And that killed him?'

'I wouldn't have thought so,' Doctor Marcos snapped. 'As I said, we still need to check.'

Declan took an involuntary step back at the outburst. This was definitely not like Doctor Marcos - and she obviously realised this too, as she held up a hand.

'Sorry, long day.'

'We get that. Can you keep us updated?' Anjli asked.

'De'Geer's turning up in a minute. He'll have some more stuff for me,' Doctor Marcos nodded. 'And I'll be able to give you more of an idea by morning.'

Declan turned to Anjli.

'Let's go speak to some witnesses, see what we can find out,' he suggested.

'We still have the protester,' Cooper replied.

'I'll speak to the owners, you speak to the protester,' Declan added, and Anjli nodded, walking off with Cooper to a side room as Declan looked around the gallery, trying to visualise how it would have looked at the height of the party. What he should have done was ask somebody where the owners were, but he didn't need to wait long because as he glanced about, a man and a woman, looking anxious and loitering beside the wall of the next gallery along made their way towards him.

'Are you the detective in charge?' the man asked nervously.

Declan nodded. 'Detective Chief Inspector Walsh,' he said, 'City of London Police. Are you Miles and Veronica Benson?'

The two nodded.

'How well did you know the victim?' Declan asked.

'Not really that well, I'm afraid,' Miles replied. 'I mean,

my brother sourced him in Austria, and he's quite well known there, but he'd never been over to England, as far as I know. We had maybe five, six meetings with him over the time. I saw him in half of those. Mainly, we were just buying the items.'

'And this is all of his stock?' Declan asked, looking around the gallery.

'Yeah, well, most of it,' Miles replied. 'We put the best stuff out, and there's probably a handful of items that were kept in the back room – that's the room where the body was found.'

Veronica pointed at one room.

'The others are in there if you want to look,' she said.

'No, we'll look into that later,' Declan replied. 'At the moment, I'm just getting an idea of what happened. It sounds like someone came in, killed Lukas Weber, and disappeared.'

'Well, that and the painting,' Miles muttered.

'Painting?' Declan looked at him, confused at the comment.

'You know, the painting that was stolen.'

'No one said anything about a painting being stolen ...'

'We've got a photo of it here if you want to see it,' Miles frowned now, pulling out his phone and scrolling into his photo section. 'We took a picture of all the paintings for the website, so we have good quality ones here.'

Swiping left a few times, he paused and started showing images to Declan.

'These are the ones that aren't out,' he said, eventually pausing while showing a picture of a corner of a storeroom with seven paintings around it, all resting against the wall. 'My brother said we might have a private buyer for them, so we held back.'

Declan nodded knowledgeably, glancing down at the photo. He didn't really understand much about art, but even he could see that these weren't quality paintings, like the ones on the wall. These looked rushed, compared to the ones he'd seen walking through the gallery, and Declan wondered if Andrew Benson had held them back because of their lack of quality, rather than this mythical new buyer.

'And you told someone the painting had been stolen?'

Veronica looked at Miles, and Declan was sure they both paled.

'We, um ... with the confusion ... we might have forgotten.'

'Well, at least you told us now,' Declan returned to the photo on the phone. The paintings were all the same size, approximately, and six of them were in a generic black frame, like the ones on the walls of the gallery, while one was still in a walnut wooden frame.

'Why's that one different?' he asked.

'It's not so much different, more "not the same,"' Veronica replied.

'Isn't that what different means?' Declan asked, and Veronica, in response, shrugged.

'When we got the paintings, they were in a variety of different frames,' she explained. 'What we do is take the paintings to a professional framer, and they provide us with a signature look. So, as you can see by looking around the galley, all the frames have an inch-wide black border to keep them simple and unified.'

'So why didn't you do this one?' Declan pointed back at the picture.

'Because Mister Weber didn't want to sell it,' Miles replied, and Declan could detect a hint of annoyance in the voice. 'It's one of his earlier pieces, and after we brought everything across, he was furious. He said it wasn't supposed to come over, it was supposed to stay in his studio in Austria, and that it wasn't going out. Andrew had screwed up, you see. We put it aside, and it never got reframed. Sometimes this happens. It's not uncommon.'

Declan played a hunch.

'That's the one that got stolen, isn't it?'

'Yeah,' Miles gave a rueful smile. 'Which makes me think that maybe there was something more to the painting.'

'Can you send that to me?' Declan asked, and Miles nodded, swiping it.

'I can AirDrop it now,' he said. 'Or WhatsApp it?'

Declan wasn't a complete Luddite, and could accept the photo on his phone, the gallery's Wi-Fi sending it over.

'Tell me about the woman,' placing the phone away, Declan had pulled out his notebook now, and was writing this down with his tactical pen. 'The one who shouted during the welcome speech.'

'She stood up and started asking if people knew he used to be a Nazi,' Veronica's face reddened with anger. 'It was bollocks. Lukas was never a Nazi. He hated the Nazis. He didn't speak to his grandfather in the last twenty years of his grandfather's life once he found out what he'd done during the war.'

'And what had his grandfather been doing in the war?' Declan asked, wondering if the Benson's idea of "what granddad Weber did in the war" matched what Cooper had stated.

'We never asked,' Miles said. 'It's ancient history. But, as somebody who deals with medieval paintings and such, I've learned that history can often be rewritten. Look at Richard the Third.'

'The king?'

'More the painting of Richard the Third, the one that everybody knows, of a slightly hunchbacked man with a scowl on his face. It's been proven now that it was over-painted.'

'Over-painted being ...'

'It's an art where someone who comes in, matches the previous person's painting style and changes the image slight-ly,' Veronica explained. 'It's a common thing, changing parts of it, making it look the same. Often, it's not the original painter who did it, and is someone later who arrogantly believes they can better it. Usually, it's given away by layers of varnish under the paint. But somebody at some point was told to take this painting of Richard the Third and make him a little more villainous.'

'Richard's right shoulder was altered, the line of his coat being raised to exaggerate or create an unevenness in the shoulders,' Miles added. 'This can be seen with the naked eye too, as the overpaint has aged differently to the original layer.'

'The eyes were also over-painted to appear steely grey, and the mouth was turned down at the corners, to make him more unfriendly,' Veronica, irritated at the interruption, continued. 'Most likely it was the Tudors, wanting to make sure people never thought Richard might have been the good guy in the whole situation.'

Declan nodded, understanding.

'So, like the woman in Spain who over-painted that image of Christ, making him look like a Muppet?' he asked.

Miles shifted uncomfortably.

'Well, sure, if you want to use that as your example ...' he trailed off, irritably.

'And you think this family history was rewritten?' Declan moved on quickly.

'Honestly, all I know is when we went to visit Weber, some villagers, the older ones, had mentioned that his grandfather was the local chief of police after the war, and he ... well, he wasn't popular.'

'So, he finished the war, came home, and took a role similar to what he had before?'

'We're unsure. A lot of Austrians don't want to talk about the war.'

'I understand that, and we're not here to talk about it,' Declan noted this down. 'But do you think whoever killed Weber might have been connected to this?'

Veronica took a step forward at this point.

'That woman was shouting out about Lukas moments before we learnt he was dead! It can't be a coincidence!' she snapped. 'I think she did it, and I think you should pull her in.'

'I think she was just protesting,' Miles replied, far calmer, as if trying to pull his wife back from an edge. 'She probably doesn't know anything. Like, literally. An airhead student, all hopped up on conspiracies and our cheap champagne. We should just let her go, like returning a fish into the water.'

Veronica didn't look as if she agreed with this but said nothing else.

'We'll look into that,' Declan put away his notebook. 'Thank you for your time. Is there anything else you can think of that might have altered anything?'

'No, but you might want to speak to Andrew,' Miles replied. 'He's my brother, the other partner in the gallery. He was the man who found Lukas, and he spends his time on the road looking for new artists.'

'And Andrew isn't here right now, is that correct?'

'He's in Romania, I believe. Back tomorrow.'

'Okay, we'll look into that.'

Miles nodded and offered his hand for Declan to shake, and Declan dutifully shook it.

'Thank you for your time,' he said. 'I know this has been a stressful day for you both. I'll get someone to contact you and get a better witness statement as time goes on.'

He wasn't sure, but it looked like Veronica wanted to say something else. She looked a little concerned, a little nervous.

'Unless there's anything else that you'd like to add?' he asked.

'No, we're good. Thank you,' Miles replied, and reluctantly, it seemed Veronica nodded as well, once more silently agreeing with her husband.

Declan pulled a card out of his pocket and passed it to Veronica.

'Well, if either of you ever thinks of anything, here's my number. Call me anytime,' he smiled.

'It says Detective Inspector on this,' Veronica frowned.

'I was promoted recently,' Declan explained. 'New cards haven't arrived yet, but the number and email are the same.'

Miles took the card from Veronica, placing it in his jacket pocket.

'As I said, Detective Chief Inspector, I think everything's been passed across.'

'Always good to check,' Declan forced his smile to stay. 'Thank you very much for your time.'

He walked away, hoping that Veronica would have taken

the hint, and whatever was worrying her would give her the impetus to phone or email him at some point. She'd stared at the card for a good few seconds before it was taken, enough time to hopefully remember the email address.

This done, Declan walked out into the main gallery once more. They had a dead artist, a stolen painting, and a volatile secret in his past that could explain everything.

Declan sighed.

Basically, for the Temple Inn unit, this was a regular weekday.

———

3

PROTESTERS

It hadn't taken Anjli long to find the girl who had interrupted the speech. She was in the second gallery, sitting sullenly in the room's corner, a security guard on either side of her, as the police and forensics continued their jobs, ignoring her.

She looked up, her eyes narrowing, as Anjli walked towards her.

'Lucy Cormorant?' Anjli asked.

'Yes,' Lucy replied, standing up.

'Cormorant – is that like the bird?' Anjli continued.

'Not exactly,' Lucy replied. 'It's French. My dad always said we were named after the bird Satan became in *Paradise Lost*.'

'Would you like to tell me what happened?' Anjli asked, pulling out a notepad and writing on it.

'Who are you?' Lucy interrupted, folding her arms defensively. 'I've already spoken to an officer. Why do I have to talk about it again? I'd really like to go home now.'

'I'm Detective Inspector Kapoor of the City of London

police,' Anjli said, looking up from the notepad and fixing Lucy with a fearsome stare. 'We're just following up with a few more questions, and currently, you're the prime suspect for the murder of Lukas Weber. So, if I ask you to tell me what happened, you'll either tell me what happened here, or you can tell me in an interview room. Either way, if you refuse, you'll still be coming back to the station and sitting in a cell until we can decide what to do with you.'

'You can't arrest me for what I did,' Lucy shook her head.

'I'm sure I can find a dozen reasons to arrest you,' Anjli replied. 'I'm the police. I'm guessing you're a student?'

At this, Lucy took the comment as more of an insult than a statement.

'You have a problem with students?' she asked, glowering.

'Not at all,' Anjli replied. 'It's just that most of the protesters we've picked up over the last few months have always been student age, which I get. This world hasn't really left much for you, and you need to argue to make sure it can be sorted. But at the same time, what did you think you would gain today?'

'I'd let the world know he was a Nazi.'

'And what do you think, by outing him, you would have achieved?'

Lucy Cormorant considered this.

'People wouldn't buy his paintings.'

Anjli chuckled.

'Yeah, this is the other problem with students,' she said. 'You have a very blinkered view of reality. I can guarantee you the moment you started spouting off that Lukas Weber was a Nazi, there'd be people in that room who'd have instantly added zeros to the amount they were paying for the paintings, and worked out who they could sell them to next. All you did was raise his status.'

Lucy didn't reply, staring off as she listened to the words, and Anjli wondered for a moment whether this information was actually new to the woman.

She didn't seem as outraged as Anjli thought she'd be, for a start.

'How do you know he's a Nazi?' Anjli asked.

Lucy didn't reply.

'I said, how did you know he was a Nazi?' Anjli clarified.

'I was told.'

'Told by who?'

Lucy shifted uncomfortably on the chair.

'I was paid to do this,' she eventually replied. 'It's a job, nothing more.'

'Go on.'

'I'm a student at UAL – that's University of the Arts London – Saint Martin's. I don't make a lot, I have a part-time job in a coffee shop, my parents fund me when they can. But there's a wall in the student union where people put jobs up. Usually cash-paying things. You know, "Hey, I need to get back to see my parents. Is anybody driving that way? Could I share your car?" or "Hey, I need to move my stuff from my shared house. Can someone help me? I'll give you fifty quid." Or "Hey—'

'I get the idea,' Anjli nodded.

'So, someone puts a post up on this notice board saying, "Hey, I want someone to publicly out a Nazi." I thought it could be fun,' Lucy smiled. 'They said that the grandson of a known Nazi was launching an exhibition, and that there were conspiracies saying his family had made their money from such things.'

'Made their money?'

Lucy gave another smile, but this time it was almost mocking, as if she was feeling smug or superior to the police officer in front of her.

'You really know nothing, do you?' she asked mockingly. 'Lukas Weber is probably a multimillionaire – *was* a multimillionaire. His family owned vast chunks of Austria. He didn't need this exhibition. The vultures who took his paintings did.'

Anjli wrote this down; if this turned out to be true, the idea of Lukas Weber being a penniless artist was rapidly disappearing.

'So, who gave you the job?' she asked, looking up from her notes.

'I don't know,' Lucy admitted. 'I applied for the job, said I could do it, that I could see the best way to do such a thing. I got an email from a Hotmail address saying I had the job. I was given the details to be here today and a printout of the PDF ticket; I was told what to wear, when to be here, and exactly when to raise the comment and awareness.'

'And then what? Leave with your head held high?'

'You always leave with your head held high when you tell the truth,' Lucy snapped back.

'And how much did they pay you for this?'

'Two hundred pounds,' Lucy replied. 'Half before, half to be paid after I did it. It might even be in my account now. I haven't looked. It was through crypto transfer, Dogecoin.'

Anjli wanted to scream. She knew little about cryptocurrency, but one thing she knew was it was almost impossible to trace.

'So, someone paid you two hundred pounds' worth of

some made-up money to shout out that someone was a Nazi, and you never knew who it was? You never contacted them?'

'I'll be honest, I quite enjoyed the cloak and dagger,' Lucy shrugged. 'You know, made me feel a bit like a spy.'

'Well, I hope you enjoyed it, because right now you're going to feel very much like a spy,' Anjli nodded. 'Because you'll be coming back to the station and sitting in a cell until we can decide what to do with you. Just like James Bond.'

As Anjli turned to walk away, Lucy grabbed her arm to stop her.

'I didn't do it,' she said. 'But I ... I can help you with finding out who did.'

'And how can you do that?' Anjli asked.

Lucy looked back at the entrance to the next gallery.

'I didn't want people to know I was here on a fake ticket, as any minute I could be removed, and I didn't want to lose out on the money,' she explained, her voice lowering as she spoke. 'So as soon as I got in, I disappeared into the back rooms, hung around in the corner of a small storeroom in there, found a place to hide until I could come out and do what I needed to do.'

'Go on,' Anjli had pulled out her notebook again. 'You're moving out of that cell.'

'There were two guys having an argument in the room next door. I didn't see them, but I think one of them could have been Weber.'

'Why would you think that?' Anjli asked.

'Because he had a slight German accent. I heard arguments about a painting not being sold, or someone not being able to buy one – I couldn't hear well. Then there was a crash, some movement, and then nothing.'

'The fight ended?'

'Everything ended. There wasn't any more noise whatso-
ever,' Lucy continued. 'It was getting close to the launch
speech at this point, so I wasn't really paying attention. I
assumed it was just something going on in the background
that wasn't really my problem. You know, common launch
party shit.'

'You've done launch parties before?'

Lucy looked uncomfortable.

'My dad's an artist, I've done a couple of his.'

Anjli didn't press on with this, but knew it was something
she wanted to look into later. Lucy, not realising her expression had given anything away, continued.

'Anyway, as it got close to "showtime," I decided to get a
spot near the front of the audience so when I asked my question, it wouldn't be missed. But, when I left my hiding place, I
found myself facing a man coming out of the room next door
with a painting in his hand, who was surprised to see me.'

'Another guest?'

'He wasn't part of the event; he was wearing an overall. I
assumed he was one of the movers for the paintings – you
know, the people who box them and send them on. He stared
at me for a moment. I stared at him. Then he just left.'

'Can you give a description?' Anjli asked.

'I can do better than that,' Lucy smiled. 'I'm an art
student. Give me a pen and paper, and I'll draw him for you.'

'You do that? You get to sleep in your own bed tonight,'
Anjli waved for Cooper to come over and instructed her to
find the sketch artist and grab some paper and a pencil so
that Lucy could sketch out the man in the overalls. As Cooper
did this, Declan walked over, Anjli now stepping away from
Lucy.

'Anything?' he asked.

'Art student paid by somebody unknown to disrupt the event,' Anjli replied. 'All she really has is there was some kind of argument next door to the room she was hiding in. She believes Weber was in the room and was possibly angry about a painting.'

'I don't think it was as simple as that,' Declan replied, opening his phone, and scrolling to the photo Miles had sent him, the one of the paintings in the corner. 'This one in the middle? Apparently, according to the gallery owner, Weber lost his mind when he realised it was here. It wasn't supposed to have left Austria, and the other brother, Andrew, had brought it over by mistake.'

It was a simple painting, that of two people, a man, and a woman, kissing on a mountaintop. It was quite simplistic, around the level of the surrounding others in the image, and definitely not to the level of the paintings on the gallery walls.

'I wonder why he wanted to keep it?' Declan mused.

Anjli noticed Lucy was listening intently.

'You know something?'

'Can I see that photo?' Lucy asked, holding her hand out. Declan shrugged and showed Lucy the image, zooming in on the painting in question.

'Do you know anything about this?' he asked. 'Did you have any accomplices here who could have taken this while you were causing a scene?'

'This has nothing to do with me,' Lucy replied. 'I'm purely on my own.'

But she trailed off as she thought about something.

'Look, between us when I was given the job, I checked into it. You know, you don't want to "out" somebody when you don't know if it's true or not. So, I did a little research, checked a couple of forums, asked a couple of tutors if they knew about the Weber family.'

'And?' Declan asked, leaning closer.

'And Weber's granddad worked for the Nazis, taking paintings from French museums and Jews,' Lucy replied. 'He was high up secret police levels of baddie, and when the war ended, he grassed his friends up and returned home to play "police" and buy up land.'

'We'd heard similar,' Anjli nodded. 'Anything else?'

'The one in the middle? He called it "The Kiss," I believe. The owners of the gallery were loudly complaining earlier about it being stolen while we waited for the police. I think everyone heard.'

'They argued with each other?'

'I think there was someone else, a bloke, but I was held in another room, so when they left the room, I didn't get anything else.'

'They just told me that painting was stolen,' Declan mentioned to Anjli. 'Seems they were too thrown by the dead body to mention it earlier.'

'Understandable,' Anjli shrugged, looking back at Lucy. 'Okay, if you can do us that sketch, you might buy yourself some goodwill.'

Lucy nodded, looking back as the sketch artist walked over with his tools. She spent a couple of moments picking the right pencil, and then walked off with the pad, placing it against the wall so she had a surface to sketch against as she started her art piece.

'Anything else?' Anjli asked.

'We'll talk in a minute,' Declan replied as De'Geer finally arrived, Doctor Marcos's bag of tricks in his hand. 'I'll catch you in a moment.'

With Anjli checking her notes, Declan moved over to De'Geer.

'Is Doctor Marcos okay?' he asked. 'She seems distracted. A little angrier than usual.'

De'Geer nodded.

'Something's on her mind and I don't know what it is,' he admitted. 'Been like that a couple of days now. I'll monitor her. Even working at half speed, she's still better than every divisional surgeon out there.'

And with that, De'Geer hurried off to give his boss her tools as Declan looked around the exhibition hall one more time.

There was more here than just a murder.

There was more here than just a stolen painting.

There was something he couldn't quite grasp.

Declan shook himself out of his thoughts and walked back to Anjli. They didn't need to be here for the moment. Basically, even though it was night-time, and nothing else was likely to be discovered that evening, in a way the case was only just beginning.

4

FIRST BRIEFING

'I DON'T FEEL COMFORTABLE DOING THIS, BOSS,' DECLAN muttered as he stood at the front of the briefing room.

Monroe, standing in the doorway, gave a little grin.

'Aye, I know what you're talking about, laddie,' he said. 'But this is how it works. The DCI stands at the front. The Detective Superintendent stands to the side, quipping here and there, looking cool and making important comments when they feel it's right. Everybody else sits in front, shuts up, and looks at you like a good little soldier.'

Declan looked back into the briefing room. It was the morning after the night before, and Doctor Marcos and De'Geer both looked like they hadn't slept yet, the latter rubbing sleep out of his eyes while the former was downing probably her third espresso of the day. Beside them was PC Cooper, and in front of them, on either side of the room to him, was Anjli to the left and Billy to the right, sitting in his usual spot with his laptop in front of him.

After they'd returned to Temple Inn the night before nothing new had come in, so Declan and Anjli had both returned home by different means, and discussed the case into the early hours. However, with no new intelligence, all they'd done was go around in circles. With luck, today would give more information on what they needed to do.

'Okay then,' Declan said. 'Let's talk about what happened.'

'No, you don't do it like that,' Anjli replied. 'You need to make some kind of Scottish quip. "Right, laddie. This is a wealth of chickadees" or "Well, this is a fine kettle of wee fishies we have here," something like that to really start the talk.'

'I never said "wee fishies," lassie,' Monroe glowered from the door.

Declan looked at them both.

'How about, "Okay, so we have a murder. Perhaps we should try solving it?"' he asked sarcastically.

'Aye, that'll do,' Monroe nodded, leaning back against the door.

Declan looked back to the briefing room.

'Let's go over what we have,' he said.

'The victim was Lukas Weber, age fifty-four, Austrian citizen, was over in London for the launch of his painting exhibition,' Anjli read from her notes. 'He was last seen around eight in the evening, when he'd spoken to one attendee, correcting them on what his paintings meant. When the speech was made just before nine pm, one of the serving staff, Stacey Nichols, entered a side room and found him.'

'Why?' Monroe asked. 'Why go in there then?'

'According to my notes, she thought she heard a noise a few minutes earlier in the room but was still serving. Once she finished, she returned and opened the door to see if everything was alright—' Cooper read from her own notes.

'And found the dead body of Lukas Weber instead,' Anjli continued. 'That must have been a pleasant surprise.'

'He was on the floor, his black polo neck had been torn, the collar removed. There was a lipstick kiss painted onto his neck, and what looks to be some kind of tattoo of initials beside it.'

'Doctor Marcos,' Declan asked, looking up to the back, 'do we have anything more about that?'

Doctor Marcos nodded, rising.

'There were no visible wounds as we looked at him, but there was significant trauma to the back of his head,' she explained, walking to the front of the room. 'It looked as if he'd fallen and hit his head.'

'Is that what killed him?'

Doctor Marcos shook her head.

'Actually, although we weren't sure about that, we didn't know until we had a good look.'

'And did you find anything?' Declan asked.

'We didn't have to check for long,' Doctor Marcos nodded. 'We'd already spotted the issue. Weber had burn marks on his chest.'

She tapped with two fingers to her own sternum.

'A shock stick?'

'We think so,' Doctor Marcos nodded to De'Geer, who rose. 'Viking boy wonder can take it from here.'

De'Geer nervously cleared his throat.

'In the past, we've seen that people repeatedly shocked can leave terrible burns, but this wasn't as severe, so we think Weber was only shocked once.'

'And then what, he fell backwards and slammed his head on a table?' Monroe asked. 'Would that kill him?'

'No,' Doctor Marcos took over again. 'But we think the

shock and the fall caused a cardiac arrest. Lukas Weber had a pacemaker and a triple bypass two years ago. But we can also tell you it wasn't an instant death, as there were traces of blood on the tattoo needle area, which if he was dead ...'

'Wouldn't have shown,' Declan nodded, shuddering at the image. Whoever killed Lukas Weber might not have meant to do it, but, as Weber lay on the floor, injured and possibly dying, they'd leant over him and started painting.

He would have been staring into their eyes as he died.

'How long would it have taken to paint the lipstick and tattoo the neck?' Monroe frowned from his position in the doorway.

'No idea,' Doctor Marcos replied. 'I'm not an artist. But what I will say is the room he was found in wasn't one that was being used. The only reason the server walked in later is because she thought she had heard a noise. If she hadn't heard anything, we would never have found the body. Nobody would have known he was dead until somebody went in there, either by the end of the event or even the next day. If he wasn't dead when they left, they were risking a lot to leave him alone.'

Declan shuddered at this.

'Premeditated,' he said. 'Has to be. The death might have been an accident, but the kiss, the tattoo... they knew they wouldn't be disturbed where they were. They knew they had time to do what they wanted.'

There was a moment of uncomfortable silence as the officers took in the information.

Okay, so what else do we have?' changing the subject, Declan looked over at Billy, who tapped on his laptop, and the sketch Lucy Cormorant had made of a man in overalls appeared on the screen.

'The art student protester did this,' Billy replied. 'It came through last night. It's superb. There's an element of photorealism in the charcoals, and I think she's captured the nature of the man quite perfectly.'

'You were a frustrated artist, weren't you?' Anjli asked.

Billy shrugged.

'Aren't we all in a manner of speaking?' he replied enigmatically. 'The fact of the matter is, her sketch is so good, I can use it with photo recognition tools. It picks up the details we need, so I can look into it, as it's far better than the average sketch.'

'Have we shown this to the Bensons?'

'Neither of them claim to recognise the man, boss,' Cooper now spoke, reading from her notes. 'Miles confirmed he didn't work for them. So, this is definitely somebody off the books.'

'So, he could have been the one who took the painting?'

'Maybe.'

'Do we have anything on that?'

Billy shook his head.

'We're still looking into this,' he replied. 'Miles Benson said Lukas Weber had been angry it'd been brought across. It was supposed to have stayed in Austria, a personal piece he was never selling. However, I've spoken to a couple of people who know his work in Austria – on a variety of internet forums – and they confirmed it's not very good compared to the others, and is definitely one of his earlier works.'

'Could this be why he wasn't selling it?' Anjli asked, looking up. 'He knew it was bad enough to affect his brand?'

'Possibly,' Billy said. 'But the impression I got was there's something more there. That it's something more than a painting.'

'And what does that mean?' Declan asked.

Billy shrugged.

'That's the problem with conspiracies,' he replied. 'It's all vagueness and explanations. Stories of a painting that could be more than a painting, or a dead artist who's been claimed to be a Nazi when he wasn't.'

'And the lipstick on the neck?'

'It's definitely brush strokes,' Doctor Marcos rose again. 'We had a better chance to examine the body last night, and as I said, the lipstick kiss is painted on with oil paints. The tattoo, however, wasn't painted. They tattooed it with something cobbled together that worked like a prison, rather than professional tattoo gun, as there's no way they're getting a professional one in there without people seeing it, and the prison devices are made to be hidden.'

Declan understood what Doctor Marcos meant by this; prison tattoos were often rudimentary ones created by a common ball-point pen ink and crude make-shift needles. But inmates could create actual machines using tiny motors from beard trimmers and small CD players, connected to a battery, the needle itself often made from a metal guitar string split in two by holding it over an open flame until it snapped in half, creating a fine point. They were classed as contraband, and often people having these in prison could contract diseases like HIV through the practice, but it was effectively a hand-held device, slightly larger than a pen, which could have been brought into the party by any of the guests.

'Do we know what the tattoo said?'

'Yes,' Doctor Marcos nodded. 'We believe it's the initials J K.'

'Any ideas who that could be?'

'Not yet. We're still guessing,' Doctor Marcos replied. 'It was a crude tattoo at best and it could have been a different set of letters, as if there was an ink blowout, and the letters had smudged during it, a T could become a J and so forth.'

'Keep on it,' Declan said, looking back at Monroe, still standing by the door.

'What am I missing, Guv?' he asked.

Monroe was scratching his chin.

'I don't know, laddie,' he said. 'It feels like it's a deliberate act. But as of yet, we have no cause and it could have been an accident. The plan may have been to taser him and paint him while he was unconscious.'

'Could it have been someone from Austria?' Billy asked. 'Someone who had followed Weber across? Maybe it's someone with a grudge in his homeland?'

'Aye, could be. We might need to look into that,' Monroe replied. He paused though, as the phone in his office rang.

'Keep going, laddie. I'll be back in a minute,' he said, walking off. Declan sighed loudly, looking back to the audience now watching him.

'Okay, so next steps,' he said. 'We need to look more into Weber and work out who'd want him dead, or at least incapacitated while being tattooed. Anjli, see if you can find out more about the brother, the one in Romania. He was the one that found Weber, so maybe he knows something more about the man. Miles said he was landing today, so go wait for him with a "welcome home" sign. De'Geer, Doctor Marcos? Keep doing what you do. Let's see if we can work out anything else about the body.'

He was pacing unconsciously now.

'Billy, look for any CCTV; let's see if we can work out where that painting went. Am I missing anything else?'

Cooper held up a hand.

'Lucy Cormorant gained her job on a university notice-board,' she said. 'The person who put it up there had to have been connected to the university to get in there to put the note up.'

'Or they paid a student to put the note in there,' Billy suggested. 'Either way, there should be CCTV I can use.'

'I think she was called in as a distraction,' Anjli suggested. 'They weren't expecting the body to be found so quickly and wanted Lucy to take the rap for it, perhaps?'

As she spoke, Monroe returned into the room, his face darker than it was when he left.

'So, laddie, we might have to change our investigation a little,' he said, now taking his original spot in the briefing room. Declan almost returned to his chair as an automatic reaction as Monroe now faced the briefing room.

'That was Berlin,' he said. 'An old friend of ours. Margaret Li, the Kriminalkommissar of the Scwere und Organisierte Kriminalität; the one who helped with Karl Schnitter. She's on a case and understands that we could be investigating something similar.'

'How similar?' Declan couldn't help himself.

'Well, it seems that there's a prominent German artist found murdered a month back in his Berlin apartment,' Monroe's eyes narrowed as he spoke. 'They know little about it, but what they do know is that the killer left a mark on his neck.'

'A lipstick kiss?'

'Aye, a wee oil painting of one,' Monroe nodded. 'She's on the next flight over. It looks like we've got the startings of a series of murders, guys, and it's up to us to work out how connected they are.'

He looked around the room.

'Get going quickly,' he said. 'I don't want our thunder being stolen. Declan? When you get a chance, my office.'

And, this said, Monroe walked out, his body language completely changed from the start of the briefing.

He was annoyed, frustrated even.

And Declan knew exactly how he felt.

5

SECRETS AND MEETINGS

AFTER THE BRIEFING HAD ENDED, MONROE WAS IN HIS OFFICE when Declan walked in, closing the door behind him.

'You rang, my lord?' Declan asked, concerned what the conversation was about to reveal.

Monroe nodded, waiting for Declan to sit down.

'Just to let you know that Bullman's back tomorrow,' he said. 'It's just for the day, and to check in on the case, but it means I'll need my old office back. You'll be back in the bullpen with the others.'

'Why can't you be back in the bullpen with the others?' Declan asked.

Monroe grinned.

'That's not how it works, laddie. I'm your superior and I need an office. So, I'll take your office. You're their superior, so you can take ...'

He paused in mock horror.

'Oh, wait. There aren't any more offices.'

'That'll be fine. I'll be all over the place this week, anyway, with this case going on,' Declan said. 'And I'm not really enjoying the office. It places you apart from the team.'

'That's the point.'

'Well, I think it's a stupid point.'

Monroe looked around his own office.

'I have to admit, I do like this slightly larger space I have here,' he said. 'The window view's nice as well.'

Declan watched Monroe for a long moment before speaking again.

'Sir, can I ask a personal question?'

'It's never stopped you before,' Monroe smiled. 'Go ahead.'

'Are you, well... are you and Doctor Marcos okay?'

Monroe's eyebrows raised at the question.

'Aye, well, I walked into that one, didn't I?' he said. 'As far as I know, we're okay. Or do you have something you need to tell me that changes everything?'

'No, no, not at all,' Declan shook his head vigorously. 'It's just ... well, she seems a little off her game at the moment. She seemed distracted at the crime scene last night, she looks like she hasn't slept—'

'She hasn't slept.'

'I get that. But she's done that dozens of times in the past, and she's never looked as vacant as she is now.'

Monroe shifted in the chair as if taking the time to consider his next response.

'There was a problem,' he said. 'I don't know what it is. A couple of days back I asked why she's been so distant. She made a point of explaining to me it was nothing to do with me, and that I shouldn't worry. But there's something that spooked her, and I don't know what it is.'

'Do you want me to check into it?' Declan asked.

Monroe shook his head, rising from the chair.

'No, laddie, you have enough to do,' he said. 'Just find this artist killer and we can move on to the next God knows what we'll get sent. I'm going to pop out and speak to the gallery owner again. He was a little shifty last night, I thought a bit of a break might loosen his tongue a little.'

'Shouldn't I be doing that while you wait for the German officer?'

'Li won't be here for hours, and I need to get out of here,' Monroe smiled. 'I'm sure you can find other ways to make yourself useful.'

'I thought you liked the new office?'

'Well, I'm not *wed* to the idea.'

Declan rose to meet his boss.

'As long as you're sure, sir,' he said.

'Solve the case, Declan,' Monroe replied, and his clipped tone made Declan remember he was prying into a personal area – Monroe's love life. So, instead he walked towards the office door and opened it.

'Declan,' Monroe said before he could leave. 'I appreciate it. I really do.'

Declan gave a tight smile before leaving and as he walked back to his own office, he wondered what was bothering Doctor Marcos.

Of all the people in the Last Chance Saloon, she was the one least likely to be spooked by anything.

If something was worrying her to the point of distraction, then it was never going to be good.

AFTER DECLAN HAD FINISHED HIS MEETING WITH MONROE, HE didn't feel like returning to his office. So, instead, he walked back into the office bullpen, intending to loiter until people got sick of him.

Billy was the only person there, sitting at his monitors, so Declan strolled casually over as if nothing was wrong.

'Have I done something?' Billy asked, watching him.

'Nothing,' Declan replied, pausing. 'Why would you think that?'

'Because you're walking over to me like you're stalking me, Guv,' Billy said.

'I was casually strolling,' Declan replied, slightly hurt at the accusation.

Billy chuckled.

'If that's your casual strolling, then you have an issue,' he said. 'You looked like the Angel of Death coming towards me.'

Declan swallowed.

'Sorry,' he said. 'I don't like the office. I'm still having problems settling in.'

'I get that, really,' Billy said, still watching the computer monitors. 'I was promoted too.'

'But you still do the things that we hired you to do. You still solve crimes using whatever internet magic you use. How is this in any way different?'

'Well, I have to use Detective *Sergeant* instead of Detective *Constable* now,' Billy said, as if it was the most obvious answer in the world. 'And some detectives look at me differently now.'

'Anyone in particular?' Declan smiled.

Billy reddened. 'No, no, I've just ... I mean, it's not ...'

Declan knew to stop questioning. The last thing he wanted was to know anything about Billy's love life. It had been painful enough for the man as it was, as the previous year he'd fallen in love with a foreign diplomat only to find out that he had been working as a spy.

'Whatever you decide to do,' he said. 'Just be careful, okay?'

'You mean don't date spies or murderers?' Billy shrugged. 'Can't promise that sir. Once you've dated one, you have to date more.'

Declan actually laughed and was about to reply when Monroe quickly exited his office, nodding at them both before leaving the room.

'Going to speak to Miles Benson,' he said as he exited through the main doors. 'Back shortly.'

Declan and Billy stared after him.

'Boss seems in a hurry. Probably forgot his lunch again,' Billy said.

'I think he's just happy to be out of the office,' Declan replied.

'Actually, while you're here, can I show you something?' Billy asked. 'The sketch of the man in the overalls that Lucy Cormorant did for us? It was very good. So good, in fact, that I put it through some algorithms to create a 3D version, and effectively use it as a headshot for facial recognition.'

Declan found this a bit concerning.

'I mean, I guess that's fine if there was a photo we could use, but if it's an artist's impression ... what if it looks like someone else and we end up arresting them?'

'I don't think so; I reckon this led us straight to the right person,' Billy said, tapping on a button. The screen lit up in front of him, showing a photo of a man in a suit, smiling in a group of similarly suited older men at some kind of event or gala. Declan could see immediately that this was the same man Lucy Cormorant had sketched.

'Who is he?' he asked.

'Gary Krohn,' Billy replied, pulling up another file. 'He's an art restorer based in Shoreditch.'

'An art restorer?' Declan asked.

'I think he's probably a forger, but he's clever enough not to get caught,' Billy nodded. 'He's been around the block a few times, shall we say. I've contacted a couple of people and asked their opinion of the man, and they both say he's very good at what he does.'

'And what's that?'

'He's a fixer for broken paintings,' Billy explained. 'He can take paintings that are badly damaged and recreate them; over-painting, stitching, whatever's needed so you can't even tell what's going on. Besides this, he trained at the Courtauld Institute of Art in the late nineties to learn how to conserve and restore paintings.'

Declan felt a chill run down his spine. He placed a hand on Billy's shoulder as he did so.

'Are you saying this guy is an expert at *removing* paintings?' he asked.

Billy thought about the question and then nodded.

'I suppose so, yes. Why?'

'Something Miles Benson said to me ... it's just ... it's there in the back of my head. I'll come back to you about it. So, this guy's legit? As in, he's good at what he does, rather than he's a legitimate business owner?'

'Oh, he's both. I contacted a source,' Billy replied, reddening. 'A source that ...'

'You spoke to a forger, didn't you?' Declan filled in the blanks.

'I put the message out,' Billy said. 'I spoke briefly to Ellie Reckless's thief guy, Ramsey Allen. He knows a lot of forgers and has worked with them from time to time. He suggested some places that might be able to help. And he recognised Krohn.'

'And then?' Declan asked, amused because Billy was now flustered.

'I ... I might have spoken to Sam,' Billy's voice dropped as he spoke. 'Sam Mansfield. Forger Sam Mansfield.'

'Sam Mansfield. Forger Sam Mansfield,' Declan smiled. 'Was that in case I forgot who he was?'

He looked around as if by saying the name, the man would appear.

'So, you've discussed this case with a known criminal?'

'Oh, come on, sir,' Billy replied. 'We worked repeatedly with Johnny Lucas.'

'Johnny Lucas was never convicted of anything. Well, yet,' Declan replied, 'But I get what you're saying.'

A sudden thought came to him, and he cocked his head.

'This conversation with Sam,' he said. 'Have you been speaking to him much since the first time we dealt with him?'

Billy reddened even more, his cheeks flushing as he went to reply.

'We hit it off,' he said. 'Well, when we were creating the forgery to take down Commander Sinclair, anyway. And after that, well ...'

His voice trailed off as he tried to explain himself.

'We had a couple of drinks. Platonic, like. It was nice.'

'Nice?' It was all Declan could do to not laugh out loud.

He was happy that Billy was getting out, but Sam Mansfield was definitely not the "booty call" he'd have expected.

'Since Andrade, I've not really been able to open up to anyone,' Billy continued.

'And you felt that opening up to a forgery con man was a good idea?'

'Well,' Billy shrugged, 'I've had worse ideas.'

Declan couldn't help it; he laughed.

'That you have,' he said. 'Actually, you might have given us a good idea there. See if De'Geer can get me Krohn's address, and call both Ramsey Allen and Sam Mansfield. Get them in, explain they're not suspects but more "helping the police in their inquiries" right now.'

'Really?'

'Yes,' Declan nodded. 'I think it's worth a shot.'

Before Declan could continue the conversation however, his phone rang. Pulling it out he didn't recognise the number and so waved to Billy, motioning that he had a call to take while walking across the office.

'Walsh,' he said eventually answering the phone.

'Is that Detective Chief Inspector Walsh?' a woman's voice asked, hesitant and nervous.

'It is,' Declan replied. He recognised the voice, but he wasn't a hundred percent sure he was right. 'Is that Veronica Benson?'

'It is,' she replied. 'I apologise for interrupting, but I wondered if we could speak at some point.'

'What's the problem?' Declan asked.

'It's my husband,' Veronica admitted. 'I ... I think he might be ... well, that is, I think he might be connected to the murder.'

'And why would you think that?' Declan asked, pressing forward slightly.

'Because I found something,' she said nervously down the line. 'And I think you really should see it ... because, Detective Chief Inspector, I think my husband is the killer.'

6

PAINT MARKS

DOCTOR MARCOS WAS IN THE MORGUE WHEN THE CALL CAME in, her phone buzzing, set on silent yet still loud enough to distract her in case something important needed to be passed on to her.

Morten De'Geer, also standing beside the body of Lukas Weber, looked up at her as she glanced nervously back at it.

'Do you need to take that?' he asked.

'I probably should. I'll come back in a moment,' Doctor Marcos replied, walking over to her phone. She caught it a split second before it went to voicemail, listened for a moment, said 'Fine, I'll be right there,' and then disconnected the call.

'More trouble?' De'Geer asked.

'Keep looking. I'll be away for an hour or so, maybe less, so keep me updated by text,' Doctor Marcos said, taking off her mask and apron and leaving the room, heading towards reception. She was so busy in fact, that she didn't see Sergeant Mastakin on front desk duty make a call as she passed by in a rush.

It was midday, and Temple Inn was quite busy, but Doctor Marcos had no intention of hanging around near the offices. She walked out of the main entrance, hurried across Temple Inn itself and down towards the main exit onto the Embankment. Once there, she hailed a cab heading towards Blackfriars. The cab journey wasn't long, taking her just to the south side of the Thames, where there was a strangely named pub called *Doggett's Coat And Badge*, named after the oldest continuous rowing race in the world, held almost every year from 1715 where the Watermen of the Thames would row upstream from London Bridge to Chelsea. She then paid the fare and entered the pub, looking around.

A man sitting at a table nodded at her. He was well dressed, his clothes fitted, tall and built like a fighter, his head shaved.

'Sorry to call you,' he said, his voice showing a slight Scottish twang as Doctor Marcos sat opposite him, waving down his offer of a drink.

'Let's just get this done. I'm in the middle of an autopsy.'

'Anyone I know?' the man asked with the hint of a smile.

'I bloody hope not, Derek. Can we just get on with this?'

Derek Sutton sat back on his chair and smiled.

'You know, he always talks about you,' he said. 'I never really had a chance to properly meet you, to see how you did under stress. But Jesus, he underestimated you ...'

Doctor Marcos smiled.

'Are we flirting now?' she said. 'Because it sounds to me like you're flirting.'

Sutton shook his head.

'I'm just stating facts,' he replied.

'Well, then let's stick to the fact of keeping him alive,' Doctor Marcos replied, leaning forward, elbows down on the table. 'Because if this hit goes through, not only will he be dead, but I'll be very pissed off and I'll tell you now, when I'm pissed off, *nobody* is safe.'

Sutton matched her, leaning forward as well.

'If Alex dies, you'd have to race me to kill the culprit because I'll be ending everyone,' he said. 'I have news. I got a wee scroat to confirm it. This is Lennie Wright's work.'

'Thought he was still in jail, awaiting trial dates.'

'Change of plan. Got his court date in two weeks. Not enough time really to set a defence, but he's had a while to prepare for it.'

Doctor Marcos nodded at this. Lennie Wright had been an old enemy of Alexander Monroe's when he lived in Glasgow and before he became a police officer, and the previous year Monroe had returned to Edinburgh and faced Wright one last time, a confrontation that ended with Wright being arrested for a variety of rather bad, rather lengthy-sentence-inducing things. However, he hadn't taken it well, and now with his trial about to happen and Monroe being the prime witness against him, Lennie Wright was planning to hit back.

'Do we know who the takers are?' she asked.

'Takers? You mean the pricks coming to kill our friend?' Sutton shook his head. 'I'll know by the end of the week.'

'I'll know by the end of the day,' Doctor Marcos replied coldly, checking her watch. 'We need to tell him. It's unfair. He already suspects something's going wrong and having me leave and travel to see you … it's not good.'

'I know,' Sutton said. 'We'll speak to him soon about this.'

'We could have spoken about this on the phone.'

'No we couldn't have,' Sutton replied, nodding to the bar. 'A man over there? End of the bar, looks like he was dragged through a hedge and beaten to shite with the branches? That's Harvey Drake. Used to run Lennie Wright's London operations. He doesn't recognise me, and he shouldn't recognise you. I've been watching him for the last two days, and yesterday ... well, he was showing your other half's picture around.'

Doctor Marcos half-rose, her eyes narrowing but Derek Sutton paused her, placing a hand on her own to keep her seated at the table.

'He won't be the one that does it,' he said. 'The chances are he won't even be connected to the one who does it. They're not that stupid. If we stop him, then someone else takes the job. Following him is our best opportunity to find out who's going to be trying this.'

'And then?' Doctor Marcos asked.

'And then we take the whole damn lot down,' Sutton said.

Doctor Marcos was staring at Harvey Drake, her eyes widening in recognition.

'Oh, shit,' she said. 'I know him.'

'Personally?'

Doctor Marcos shook her head.

'The Tancredi case,' she replied. 'A couple of years back. Four Liverpudlian crime lords killed each other while sitting at a circular table. I worked out that someone had to have started it, and Drake was a prime instigator.'

'Is this going to be a problem?' Sutton asked.

However, Doctor Marcos replied with a grin.

"Hell, no,' she said. 'I might actually get some closure on something.'

DOCTOR MARCOS HADN'T REALISED SHE WAS BEING WATCHED as she sat in the bar as outside, standing on the South Bank, the Thames behind him, Alexander Monroe watched the two of them talking, narrowing his eyes as he did so.

He'd asked Mastakin to keep him informed if Rosanna left, and he'd done so a few minutes earlier; with Monroe running out after her before she could get too far away. He had guessed something was wrong, but he had never thought it would be an affair. Now, seeing Derek Sutton with her, he knew for certain it *wasn't*. But whatever teamed both Rosanna Marcos and Derek Sutton together, it couldn't be good.

He almost entered the pub and confronted them, but he knew that whatever they were doing, the information would come to him at some point.

And so, placing his hands into his pockets, he turned, deciding instead to walk back to the bridge and a cab back to Chancery Lane and Miles Benson – but, in doing so, accidentally bumped another tourist that was standing beside him.

He was a younger man, Asian in looks, with short black hair half scrunched under a baseball cap with a *New York Mets* logo on it. He had a camera in his hand and had been taking photos of the other side of the Thames as Monroe knocked him, and now the man glared at him.

'Watch it, mate,' he said, his accent more London-based than his look. 'I almost dropped my camera. You'd have paid for that.'

Monroe held his hands up to apologise, aware his distracted nature could have caused a visible scene which would have alerted Derek and Rosanna of his presence, and before anyone inside the pub could glance out and see him, he turned the other way and left quickly.

The man, shaking his head, returned to taking photos of the Thames.

GARY KROHN WAS PACING IN HIS STUDIO WHEN THE GIRL arrived. No older than his son – well, he assumed so, as he hadn't spoken to him since he was twelve – and wearing a hoodie to cover her head, only her nose and mouth visible through the shadows.

But Gary knew he'd seen her before; the previous night in fact, at the gallery.

She'd been there in the storeroom.

She'd seen him.

'You're with Benson, aren't you?' he asked, walking back into his studio space. 'You shouldn't be here. You know it's too soon.'

'Did you get it?' the girl, not giving her name asked. 'Or did you pass it to Bauer?'

'You think I'd betray Mister Benson?' Gary gave a mock-shocked expression as he cleaned up a paint spill on his windowsill, ignoring her. 'Like you did?'

'I don't know what you mean, and you know nothing about me,' the girl snapped back, but Gary saw the hesitant step backwards. He'd caught a nerve, and he knew he could use it.

'I know you're a student at the art college,' he said. 'I saw you. At the lecture.'

'That was months ago—' the girl replied before stopping herself. 'You weren't there.'

Gary smiled, nodding.

'I was,' he said. 'That's when you met him, wasn't it?'

'Shut up,' the girl snapped. 'Mister Benson wants to be sure you don't have it, as the client is asking questions.'

'The "client" being Bauer?' Gary Krohn laughed. 'You really don't know what you've done, do you? That man's a killer. Literally. He's all smiles and business suits, but he's ex-Junta. He's first generation Argentine and his father—'

'I don't need a lesson in DNA from you, Gary,' the girl turned and walked to the door. 'I just needed to know if you succeeded or failed in your job.'

'Go tell your boss that he should come see me, and I'll tell him to his face,' Gary snarled. 'And tell Benson he didn't mention that the police would be around! That Weber would die!'

'It was an accident,' the girl opened the door about to leave, but then stopped, looking back.

'You should burn everything,' she said. 'Plans have had to change.'

'No, Bauer just made a bigger offer,' Gary snapped. 'I know what's going on here. I saw Marcel at the event. It's why I left. The brother, the idiot - he's playing too, isn't he?'

The girl smiled, without replying, and left the studio, closing the door behind her as she did so.

For a long moment, Gary Krohn stared at the door.

And then he threw a paint pot at it, the paint splattering across the wood.

'Shit,' he muttered, picking up a plastic box filled with "Big Wipes" and walking over to it. 'I thought that was empty.'

He stopped at the door, staring again at it.

And, before cleaning the paint off the door, he bolted it.

Let them come, he thought to himself. *Anyone.*

Anyone apart from Gabriel Bauer, that was.

OUTSIDE, THE GIRL PULLED OUT A PHONE, AND FOR A MOMENT stood staring at it, as if agonising over whether she should send a message.

Eventually she shook herself out of whatever torpor she was in and typed in the text.

TO: SCARY BASTARD

I think Gary Krohn has it.

Sending the message, she pulled the hoodie off, ran her hand through her hair and then walked off into Shoreditch.

7

VISITORS

MILES BENSON STOOD IN HIS GALLERY SPACE, WATCHING THE last of the forensics leave the building.

Placing his hands in his pockets, he turned and started towards his offices.

Finally, the place was empty.

Finally, he could start sorting things out for the better.

After the body had been found, everything had turned into chaos. He ordered Veronica to try to return the bids back to the buyers; the last thing he'd wanted was for anyone to have a say over the paintings now that Lukas Weber was dead. Now, with Lukas dead those paintings were worth double if not triple their value; and Miles, as the arbitrator of the sales wanted to make sure that his percentage was as high as he could get. He was sad that Lukas Weber was dead, but at the same time he had met the man a handful of times and had found him quite an odd fish.

And there was also the fact that his grandfather was a Nazi, something he didn't bother to mention when they first started talking to him.

That was something that had left Miles cold.

Not, however, cold enough to kill him.

Miles stopped walking towards the office, realising that now the police were gone, anybody could just walk in, and instead made his way up to the glass doors at the front of the building to lock them. But a figure appeared in a doorway, pushing the door in, knocking Miles backwards into the gallery space.

It was a face he recognised; Gabriel Bauer, one of the high bidders from the previous night. He was tall and muscled with short dark hair, in his late fifties at best and Argentine in looks. Bauer had been at several of Miles's previous purchases, and he always spent high. He wasn't a fan of art; he was an investor. He'd been personally invited by Andrew, and Miles knew that this was going to be an argument about pricing.

'Mister Benson,' Bauer said, his voice calm and measured. 'We need to have a conversation.'

Miles held up his hands apologetically.

'The police have only just left. It's been a hell of a time, and I've been up all night. Can we do this later? I don't have any paperwork yet.'

'I was promised my opportunity for them last night,' Bauer replied. 'And for the amount of money I've spent, I think you should at least be giving me that.'

Miles frowned at the statement.

'We cancelled all bids,' he said carefully. 'You spent nothing.'

'You cancelled the bids?' Bauer stared at him, narrowing his eyes as he did so. 'Every painting on these walls had a bid. Are you telling me you refused to sell?'

Miles flustered. He didn't know Bauer's background, but

he knew he was probably some kind of Argentinian Cartel leader, if they even had Cartels there.

He was definitely somebody you didn't want to piss off.

'Gabriel look, bear with me here,' he said. 'Lukas Weber was an upcoming artist. He wasn't a name—'

'Lukas Weber had been working in Austria for twenty years or more,' Bauer replied. 'We'd heard of him in Argentina. We knew about his work. Why else did you think I turned up?'

'Because you've come to all of my other gallery openings,' Miles replied, confused, 'I just assumed ...'

'Assume, making an ass out of you and me,' Bauer interrupted. 'Are you making an ass out of me, Miles?'

'No, of course not,' Miles shook his head vigorously. 'But I need to check with Lukas Weber's estate. They might not want to sell now, and—'

'And the paintings are worth double what they were yesterday,' Bauer leant threateningly closer. 'That's the case, isn't it? You've realised you're not making the money you wanted; if you were to sell them at the bids you took last night, every single person would make a fortune and you would make nothing. This is why you sent your wife out to cancel everything.'

'Yes,' Miles gave a reluctant shrug. 'The estate could go into probate for months, but if we could show these were purchased before his death we should have a case to keep the sales rights, which would obviously be higher. You can't blame a man for trying.'

'What I can blame a man for is taking money and running,' Gabriel Bauer replied. 'For taking my "buy in" and not allowing me to purchase the paintings I really came for.'

At this, Miles straightened angrily.

'I took nothing from you! If anything, you ate my free food and drank my free champagne,' he said. 'And nobody told me about any "buy in," whatever that's supposed to mean!'

'It was cheap champagne, the canapes were cold, and it sounds like your brother is the more intelligent one of the two of you,' Bauer cocked his head to the side as he replied. 'Even so, I gave your man a wire transfer of just under a quarter of a million pounds for my paintings.'

'You gave *what?*'

'Your man,' Bauer repeated. 'The slim one with the greying hair. He came out when we were standing outside, came to me personally, said the "buy in" was still valid but only if we paid there and then so we could claim we sealed the deal before the... well, before Weber died.'

Miles frowned and shook his head at this.

'I don't have anybody like that,' he said. 'It's just me and Veronica, and I don't have a bloody clue what you're talking about!'

His voice lowered, barely a whisper.

'Unless Marcel ...'

Gabriel Bauer didn't reply, staring coldly at the gallery owner as Miles knitted his eyebrows in thought.

'I gave this man two hundred and twenty-five thousand pounds,' he said. 'Payments for the paintings that I won, and an introduction for the purchase of the other seven. I would like my receipt.'

Bauer leant even closer, his tone more menacingly.

'I would also like my paintings. *All* of them.'

Miles swallowed, realising something had happened here he wasn't quite in control of.

'Gabriel, please,' he said. 'I don't have your money. I didn't take it.'

'Then you had better sort something out,' Bauer hissed. He was going to speak some more but there was a gentle clearing of a throat beside him, and as Bauer looked to his side he saw an old man, white-haired, with a goatee beard.

'Am I interrupting anything?' the man said, his voice broadly Scottish.

'I'm asking for my property.'

'I got that. I caught the end of your conversation,' the man showed his warrant card. 'Detective Superintendent Monroe. I think you might want to have your little chat later on, laddie, because we have dibs on Miles Benson before you do.'

He gave a dark smile.

'And I would suggest you hold back on your ideas about ownership of any paintings, because we might just be taking them as evidence.'

Bauer returned the smile. It wasn't warm, but it was a motion of acceptance... and then his phone beeped.

He pulled it out, read the message, and smiled.

'I'll speak to you soon, Miles,' he said, nodding to Detective Superintendent Monroe. 'And I'll be speaking to you as well. The gallery has taken my money.'

'Are you thinking of making a statement?'

'If I don't get my money back, I'm thinking of pressing charges. Or I might just take things into my own hands.'

'Yeah, I'd think twice about doing that on our patch, laddie,' Monroe's eyes flashed.

Bauer turned and walked away, heading towards a Mercedes parked down the street. After a moment, Monroe heard a weird deflating sound, and turned to see Miles releasing a long-kept breath, almost as a whimper.

'I'm really glad you came,' Miles said, staring after the car as it drove off. 'That's a man you don't want to piss off.'

'So why do it?'

'I didn't take his money,' Miles whined. 'I don't know how much you heard—'

'I heard most of the end,' Monroe said. 'I was just around the corner; thought I'd wait until a suitable moment to make an entrance.'

He looked around the gallery.

'So, let me see if I got this right, laddie,' he continued. 'Are you telling me there was somebody walking around your gallery last night, taking money off people without your knowledge?'

'I don't know anymore,' Miles leant against the wall, shuddering. 'It was chaos when Weber was found. Somebody must have realised there was an opportunity here.'

Monroe nodded at this.

'You have any suspects?'

Miles paled.

'No,' he replied. 'I ... no, I can't think of anyone.'

'So, whoever did it had to be at your party and knew what was going to happen?' Monroe asked. 'I think we need to have a look at that list.'

And, this said, Monroe invited Miles Benson to return into his gallery, indicating for them to head, finally, to his office.

FOLLOWING THE PHONE CALL FROM VERONICA BENSON, DECLAN had hurried to the address they had on record for the couple, an apartment slightly north of Stratford International

Station, and beside what was known as the Olympic Park. This area had undergone gentrification and revitalisation a decade earlier, during the 2012 London Olympics. Thinking about this, Declan couldn't help but smile, recalling a case a year earlier he had been involved in, one centred around a money laundering scheme from back then, utilising cheap real estate properties purchased by gangland criminals before the Olympics solely to profit from the upcoming gentrification. Declan even wondered if the apartment he was walking towards had once belonged to the Seven Sisters, the Simpsons, the Twins or the Tsangs.

The apartment was one of many similar buildings along a wide and eerily empty street, seven-storey apartment blocks built out of varying shades of grey brick on either side. Walking up to a ground floor door, a black one with the number "43" on it, Declan took a moment to examine the area. The apartments here probably ran to three quarters of a million each, so basically, the Bensons weren't struggling.

Knocking on the door, Declan waited a couple of moments and greeted Veronica Benson with a smile as she opened it. She was dressed in jogging bottoms and a sweatshirt, looking hot and flustered, as if she'd been for a run. Declan wondered however, if her perspiration was because of nervousness, commonly known as "flop sweat." After all, she had mentioned on the phone she thought Miles was a killer. That was enough to make anyone nervous.

'Detective Chief Inspector,' she said, stepping back. 'Please come in.'

Declan followed Veronica into the building, instantly reassessing his estimation of the mortgage value; this wasn't a two-bedroom maisonette, this was a four-bedroom townhouse. If they'd spent less than a million on this when first buying, he'd have been surprised.

As she spoke, mainly small talk about the area, filling the dead air as they moved through the house, Declan noticed she hadn't led him to the living room where most home interviews started. Instead, she guided him down a corridor towards a door with big red letters saying, "The Studio," painted on a mock easel cut out, and hung off the door.

Cutting to the chase, I see, he thought to himself.

'Okay, so can you explain to me what's going on?' he asked. 'Your phone call gave me the impression that you believe your husband ...'

He trailed off, hoping Veronica would continue.

'I found something yesterday,' she replied nervously. 'And I don't really know what it is. I was going to confront him about it, but then, last night ...'

Declan nodded, understanding the previous night probably wasn't the best time for personal chats.

'I get that. So, what are we looking at exactly?'

Veronica went to open the office door but encountered a problem – it didn't want to open.

'I don't understand,' Veronica muttered nervously, applying pressure and trying to open the door. 'He never locks his office.'

She rummaged through her pockets, still muttering to herself, although it was too soft for Declan to make out. Eventually she pulled a small keyring filled with door keys from her pocket.

'I think there's a copy on here,' she explained. 'We keep everything on it in case of emergencies.'

'Did you tell him you'd been in his office?' Declan asked while Veronica searched for the correct key.

'Do you think he locked the door because I told him I'd been in here?' she replied, her voice filled with uncertainty.

'Maybe,' Declan nodded. 'And this means whatever you were going to show me might be gone now.'

Finally, Veronica found the key she was looking for and opened the office door. As they walked in, Declan allowed Veronica to take the lead as she looked around the room.

'He hasn't changed anything,' she remarked with what looked to be a little relief. Declan wondered what Veronica had expected to be changed, but he didn't question further.

Walking over to the corner, Veronica pointed at a painting on an easel, but didn't approach it too closely, as if scared to be next to it.

'You need to look at that,' she said.

Declan approached and examined the painting – it looked to be a brutalist industrial design, or at least that's what he thought it was. It could have been anything if he was being honest with himself.

'What seems to be the problem?' he inquired, inspecting the edges of the frame.

'Turn it over,' Veronica urged.

Declan did as she said, and as he looked at the back of the painting he paused. The thick card was still inserted into the frame, and contained cut-out notes, newspaper clippings, and pieces of paper with interconnected scribbled down words, all linked with pieces of string. Declan recognised it as a crime board immediately. He had spent enough time with his father's own one to recognise it.

'Let me guess,' he said. 'You're worried your husband is a killer because of what's here?'

Veronica hesitated, unsure of what to say.

'I don't know what it means,' she finally replied. 'If you look, there's information about murders and ... and Lukas.'

Declan held up his hand, interrupting her as he examined the board – the last thing he wanted was Veronica guiding his eyes. He needed to take this all in before he focused on the minute details. Pulling out his phone, he opened the camera app and started taking photos. As Veronica had said, there were newspaper clippings about Lukas Weber, written in his native Austrian. Another piece, from an English paper, discussed war crimes committed by the Nazis in World War Two, and another appeared to be a torn page from a reference book, with selected text highlighted. As Declan leaned closer and read it, he realised it was about the ERR confiscating paintings from Jewish families during the war.

Aside from that, there were more newspaper clippings. One reported about a lady found dead in her Paris house a couple of weeks earlier. Another mentioned a murdered Salzburg university professor found in a car. To the side, there was a month-old piece, written in German, about another prominent artist being murdered. Declan couldn't read the text, but he noticed the word 'Berlin' and wondered if it was related to the case Margaret Li had been working on.

'Do you see what I mean?' Veronica asked. 'Do you think he killed them? Is this his trophy wall?'

Declan shook his head.

'I've worked in this business for a long time, Mrs Benson,' he replied. 'I can tell you now, this isn't normal and it seems to be related to the investigation. But it feels like there's something else going on here. I think your husband needs to explain how he knows more about Lukas Weber and the murders than he's let on, but currently, I don't think he's the killer.'

He pointed at the string.

'This is a common tool used to link things together when investigating,' he said. 'If he'd done the killings, he wouldn't need to.'

Veronica didn't seem convinced as she looked at the newspaper clipping dates.

'What about them?' she asked.

Declan frowned at this.

'The dates?'

'They match when he was abroad,' Veronica replied quietly, nodding. 'He was in Paris around the same time, Salzburg too ...'

Declan glanced back at the paintings. If Miles had been present in the same locations as the murders, it meant Miles was either hunting the killer ... or he was the killer himself.

And that changed everything.

8
———

BACK ROOMS

Monroe paused as he entered Miles's office, looking around as he did so.

It almost looked like a tiny version of the gallery space, with white walls and paintings on all sides, although this one had what looked to be a black onyx-topped desk at the very end.

On the desk was an Apple MacBook, a separate monitor and a few knickknacks, and apart from a small filing cabinet at the back – one that looked wide enough to place A2 sheets in – there wasn't much else here.

'I like what you've done with the place,' Monroe said, walking over and examining a painting.

'I wish I could do this with my other office, I'll be honest,' Miles smiled as he walked over to his desk, sitting down. 'I have a home office back in Stratford, and that's a lot messier. This is more for the day to day, the things that need to get done.'

Monroe nodded, taking the office chair in front of the desk and settling into it, facing Miles.

'I hope you don't mind my interruption,' he said. 'It's just we had a few more questions we wanted to ask.'

'No, I get that,' Miles smiled. 'And you saved me from a close call so please, anything we can do to help.'

Monroe pulled out his notebook.

'You spoke to my colleague last night about Lukas Weber,' he said. 'I was hoping, with time passed, that newer thoughts came to mind in the early hours of the morning?'

'I didn't really meet him that much,' Miles leant forwards, resting his arms on the table. 'Andrew, he's the one who dealt with him. He's back later today if you want to speak to him.'

'Aye, I'll be speaking to him later,' Monroe nodded. 'But I want to hear about him from you.'

'He's quiet – well, he *was* quiet – kept to himself, and I kind of felt like he was on the spectrum, you know?'

'Let's pretend I don't know.'

'He was socially inept. You know, twenty years ago someone would have said he was eccentric. Now people just say he's autistic.'

Monroe wrote this down.

'I thought only rich people could be eccentric?' he asked.

'He is rich,' Miles replied. 'He wasn't a penniless artist that we brought over. The Webers have family money. Although, I think he's ostracised, so maybe he is poor.'

'Oh, aye?' Monroe raised an eyebrow.

'I don't know much about it. I don't really *want* to know much about it. I'm guessing it's probably family money made from when granddad was a ...'

Monroe understood very well what Miles was talking about.

Miles, however, continued.

'All I know is that Andrew found him in Austria, realised

his artwork was good enough to get us some solid commissions, and he has a bit of an underground reputation for his work.'

'But he's unknown?' Monroe asked.

'Well, he's kind of Austria famous,' Miles replied. 'But let's be honest, Austria is only famous for things like strudel and Arnold Schwarzenegger, so there's not much of an audience for his paintings, and the fact he agreed to have his paintings sold in London should give you an idea of what he thinks they're worth.'

Monroe nodded, noting this down.

'You were at the event from the beginning,' he said. 'Was Weber off at all? Did he look worried? Like he knew someone was after him?'

'He was around near the start,' Miles nodded. 'But he kept to himself. He didn't really want the people to know he was the artist. So, he stayed around the back, pretended to be a buyer.'

'Did you see him talk to anyone?'

'A couple of people here and there. Someone might have asked about a painting or given their opinion and I saw him at one point correct someone, saying one of his pieces was more to do with the futility of life than what the critic thought it was.'

'What did they think it was?'

'Something to do with farmyard implements. I didn't quite get the full conversation but I think he gave himself away at that point and realised it, so before anybody could catch on the artist was in the room, he disappeared quickly.'

'Did you see him again?'

'I glimpsed him.' Miles nodded. 'I was in the office picking something up, and he walked in. He was annoyed at some of the painting placements. We sat down and I went through every single piece with him. He knew what was being displayed from the very beginning, but he was right, we swapped it quickly, and he was fine.'

Miles sighed.

'There was a painting that he was annoyed had been brought across. But do you know the funniest part? Andrew, my brother, claimed Weber did know. Bloody Lukas Weber was the reason it was there.'

Monroe noted this down.

'Tell me about the painting that was stolen.'

'I don't know much about it,' Miles admitted, 'I can tell you it wasn't very good. He's done better. But some of those paintings were going for crazy money. We had early bids for ten, even twenty thousand pounds on some of the cheaper ones. We knew that some of his bigger paintings would easily hit mid five figures. Maybe even six.'

'This was an auction?'

Miles nodded.

'And the painting he didn't want out?'

'I think there were seven paintings in total he'd put aside, and I think he had a private buyer for them, something Andrew was sorting, but Andrew wasn't about to keep us in the loop.'

'Could that have been the "buy in" your friend outside mentioned?'

Miles Benson stroked his chin for a moment.

'Oh, that stupid bastard,' he muttered. 'Always lining his own pockets, not bothering to tell me, and allowing me to clean up the shit when he's not here.'

'But he's here later?'

Miles smiled, but it was a thin-lipped, humourless one.

'Until I kill him,' he muttered, paling as he realised what he'd said. 'Sorry, bad joke.'

Ignoring the comment, Monroe pulled a sheet from his pocket, unfolding and passing it across.

It was a printout photo of Krohn.

'Do you recognise this man?' he said.

'I told your officer; we don't have anyone like that on our books—'

'I didn't ask that,' Monroe leant closer. 'I asked if you *recognised* him.'

Miles's face darkened as he realised Monroe already seemed to know the answer.

'Yeah, I know him,' he eventually said.

'You told our officer you didn't recognise the sketch of him.'

'That was a sketch. This is a photo.'

'Apparently it was a photorealistic sketch.'

'Whatever. I didn't recognise him then. I recognise him here. He's banned from our events.'

'Really? Then why was he here last night?'

'I can't answer that, because if we'd seen him we would have blocked his entrance. He claims he's a restorer, but he's a middleman for forgers.'

'You think he could have taken the painting?'

'I don't know. It was chaos after Weber died. Just look at Bauer, claiming he'd given money to someone. Krohn could have got in, taken the painting ... hell, he might even have brought the guy who ripped us off in with him.'

'I wanted to ask you about that,' Monroe said. 'Do you usually take the money at the end of the night?'

'Christ, no!' Miles almost exploded. 'And we weren't taking it last night, either. I told Veronica to stop the bids, not get payment for them. We knew we'd be out a ton of money the moment Weber died.'

'Not when he was outed as a potential Nazi?'

Miles smiled slightly at this.

'There's a darkness in the soul,' he replied carefully. 'It gives us a morbid curiosity. The "outing" of Weber, whether or not it was true actively helped us. But we didn't know at the time Weber was dead.'

Miles got up, walking over to the painting Monroe had examined when he arrived, staring at it.

'This is a Marsdale,' he said, tapping the frame. 'You won't have heard of him, nobody has. I bought this at a car boot sale for about fifty quid. A year later, he died of a terrible drug overdose, and he was all over the papers. I saw a painting just like this go for forty grand at auction last month. Death is always good for sales.'

Monroe wrote this down.

'So, if I'm right, you didn't want to sell anything but someone was going around doing it anyway?'

Miles nodded.

'It's usually given that at the end of our events, the highest bid at a set time wins and before they go home, depending on our relationship with them they'll give a deposit, usually a quarter of the cost. It's a proof of intent. That way, if someone got too excited about bidding and now can't afford it, it drops to the next highest bidder.'

'But you didn't do that last night.'

'No,' Miles replied. 'The moment Weber died, we cancelled all bids. We said nothing was going through. We didn't know who would run the estate. They might want everything back; if we sold low, they could claim we owed them.'

Monroe shifted in his chair, watching the art dealer.

'Is that really why you did it?' he asked.

Miles didn't answer the question, staring coldly at Monroe.

'We had the wishes of his family in mind,' he said eventually.

Monroe wanted to argue the case, but the day was moving on, and he had a German police officer to meet later.

'We asked about CCTV last night,' he said. 'We haven't received anything yet.'

'As I said to your people, we only really have the exhibition space watched because that's where the paintings are,' Miles walked back to the desk. 'That's where the product is. We're not bad people, Detective Superintendent. We just want to make our way in the business, introduce new artists to the world while at the same time making a little profit.'

'I never said you were bad,' Monroe said, placing his notebook away. 'We'll have more questions for you later. But for the moment, have a think about what you've forgotten to tell me. Things always pop up down the line.'

'I told you everything I told your colleague,' Miles muttered. 'This feels a little like harassment.'

'Aye? Well, if it is, it's harassment that confirmed you knew Gary Krohn, and had a mysterious seller taking money from clients, so it's not all bad, is it?' Monroe gave a smile. 'And I'd suggest asking around and seeing whether this seller convinced anyone else to part with their money.'

And, with this spoken, and Miles now blanching at the thought, Monroe rose from the chair, walking to the door of Miles's office.

'One last thing,' he said, looking back. 'Lucy Cormorant,

the one who stood up and shouted at you. Did you know she was turning up?'

Miles frowned at this.

'Why would you think it was something I knew about?'

'As you said, something like this would probably pique the morbid curiosity of your buyers. It could have helped you make a pretty penny.'

'Her appearance was completely surprising to everyone watching me,' Miles replied, irritated now. However, Monroe noted Miles's changing of the question when he gave his answer.

'And her ability to gain an invitation to the event?' he asked.

Miles shrugged, refusing to answer, his lips thin and angry and Monroe gave a last nod and left the office, exiting the gallery through the front entrance.

Monroe had wondered about Lucy Cormorant; it seemed too easy for her to get in, to know when to be there, without someone on the inside guiding her along.

But could Gary Krohn have brought her in to divert from his theft?

Monroe didn't like the questions this gave him. A murder, a theft, a diversion; were they connected, or just coincidentally on the same night? He'd wondered whether this was more of a plan than he thought it would be, and whether Miles Benson had been more involved than he'd claimed. Pulling out his phone he was going to make a call as he started his five-minute walk back to Temple Inn; it was a nice day ... but as he did so something out of the corner of his eye stopped him.

There was a motorcycle moving up behind, but it was

slow, moving as if the rider was lost and trying to read street markings.

In the building's mirror window beside him, Monroe saw the rider, in black leather and a blacked-out visor pull a gun from their jacket.

It was instinctive – Monroe ducked to the floor, diving forward, a car parked at the side of the road now between him and the passing motorcycle. He heard three *pop* sounds, sounding like nothing more than compressed air, really. And then the bike, nothing more than a 125cc sped off, screeching away.

When Monroe rose, looking at the building beside him, one window had been broken, a visible bullet hole within the glass. The wall beside it had two pockmarks in it where the other two rounds had struck.

Brushing himself down, Monroe stared after the bike, trying to remember everything he could about it.

Someone had just tried to kill him.

For a surprising moment, and for a not-so-welcome change, Monroe didn't know why.

9

FOUND FOOTAGE

As Andrew Benson arrived at customs at Stansted Airport, the one thing he probably hadn't expected was to be held to the side as police officers arrived.

'What have I done?' he asked, confused as a door to the side opened, and Anjli walked into the hall, showing a warrant card to him as she approached.

'Andrew Benson? I'm Detective Inspector Anjli Kapoor,' she said, offering a hand towards the door she'd appeared through. 'We need to have a quick chat about Lukas Weber.'

'Am I in trouble?' Andrew asked nervously, glancing around. 'The art I have, it's legit. I have paperwork.'

Anjli paused.

'Have you not spoken to your brother yet?' she asked. 'Or seen the news?'

Andrew's blank expression gave her all she needed.

'Lukas Weber? He was murdered last night.'

Andrew didn't seem surprised; if anything, he seemed relieved.

'Thank God,' he said. 'I thought I was in trouble.'

Anjli raised an eyebrow at this.

'Your compassion knows no bounds, Mister Benson.'

Now in the side room, and away from the gawking travellers and holidaymakers, Andrew Benson slumped into a chair with relief.

'Guy was a Nazi, deserved it,' he said. 'I never wanted him in the gallery. Miles did, and we both knew he'd make us money. I suppose he'll make us more now.'

He smiled.

'And as you said, he was murdered while I was in a different country. So, I can't exactly be a prime suspect now, can I?'

'But your brother is,' Anjli replied, standing over Andrew now. 'Doesn't that worry you?'

Andrew shrugged.

'What he does in his own time is his concern,' he said, completely unconcerned. 'And, more importantly, am I under arrest for anything?'

'What do you know about a painting Mister Weber didn't want brought over?' Anjli ignored the question.

At this, however, Andrew laughed.

'Oh, God, is this what everything's about?' he asked. 'If you bring it to me, I can explain everything.'

'That might be a little more difficult than you expect,' Anjli smiled darkly. 'It was stolen last night.'

If Andrew had expected this as an answer, he made a damned good show of not looking so. His face purpled in anger as he shot to his feet.

'The painting's gone?' he snapped. 'You need to get it back! Who took it? It was... they don't know what they have!'

'Then why don't you tell me what they have first, Mister Benson?' Anjli rested a hand on his shoulder, guiding him back into the chair. 'And tell me about these arrangements? Because we have all the time in the world—'

She stopped, frowning as her phone buzzed. Glancing down, she saw a message from Billy.

> 9-9-9 - Monroe shot at - all hands on deck
> we could all be targeted

Quickly she typed a reply:

> Was he hit

A moment later, the reply came through from Billy:

> No but it was pure luck he saw it

'Shit,' she muttered, placing the phone away and looking at the officers. 'Okay, we're heading back to London.'

'Wait, am I under arrest or what?' Andrew grumbled as one officer helped him to his feet.

Angry now, mainly because of the contents of the text, Anjli spun to face the man.

'Of course not,' she said sweetly. 'We know how much of a pain it is to get from Stansted to London, so we thought we'd give you a lift. After all, I'm heading back there anyway.'

Before Andrew could say anything else, she leant closer.

'But, if you decide to refuse our ever so kind offer, I'll leave and go alone, while my colleagues here check every piece of your luggage to see what exactly you brought home with you.'

'I have receipts and visas,' Andrew muttered back, but it was uncertain, like he was trying to use bluster and bravado to back the police off.

'Let's hope so,' Anjli smiled. 'It'd be such a shame if you didn't.'

Sighing with resignation, Andrew nodded.

'I'd love a lift,' he mumbled.

'Excellent,' Anjli waved for one officer to open the door. 'We can have a pleasant chat on the way there. Oh, by the way, do you know a Gary Krohn?'

Grabbing his bags, Andrew nodded.

'Yeah,' he replied. 'Why?'

'Because we think he stole the painting. Do you know anything about that?'

Andrew's shoulders slumped even more.

'Yeah,' he sighed. 'I think he misunderstood a request I gave him.'

Anjli nodded, holding the door open.

'Oh, we're going to have such a fun chat,' she said. 'And then we're going to chat to Mister Krohn, too.'

DECLAN HAD RECEIVED THE CALL ON HIS WAY BACK FROM Stratford. There had been little else for Declan to see in the home office; he'd tried his best to look around a little more, but Veronica was only happy to show him the painting - or rather, the collection of clippings hidden behind it. So, with Veronica no longer answering questions now she knew her husband might not actually have been a murderer, he had left, deciding to contact Monroe. The last time they'd spoken was when Monroe left the office in a hurry and had shouted, while leaving that he was going to see Miles Benson, so Declan wanted to check if he was still there, and if so whether they could bring Miles in for a moment or two, if only to answer why he had such a disturbing collection of clippings in his office.

He'd also sent the photos to Billy, asking if there was any way to translate the clippings, but Billy had replied with some snarky comment about how *the photos weren't high enough definition*, before sending a second one a moment later saying *not to worry, he'd found another way*, and *yes, Declan could feel smug for being right.*

Declan *had* felt smug.

However, before he could call his boss Billy had sent another message, a 9-9-9 one that wasn't connected to either of his earlier ones, and less than fifteen minutes later Declan was outside the Benson's Chancery Lane Gallery, which once more was surrounded by crime scene tape.

This time however, it wasn't to do with the gallery, but more to do with an area of building around thirty feet to the west where three bullet holes could be seen, with one having shattered the glass of a nearby building looking out onto the lane.

Doctor Marcos was there, already investigating the wall, poking at the holes in the brickwork with what looked to be a pair of tweezers. Monroe, meanwhile, was standing to the side surrounded by uniformed officers, De'Geer front and foremost, and glaring angrily at everybody who walked past.

'I'm fine, laddie,' he said angrily, holding his hand up to stop Declan before he could speak. 'I don't need you checking up on me.'

Declan shrugged.

'You've had worse,' he said. 'I assumed you were fine.'

He looked back at the gallery, only a few yards to the right.

'What I can't work out is whether they were trying to kill

you, or someone coming out of the gallery,' he asked carefully as if not wanting to rock the boat or say something wrong. But it was the expression he gave that was the important part; an expression that said *would you like to tell me if someone was trying to shoot you, and why they were doing it this time, boss?*

Monroe pursed his lips together.

'I don't think they were after anybody connected to the case,' he said. 'I think they were looking for me.'

'Why would somebody want to kill you?' Declan asked before shaking his head. 'I mean, apart from all the usual suspects and obvious candidates?'

'Well, I was wondering that myself,' Monroe replied, glancing over at Doctor Marcos, who was now stepping away from the wall and watching them both. 'Maybe Tweedle Dum and bloody Tweedle Dee can explain it.'

Doctor Marcos sighed, looked across the road and waved.

Declan glanced across Chancery Lane and saw Derek Sutton standing there, keeping out of the way.

'What the bloody hell is he doing in London?' he asked without thinking.

'Aye, that's my question as well,' Monroe grumbled as Sutton straightened, adjusted his cuffs, and walked across the street. 'Because these two eejits have been having secret meetings.'

'And keeping you out of the loop for a reason, Ali,' Sutton said as he approached. 'We didn't want you going off half-cocked and trying to sort something out that could get you killed.'

'Oh, aye?' Monroe said, pointing at the bullet marks on the brickwork. 'And how's that working out for you?'

Doctor Marcos pulled off her blue latex gloves, running her hand through her hair.

'Lennie Wright is going to trial,' she said. 'Derek heard up in Glasgow there was a hit on you.'

Monroe looked quizzically at Sutton, who shrugged.

'I'm out, I swear,' he replied. 'But you know how it is. I hear things.'

'Do we know who's brokering the deal in London?' Declan asked.

'We think it's Harvey Drake,' Doctor Marcos replied. 'We were trying to work out who he'd booked for the job—'

'And you didn't think of bringing me in on this?' Monroe was both angry and hurt at the same time.

'We didn't think it was important enough at this point,' Doctor Marcos explained. 'We didn't even know if it was going to happen.'

'We were hoping we could find out who it was, Ali - and scare them off before they even tried,' Sutton added.

'Well, now we know you didn't do either of these things,' Monroe mused, as he stared back at the bullet holes. 'Aye, so there's a hit on me. Perhaps we can do something different to how you planned it? Perhaps like arresting Harvey sodding Drake before they try to do it again?'

Declan frowned, looking around the street.

'How did they manage to do it in the first place?' he asked to a wealth of blank faces. 'Think about it. How did they know the Guv was here?'

He looked back at Monroe.

'Did you tell anybody you were coming here?'

'Only you and Billy, and that was as I left,' Monroe admitted. 'But I didn't come straight here. I was following Rosanna.'

'You were what?' Doctor Marcos was livid at this. Monroe, however, was unrepentant.

'I'd asked Mastakin, who was on desk duty to keep me informed if you suddenly left the building,' he explained. 'I bloody knew something was going on, and that you were too bloody stubborn to tell me so I followed you to the South Bank and watched you talking to Sutton in the pub.'

'That still doesn't explain how they knew you were here,' Declan shook his head. 'Could you have been followed?'

Monroe paled.

'There was a man - well, only a lad,' he said. 'He was snapping the Thames as I was watching outside, and as I left I bumped into him, almost knocked his camera into the water. It was a split second. I wasn't even thinking about it.'

He rummaged in his pockets.

'Makes sense Drake had someone outside watching,' Sutton muttered.

'Aye well you could've warned me, you bampot.'

'How were we gonna warn you, Ali, when we didn't bloody know you were even there?' Sutton reddened.

Monroe didn't reply, still rummaging through his jacket pockets.

'You think he pickpocketed you?' Declan narrowed his eyes as he watched.

'No, laddie, I think he gave me something instead,' Monroe replied, pulling out a small grey piece of plastic. 'This, for example.'

Doctor Marcos took it, examining and holding it up to the light.

'Could be some kind of tracking device,' she said. 'You know, like an AirTag, or the ones Billy always sneaks into our pockets because he's scared we'll all leave him one day.'

She slammed the piece of plastic back into Monroe's hand.

'This is why we weren't telling you anything,' she retorted. 'If you hadn't followed us, he wouldn't have spotted you. He wouldn't have placed the tracker on you. He wouldn't have tried to kill you.'

'Aye,' Monroe said. 'Or Drake knew you were following him and set up a fake meeting at a place he needed you to be at. If I hadn't turned up, one of you would have been tracked.'

He sighed, looking up at the sky.

'If it wasn't me being shot at, it would have been you.'

As Doctor Marcos's face darkened and she went to open her mouth, most likely to give Monroe another piece of her mind, Declan held a hand up.

'Arguing isn't really going to help anything here,' he said. 'All we know now is that *they* know you're looking for them, and they have a hit on *you*.'

He aimed this last piece at Monroe.

'So, we need to get you somewhere safe.'

'To hell with that,' Monroe exclaimed. 'We're in the middle of a murder case.'

'Guv,' Declan replied carefully. 'You're a Detective Superintendent now. Your job is to stay in your office. Perhaps, for a change, you could do that?'

'Fine, I'll liaise with Margaret Li when she turns up,' Monroe deflated, passing Declan the piece of plastic. 'Give this to Billy, see if he can find anything else. Maybe we can get an idea of where it comes from, or even who it was that gave it to me.'

This said, he turned and walked away.

'Guv—' Declan spoke, and Monroe stopped and looked back.

'If you're about to tell me I need to have some kind of police escort to go twenty yards down the street, we're going to have a wee chat,' he said.

Declan shook his head, passing Monroe back the tracker.

'I was just going to say that they could be watching,' he replied. 'I suggest you take someone more expendable who could jump in front of your bullet.'

Monroe looked over at Derek Sutton.

'Aye, I'll take this useless bastard,' he said. 'And why do I have the tracker again?'

'Because you'll be seeing Billy first,' Declan replied, already heading towards the gallery. 'I need a wee chat with Mister Benson.'

'A wee chat, you say?' Monroe laughed for the first time during this whole conversation. 'Now you're sounding like a DCI, laddie.'

10

BROTHERLY LOVE

THE FIRST PROBLEM DECLAN HAD WHEN TRYING TO CONTACT Miles Benson, was that Miles Benson didn't want to be contacted.

As the police started tidying up, removing tape and returning to Temple Inn, Declan found himself hammering repeatedly on the glass doors of the Benson Gallery.

'Come on, Miles, open up,' he shouted through the letter-box. There wasn't any kind of speaker system, and the buzzer didn't seem to work. After a couple of minutes, he was about to give up and phone the gallery directly when the door at the back of the main gallery opened, and a confused and nervous Miles Benson started walking towards the door, speeding up when he realised it was the Detective Chief Inspector standing outside.

Opening the door, he gave an apologetic smile.

'Sorry,' he said, 'I didn't realise it was you.'

'Who did you think it could be?' Declan asked.

'Creditors,' Miles replied honestly. 'It seems somebody was selling our paintings when we weren't aware of it. An angry Argentine at the door before your boss turned up added to that. Then, having three gunshots outside and a whole load of police wandering around made me a little twitchy. So, I closed the door and hid in my office.'

'I get that,' Declan nodded. 'But I'm afraid you're going to have to answer a few quick questions for me.'

'Can we do it later?' Miles asked nervously, looking around, 'It's just that ...'

'No,' Declan interrupted. 'We do it now. I'd like to know why you have a crime board hidden on the back of a painting in your office.'

At the words Miles seemed to sag, his legs giving way underneath him as he leant against the door.

'Oh God,' he said, 'I thought she might have seen it. Oh, God. Oh, oh, no. Oh, God.'

He started wringing his hands together and Declan, feeling a little sorry for him, placed a reassuring hand on his shoulder.

'Look, I'm sure it's not as bad as it looks,' he said, 'I mean, you weren't killing the people, were you?'

Miles shook his head.

'But you knew more than you let on,' Declan continued, his voice ice cold. 'In fact, looking at it, you seem to know more about the killer than we do.'

Miles nodded quietly.

'So why don't you tell me about your crime board?' Declan continued. 'In particular, who you think is doing the killings?'

Miles paused, as if unwilling to reply and then, as if a weight was removed from his shoulders, he slumped.

'Andrew,' he replied simply. 'I'm worried it's Andrew.'

'Your brother?' Declan hadn't expected this answer. 'Why do you think your brother could be the killer?'

'Because I've seen where the killings were,' Miles shot back. 'There was a man in Salzburg, there was a woman in Paris, and both times we were there and I know it wasn't me. Even the Berlin murder, I think Andrew was there then.'

'So, you instantly think it's your brother,' Declan was quite surprised at the heartlessness of the situation, even if Miles could be correct.

Miles said nothing, looking at the ground as if ashamed.

Eventually he looked back up.

'As I said,' he replied. 'It seems the obvious answer.'

'You knew what the lipstick kiss meant, didn't you?' Declan asked.

'I knew people had it when they were found,' Miles replied. 'But I don't know why. I swear I was just picking up clues and pieces about the murders.'

'Because you thought your brother was killing people?'

'Yes.'

'But what about now?' Declan asked, 'Do you still think he's killing people?'

'He wasn't here yesterday,' Miles shook his head.

'There's no way he could have hired someone or paid someone on board to do it for him?'

'We might have had our differences, but we always paid attention to what was going on,' Miles continued to shake his head.

'Would Andrew have used Gary Krohn?' Declan asked, playing a hunch. At this, Miles shook his head even more vigorously, and Declan wondered if it was about to fall off his neck with the force.

'He hated Weber. More than I did,' he said. 'He was the one ...'

He trailed off as if something terrible had come to mind.

'Hold on,' he continued. 'The last time Gary was here was an event Andrew had run. I'd been angry that he'd been there, but Andrew said he'd been doing some work for him. I didn't know what the work was. Maybe you should ask him.'

'Andrew?'

'No, Gary,' Miles replied. 'I can give you an address.'

'There's no need,' Declan replied. 'We have it, and we'll be making our way to him next. In the meantime, don't go anywhere. We'll be coming to speak to you very soon.'

Miles, almost relieved this was over, nodded. Declan was about to leave when the door to the gallery opened, and Anjli stood in the entranceway.

'I bloody missed everything, didn't I?' she asked. 'Someone shot at the Guv and I missed it?'

She looked at Miles, and a dark smile appeared at the edge of her lips.

'Mister Benson,' she said. 'I've just been talking to your brother. He was quite the talker.'

'Is he with you?' Declan looked behind her. Anjli, however, shook her head.

'Let him go home before he comes in to sort a statement,' she replied. 'He was telling me all about Gary Krohn. I was thinking about paying him a visit.'

'That's interesting,' Declan gave Miles a smile. 'We were just deciding the exact same thing.'

He walked past Anjli and into the street.

'Your car or mine?' he asked.

'Yours,' Anjli grinned. 'I just had to drive back from Stansted in afternoon traffic.'

BILLY HAD FOUND AN ADDRESS FOR THEM; A GALLERY IN Shoreditch, and with Monroe in a bad mood, Declan really didn't want to go back to the office right now. So, instead of entering the Temple Inn unit they climbed quickly into Declan's Audi and headed north east before anyone could stop them.

The studio itself was an office space on the fourth floor of a red-brick building to the right of Shoreditch High Street, away from the overground station and bordering on the north end of Brick Lane. It was a mishmash of old and new with chrome buildings next to older revitalised ones, and Declan walked up to the main entrance, trying the door, realising it was locked.

There was a selection of buttons beside the door, each one with names written on them. One button said "Krohn Restoring" so assuming that was the correct one, Declan buzzed.

After a few moments, Declan buzzed again.

'Maybe he's out,' Anjli suggested.

'Yeah, I'll give him one more go,' Declan replied, but before he could do so there was a click as the speaker in the wall came to life.

'Hello?' It was a man's voice; middle-aged, with a strong East End accent showing through.

'Is that Mr. Krohn?' Declan asked.

'Not today. Thank you.' There was a slight wavering in Gary Krohn's voice, if it even was the man himself.

Declan glanced at Anjli.

'Mr. Krohn, we really need you to open this door. You said—'

'No thanks.'

'This is Detective Chief Inspector Walsh and Detective Inspector Kapoor of the City of London Police,' Anjli leant closer to the speaker now. 'We'd like to talk—'

'Not now,' Gary Krohn's voice interrupted through the speaker. 'I'm in the middle of something. Can you come back later?'

Declan tensed. The voice was nervous. Worried, even.

'Mr. Krohn, I don't think you under—'

'Oh, I understand very well,' the voice replied. 'I think you should leave.'

And then suddenly, as if changing his mind, Gary Krohn's voice rose in pitch and tone.

'They've got a knife—'

There was a click as the speaker was turned off, someone on the other end disconnecting the call.

Declan glanced back at Anjli.

'Someone's with him,' he said, trying the door again. 'Dammit, we need to get up there.'

Before he could do anything else, though, there was a crashing sound four floors above them, and a human-shaped figure smashed through the glass of one of the building's office windows, falling and slamming to the ground only seven feet away from them.

Declan and Anjli jumped back instinctively, but they were still close enough to see with no doubt the body was Gary Krohn, his obviously dead, glassy eyes staring blankly at them in return.

Anjli was already pressing every single button on the pad as Declan looked up at the now shattered window. After a couple of seconds, several irritated people answered.

'City of London police!' she shouted down the line. 'Open this door now!'

Usually, people would be less trusting, asking for proof of identity, but this time, perhaps the loud crash followed by the urgency in her tone stopped this, and half a second later, the door opened.

'Go around the back!' Declan shouted as he ran through it. 'Check for fire escapes!'

'Fourth floor, third on the right,' Anjli shouted back as she started down the side road.

But Declan was already sprinting up the stairs. A dead sprint up four storeys was exhausting, but he liked his park runs, and if anything, all this would do was build up a small amount of lactic acid in his legs. That said, by the time he got to the fourth floor, he was having to stop and hold his sides for a second, realising he'd woefully underrated the effort.

The door to Gary Krohn's studio, the third on the right was open, and Declan glanced quickly in, seeing that there had been some kind of scuffle. The furniture was knocked over, there was paint all over the doorway, and a broken lamp was on the floor next to the more visible broken window. From the looks of things, Krohn had fought back, maybe even tried to escape, resulting in his death.

There was a slamming of a door to his left and Declan turned, seeing down the other end of the corridor where a fire escape door had just closed. Sprinting for it, Declan knew the killer had just used this as his escape.

Breaking through the emergency exit, he found himself on a stairway. Looking up, he could see a black-clad figure hurrying towards the roof. They were half-blocked by the banister, so he couldn't get a good look, and they were looking away – but he could see they wore a black bomber jacket over a black hoodie, the hood up and covering the killer's hair, and what looked to be black neoprene gloves.

'Stop right there!' he shouted. 'City of London Police.'

If anything, all this did was spur the black-clad figure on harder, and Declan grumbled as he started up the stairs, pulling out his extendable baton as he did so, flicking it open. He didn't know what was going to happen here, but the last thing he wanted to do was start a fight with a killer with nothing in his hands. The extendable baton had helped him many times in the past, and this, added to his military training meant whoever was heading towards the roof was about to have a very bad time.

He didn't catch the black-clad figure before they got onto the roof though, and as Declan followed through the door, finding himself now on the rooftops of London, he paused for a moment.

They were six, maybe seven floors in the air now, with a large drop to the Shoreditch streets beside them. Ahead, he could see the black-clad figure better now as they carried on, stepping carefully across the rooftop. They were slim, and he'd say about the same height as him. They wore black trousers under the bomber jacket and hoodie and had some kind of face mask and sunglasses combo on to hide their face.

'Freeze!' Declan shouted again in a vain attempt to halt the black-clad figure. However, the figure was concentrating more on not falling off the roof, something that had slowed them down. And, importantly, something that gave Declan an advantage.

This wasn't the first time he'd run across the roofs of London in a hurry. It was, however, the first time he had been chasing someone rather than being chased. But this meant that Declan could pick up a little speed here, using his prior experience to give him a slight edge as he continued rushing after the mysterious figure as they ran along the building's line.

There was an alley between the buildings, and the mysterious figure stumbled as they reached it, pausing, glancing back at Declan before reluctantly making a jump, landing easily on the other side and carrying on. Declan, having seen the jump knew he could make it, and so didn't pause as he ran after the killer, leaping the gap between buildings, landing carefully on the other side and continuing on. The pause of the figure and the stumble they had given the other side of the building was enough to give Declan more of an advantage, and now he was almost on them as they ran towards another set of stairs.

There was another door leading down into the new building here, and Declan realised if the killer got through, then they would have an advantage heading downwards; this spurred him on to run a little faster as he caught up to the killer. However, they weren't aiming for the door now. They'd realised that Declan was going to catch them and had decided to fight him instead, pulling out what looked to be a machete, waving it viciously in front of them.

When Gary Krohn had mentioned a "knife," he'd *seriously* understated it.

'Back off,' they said, their voice strangely melodic, and audibly male.

Declan batted aside the machete with his baton.

'Give up,' he said. 'I'll make this easy for you.'

The figure, now definitely a man, laughed and lunged, the machete swiping at Declan's chest. But Declan had been waiting for this and spun to the side, letting it go past him, grabbing at the killer with his free hand as he stepped closer.

The black-clad man stumbled, overbalanced, his face still hidden. Declan wanted to grab the sunglasses, pulling them off – but before he could do so, the man had spun, making a second attack. This time, however, Declan could swing viciously with his baton, catching the killer's wrist hard on the knuckles, knocking the machete flying away from the attacker's hand, clattering down the side of the building and tumbling off the edge, as the attacker yelped in pain, grabbing his possibly broken wrist.

No longer armed, the black-clad attacker realised there was no way he could beat the detective chasing him, and before Declan could grab him, he had already pulled open the door and started towards the stairs. However, Declan once more grabbed the black bomber jacket, his hand grasping onto one pocket.

But the black-clad man hadn't been going down the stairs. It had been a feint, and as Declan grabbed him, the man spun, sending Declan's momentum forward.

For a split second, Declan realised he was about to fall down a flight of stairs and was unable to stop himself ...

And then he fell.

It wasn't a full set of stairs, only ten or twelve steps at best, but it was still enough to wind him as he tumbled to the bottom, staring dazed up at the door.

The man stared at him, his jacket pocket torn from the force of Declan's fall.

'Stay down, detective,' he said.

And then the man shut the door, continuing along the rooftops.

Declan reached up and touched his forehead, feeling the slickness of blood from a wound he'd gained from the staircase's stone edges, as he'd slammed his skull against one of them. His vision was wavering as he stared blankly around and rose gently to his feet. He fought back an urge to vomit, partly because he didn't want to be sick, but more importantly, because he didn't want to be sick until he had examined the item of paper that was in front of him on the floor.

There was an old receipt, some kind of slip of thermal paper, the text almost unreadable that had been in the black-clad man's jacket, and which had fallen out when Declan had torn the pocket's side. Reaching shakily into his jacket pocket, Declan pulled out a baggie and a pair of tweezers, using them to place the almost faded receipt into the bag.

He sealed it and placed it back into his pocket, settled against the wall ...

And then passed out.

11

POST-RACE TRAUMA

'YOU'RE A BLOODY IDIOT,' ANJLI SAID AS DECLAN SAT AT THE back of an ambulance, the paramedic bandaging his head. 'You could have been killed! What do you think you were doing, running across the roofs?'

'I thought I was catching a killer,' Declan said, leaning back, still fighting the urge to be sick. 'Could you not shout at me for a second? It's really hard to keep focus.'

'You need to go home,' the paramedic added, finishing up. 'You've probably got a concussion.'

'Did they find the machete?' ignoring the paramedic's advice, Declan looked back at Anjli who nodded, pointing at De'Geer, currently standing with some other forensics officers outside the blue tent which had been hastily erected over the body of Gary Krohn.

'It was down an alley to the side of the building,' she said. 'It was pretty battered after the fall, but they reckon they've got enough there to hunt for prints, or at least work out who owned it.'

'That's something at least,' Declan groaned as a band of

pain squeezed his forehead. 'Maybe we'll be lucky, and he picked it up before he put gloves on. The receipt?'

'Checking into it now,' Anjli said as Declan looked back up at the shattered window. 'They'll let us know if they find anything.'

'Has anybody been in the office yet?' he asked.

'Doctor Marcos is still giving it a sweep. And no, we haven't found the painting, if that's what you're about to ask. In fact, she said it looked like nobody had even looked for it.'

Declan swallowed, looking around.

'Anyone have some water?' he asked. 'I'm feeling a little ...'

The paramedic passed him a small bottle. He unscrewed the top and downed half of it in one go. He felt like he'd never felt so thirsty and ignored Anjli's concerned expression as he did so. Finally, leaning back, he turned to her.

'Could he have hidden it?' she asked. 'Before you reached him?'

Declan shook his head gingerly.

'He didn't have it,' he replied. 'I think he was there to take it, though. The mask and hoodie were a bit of a giveaway.'

He stared off into the distance.

'Why would he kill him?' he said. 'It doesn't feel right.'

Anjli nodded as De'Geer walked over to them.

'You okay, Guv?' he asked, and Declan gave a weak smile.

'I've had better days,' he replied. 'But then I've had worse ones, too.'

'When you fought him, did you catch anything about the attacker?' De'Geer asked, and Declan leant back against the wall of the ambulance.

'He had a face mask, sunglasses, a hoodie on his head, and a cotton black bomber jacket over the top,' Anjli replied for him. 'The pocket was, from the looks of things, easily tearable.'

Declan held up a wavering hand to pause her.

'There was one thing, though,' he said. 'His accent when he told me to back away. It was strangely melodic. Like South American. Somehow, it reminded me of Andrade when he dated Billy.'

'The killer was Colombian?'

'No, but there was a similarity,' Declan closed his eyes, mainly to stop the world spinning. Even concentrating wasn't a good idea right now.

'You're thinking the Argentine, Gabriel Bauer?' Anjli asked. 'South American might sound similar, especially as you've never really been out of Europe and we're relying on your uneducated ears.'

'Maybe,' Declan winced as he tapped his bandage, deciding not to do that again. 'There's no way he knew Krohn was at the event unless he saw him, was told about him, or sent him. From what we can see, Krohn never walked out into the gallery, in case he was spotted by Miles.'

'That's not quite true, sir,' De'Geer replied. 'The sketch Lucy Cormorant did was shown around to anyone still hanging about. If Bauer was still there, or anyone connected to him, and they recognised the image ...'

Declan whispered an expletive.

'If he did, then we aimed Bauer at Krohn by showing him the picture, and the murder's on us,' he muttered, closing his eyes as a searing pain passed through his temples. 'Bloody amateur hour.'

'We should get him home,' De'Geer said to Anjli. 'The paramedics have cleared him, but that was a nasty fall—'

'I'll rest on the sofa in my incredibly boring office,' Declan muttered, rising shakily to his feet. 'In the meantime, can we get out of this bloody place?'

And, with Anjli and De'Geer offering support, which he stubbornly waved off, Declan walked away from the ambulance and the blue tent hiding from view the dead body of Gary Krohn.

He'd been a potential suspect ... but now he was just part of the confusion.

BILLY GAVE A SMILE AS DECLAN AND ANJLI RETURNED TO Temple Inn's main office.

'Hail, the conquering hero,' he exclaimed, giving Declan a mock salute as he did so.

Declan glowered at him in return.

'Anjli, Billy seems unnaturally smug, wouldn't you say?'

'I think he's just as smug as he usually is,' Anjli replied. 'He's probably got some kind of very clever thing he wants to tell us, and he's just begging for the moment to do so.'

Declan considered this for a moment.

'We should probably delay him as long as we can,' he then said, giving Billy a smile. 'Where's the boss?'

Billy looked over at Monroe's office. It had the same glass walls as the others, although the privacy blinds hadn't been pulled, showing that nobody was in there.

'He's up in one of the interview rooms,' he explained.

'Why's Monroe in an interview room?' Declan asked, glancing back at De'Geer who, once he brought Declan into the main office, was now loitering uncomfortably by the door. 'Who is he interviewing?'

'Nobody, really,' Billy replied. 'He just headed there. He

said he'd rather go there with Derek Sutton because that way nobody would see him murdering him through the glass.'

'Yeah, I can understand that,' Declan said. 'I heard what happened.'

'I think that's why Doctor Marcos was first on the scene when Gary Krohn fell,' De'Geer added. 'It gave her an excuse to not be in the same room.'

Declan nodded. He understood why she'd kept the hitman information from Monroe, but that was going to be an uncomfortable relationship for a few days.

'Anyway, murders or attempted murders of Guv'nors aside, I think I have something,' Billy leant back in his chair proudly, linking his hands behind his head.

'Go on, tell us what it is,' Declan urged.

'No,' Anjli interrupted, placing her hand on Declan's shoulder. 'You're supposed to be getting some rest. Remember going home? I was going to get someone to drive you back to Hurley.'

'Honestly, I'm fine,' Declan complained. 'I'm just going to go lay down in my office and shut my eyes. But if Billy's got something, well, I'm not exactly doing much, am I? It's going to be all show and tell, where he explains how clever he is. I don't really have to be totally focused on that point.'

'You're right,' Anjli smiled as Billy, unsure whether he was being mocked or not, gave the slightest of pouts. 'Go on, then. Tell us what you found.'

'Right then,' Billy nodded as he leant forward, returning to his bank of computer monitors, already typing on the keyboard as he spoke. 'So, I started looking into the woman who disrupted the speech, Lucy Cormorant. Even though her statement seemed legit, it seemed too well timed, and there was something a little off about her statement. I looked into her background, and as we know, she's a student at St. Martin's College, like the Pulp song, so I started there.'

Billy was tapping on the keyboard, as student records for Lucy Cormorant appeared on the screens.

'I checked if any other names came up, any students or alumni that might ring any bells.'

'This is because of the note?'

'If her story is true, and she was given this job by an anonymous note on a board, then somebody had to come in to place that note,' Billy nodded. 'And I know there's every chance that whoever did this paid a student to place it. But then that's just another stage of Kevin Bacon because *that* person must know the person who did it.'

'Do you think *you* know?' Declan asked.

'I've got an idea,' Billy pulled up a list of visiting lecturers, scrolling down it. 'I found someone who has a current connection to the college. Someone we weren't expecting. I found that just under a year ago, at the start of the last term, Miles Benson was a guest lecturer during a week of talks.'

'Benson taught art?'

'Well, it looks like he was there to talk about the business side of art – you know, how you deal with people when you're selling paintings and things like that. He turned up and did a few talks, like a mini course, or something. Once I saw this, I checked with UAL Saint Martin's, and found out he still has access.'

'His pass was never stopped?'

Billy shook his head.

'I'm guessing they didn't bother because he's still available for lectures, and it's a ball ache to reinstall his credentials.'

'So he could have come into the college at any point,'

Declan pursed his lips as Billy stopped at the name MILES BENSON on the list of current lecturers.

'And more importantly, he could have left that note,' Billy replied. 'They're looking into when he last came in, but while I waited, I checked into his lectures, and his last one was nine months ago.'

'Let me guess. Lucy Cormorant was one of the students,' Anjli already knew where this was going. 'That's how they met.'

'Actually, no,' Billy replied. 'Well, I mean yes, she was in the class, and yes, they might have reconnected there, but Miles and Lucy knew each other from before.'

'Oh aye?' Declan asked before wincing. 'Sorry, force of habit. Usually Monroe's here to say it.'

Billy tapped on the keyboard, and a selection of oil painting landscapes appeared on the screens. They were contemporary and looked recent.

'Her father is Marcel Cormorant,' Billy explained as he pointed at the paintings.

Declan stared blankly at him.

'Am I supposed to know the name?'

'No,' Billy sighed. 'Because you're an art Philistine. The pair of you are. Marcel Cormorant is a French landscaper in the style of Turner or Constable.'

'Aren't they two completely different art styles?' Declan leant back as he eyed Billy. 'I believe Turner travelled extensively, which meant he infused his dramatic seascapes and landscapes with literary or historical allusions, while Constable, who never left England, preferred more straight-forward depictions of placid rural scenery.'

Billy watched Declan in return, narrowing his eyes.

'There's no way you know that Guv,' he said. 'No way.'

Declan grinned.

'DCIs are created to surprise you,' he replied.

'And Jess is doing an A Level in art,' Anjli added with a wink. 'She's been talking about the Turner-Constable rivalry for months.'

'Constable was a happily married man, while the promiscuous Turner was an outspoken critic of marriage,' Declan continued. 'But sure, tell me I'm a philistine again. Prove to me your knowledge of Marcel Cormorant is more than a google search before we arrived.'

Billy shook his head, smiling.

'My parents told me never to argue with a man with a vicious head wound,' he replied simply. 'Either way, according to google, Cormorant paintings, up to five years ago when Marcel stopped painting, were apparently regularly sold at the Benson Gallery.'

Declan sat up, instantly regretting it, as his head pounded.

'Miles Benson sold Lucy's dad's artwork?' he asked.

'Yes,' Billy replied. 'And he taught her in that class. They must have known each other. Lucy would most likely have attended her father's events, especially if she wanted to follow in his footsteps.'

'Marcel Cormorant's French?' Anjli asked.

'Came over when he was a kid,' Billy nodded. 'Marcel's obviously French, but Cormorant was changed from something even more French and probably unpronounceable. We're getting that now.'

'Miles Benson has to have been the unknown face that booked Lucy,' De'Geer spoke from the back of the room, and Declan almost physically jumped, having forgotten once again he was even there - which was impressive considering De'Geer was a seven-foot-tall blond Viking of a sergeant.

Declan looked back at him.

'But why?' he asked. 'Why send someone to tank your own sale?'

'We wondered if it was to raise sales through morbid curiosity,' Anjli suggested. 'You said Miles would come in soon. We can check then.'

'There's more,' Billy spoke now, returning everyone's attention back to him. 'I found CCTV of Gary Krohn on the night of the murder. Not the gallery, they didn't have cameras in the back rooms or outside the venue, but a building on the other side of the alley had one trained on the road.'

'Alley?'

'He entered the building through the back,' Billy pulled up an image onto one of his screens, a CCTV image of a man in overalls, walking to a van. 'There's a loading bay at the rear of the gallery. You have to go down an alleyway to get to it, but it's easy enough to do if you've got a small van.'

'Holding a painting in his hands?'

Billy shook his head.

'Nope, just walking,' he replied.

'So, he either took the painting another way, and between then and his death someone took it from him,' Declan mused. 'Or he gave it to someone else and walked out, clean. But how did he get in if he's barred?'

'I might have the answer to that,' De'Geer pulled out his phone. 'A few minutes ago I had a text from Doctor Marcos. It's a heads up one, just to say in the studio, there's no sign of the painting. But she found one A4 printout still on the printer. Apparently, it was the details for last night's event as well as the door password to get in, similarly printed in the same way that Lucy Cormorant's one was. It was on an email chain that came from Andrew Benson.'

'Who's also coming in soon,' Anjli growled. 'So, what, he sent Krohn in when he knew he couldn't be there? Or *because* he knew he couldn't be there?'

'Curiouser and curiouser,' Declan looked back at Anjli. 'One brother steals a painting, while the other brother tries to scupper the launch – or possibly tries to gain more money.'

He rubbed at the bandage. It was feeling a little too tight.

'Anything on the crime wall that was on the back of Miles's painting?'

Billy nodded.

'I've translated it through some AI systems and investigated it, and it's definitely connected to some mysterious murderer with a thing for painting kisses. What's interesting is that Borge Pedersen, the professor killed in Salzburg? His father was in the same unit as Lukas Weber's *grand*father. That can't be a coincidence.'

Declan leant back on the chair, trying to force back his approaching migraine by sheer force of will.

'Miles was deep diving here, he has to have known this before he brought Weber over. Especially if he thought his brother was the killer.'

'I agree,' Billy said. 'But now we have a problem. Because if Lukas Weber *was* killed because of his connections to something his grandfather did, then why was Miles Benson telling everybody about it through Lucy Cormorant, and why was Andrew Benson trying to steal his painting first?'

'And, of course, the obvious question,' Anjli added. 'Who actually *killed* him, and were they also the killer of Gary Krohn?'

There was movement at the door, and Declan looked

around to see a new arrival. She was short, in her thirties and Asian in looks, with short spiky hair. She wore a black suit, had an overnight bag over her shoulder, a leather briefcase in her hand, and was looking around the office with a mixture of horror and disdain.

'I am Kriminalkommissar Margaret Li,' she said, her accent strong as she spoke the words. 'Have you caught my killer yet?'

12

A MIXED CROWD

AFTER A QUICK INTRODUCTION TO ANJLI, BILLY AND DE'GEER, but done under the more formal monikers of DI Kapoor, DS Fitzwarren and Sergeant De'Geer, Declan brought Margaret Li through into his office, while De'Geer ran upstairs to inform Monroe that his German guest had arrived.

A few minutes later, followed by a grim-looking Derek Sutton, Monroe came down the stairs and entered Declan's office, all smiles.

'Margaret,' he said, shaking her hand as he did so. 'It's been a while.'

'It has, Detective Superintendent,' Margaret replied, her accent strong and clipped. 'Congratulations on your promotion.'

'Thank you,' Monroe replied.

Margaret looked around.

'Your friend,' she said. 'The woman with the white hair. Bullman, I believe her name was?'

'Ah yes, DCI Bullman,' Monroe nodded. 'She was promoted to Detective Superintendent before I was.'

'I heard, and then I heard she has been promoted again, to Detective Chief Superintendent?'

'Aye, she was,' Monroe's smile faded a little.

'So, in the time since we last met, you have been promoted once while she has been promoted twice?'

'She's better at her job than I am,' Monroe quipped.

Margaret, however, didn't take it as a joke.

'She gave that impression when we were in Berlin,' she said. 'So, can someone tell me what you have found out? I want to see how similar this is to my murder.'

Monroe's smile had completely faded by now and Declan couldn't help himself, fighting back a laugh, exploding as a slight snort as he did so.

Margaret Li looked over at him.

'Are you all right?' she asked, more questioning than concerned.

'Aye, the lad has a head wound,' Monroe said. 'Makes him a bit simple I'm afraid. So, let's go over your similarity to our case.'

Margaret nodded, placing the leather briefcase she'd been holding onto the desk.

'Actually, as mine was chronologically first you have a similarity to mine,' she said.

The smile Monroe had attempted for a second time when he'd stated that Declan was simple had still been on his face, and now it was frozen there as his eyes gave away a desperate intent to stab the Berlin officer.

'I'd ... I'd forgotten how blunt you could be in Berlin,' he eventually replied.

Margaret was already rummaging through her briefcase.

'Blunt? I hardly think so,' she said, pulling out a folder. 'I was simply stating facts. Are you sure your companion Bullman won't be joining us?'

'No,' Monroe replied as Margaret passed him the folder.

'Stefan Bierhof,' she explained as Declan moved closer to look at the paperwork. It was all in German but a photo stared out at them. 'Berlin native, lived there since the wall was up. Lived in East Berlin back then. His family had connections.'

'What sort of connections?'

'His father and his uncle were both in the German secret police,' Margaret gave a slight smile. 'It seems once more this unit brings us together, yes?'

Declan knew where Margaret was going with this; the last time Monroe had spoken to her they were hunting East German informers and secret police officers.

And serial killers, but that wasn't on today's menu.

'And Stefan was?' he asked.

'Stefan Bierhof was a picture framer,' Margaret looked at him. 'A good one, and then four weeks ago he was found dead, with a painted lipstick kiss on his neck. Similar to the ones in Salzburg and Paris.'

She waved around the room.

'And now London.'

'It doesn't mention anything about a tattoo?' Monroe said, flicking through the pages.

'How do you know that?' Declan asked. 'Unless you magically learnt how to read German?'

Monroe paused.

'I thought "tattoo" was a universal spelling?' he replied, looking over at Margaret.

'The word you look for is "tätowieren," but there is no

mention of it as Stefan did not have one,' she replied. 'Does yours?'

Monroe nodded.

'Two letters, J – or T, we're not a hundred percent sure – and K,' he replied. 'We haven't heard if the Salzburg one had a tattoo, but the Paris one didn't as far as we know. That said, we're still waiting for the intelligence to arrive.'

'And how does it arrive here?' Margaret asked. 'In Berlin, we have a department purely tasked with working on cases such as this.'

'Oh, here we have Billy,' Monroe smiled.

'Billy? Is this like your *Holmes2* network?'

'No, I mean Billy,' Monroe pointed out of the window. 'Wee laddie there. Come with me, I'll introduce you to him. He can tell you what else is happening.'

And with this done, and a glare at Declan as he passed, Monroe took Margaret Li out of his onetime office, walking her over to Billy, the one-man version of an entire German department.

Declan didn't want to spoil the moment, so he didn't mention she'd already met their cyber-expert. He thought it'd be quite funny for Monroe to find out in person, if only to make up for the "simple" comment.

There was something niggling at him however, something he'd need to look into. For a series of copycat crimes, they seemed to be changing the M.O. Surely, if you were taking the time to paint a perfect replica of a kiss, one shown on other bodies, you'd take the time to also create the tattoo? Or was this a recent or more personal addition?

There was more to this than Declan knew, and it was irritating the hell out of him.

Derek Sutton was still hanging around the doorway, and

seeing him was a welcome break from the concerns of the case.

'So, what's the plan?' Declan asked, moving on to the current situation with Monroe. 'How are we hunting this guy down?'

'We're checking into things, off the books so to speak,' Sutton walked into the room, checking behind him as he did so, as if expecting someone to be listening. 'But we need to find a place for Ali to lie low.'

'Usually it's Johnny Lucas's boxing ring, isn't it?' Declan laughed at his own joke.

Derek Sutton didn't respond, staring directly at Declan for a long moment, before finally speaking.

'He's gone legit,' he said. 'Like me.'

Declan didn't have the heart to state he seriously doubted that Derek Sutton was legit, so he proceeded to simply nod.

'We need to find a place that people won't expect Monroe to be staying at,' Sutton continued. 'I seem to recall you have a place somewhere in Berkshire.'

'Hurley, actually,' Declan straightened in his chair. 'He's crashed with me before but the defences aren't great.'

'We don't need defences,' Sutton replied, and Declan realised that by inviting Monroe to stay with him, he had effectively invited his large Scottish bodyguard to arrive as well. 'We just need a place off the grid where we can strategise.'

'Well, Jess isn't at home at the moment, so there's a spare bedroom Monroe can use and you can crash on the sofa,' Declan said.

'I've had worse,' Sutton grinned. 'How's the head?'

Declan resisted the urge to tap at the bandage around his skull.

'Hurts like buggery,' he said.

'I've had a few head wounds in my life,' Sutton replied with what felt like mock wisdom, but was probably quite genuine. 'Give it a day. Take some ibuprofen and try to get some sleep tonight.'

Declan considered the advice and quickly realised that "getting some sleep" was something that wouldn't be happening if he was babysitting both Monroe and his Scottish friend.

'De'Geer lives near you, right?' Sutton continued, looking back to Declan as he went to leave the office.

'Down the road, a few miles away,' Declan replied. 'He transferred over after we worked on a case together.'

'We should bring him in as well,' Sutton said. 'I worked with him in Edinburgh. He's a solid man.'

Declan nodded. As much as the idea of his house being even fuller didn't appeal to him, he also knew Sutton was right. If someone was trying to kill Monroe, the more people they had waiting, the better.

This decided, Sutton gave a brief "good man" and headed over to Monroe where he could loom behind him menacingly. Declan watched this, and for a moment saw a world that could have been, where Alex Monroe was a gangland boss and Derek Sutton was his loyal enforcer.

The thought was terrifyingly possible.

However, now finally alone in his office, Declan leant back in his chair, shutting his eyes for a moment. Maybe Anjli was right and maybe he needed to have a break back at home. But for the moment, all he wanted to do was try to relax, to let the headaches go away.

He heard rather than saw Anjli pop her head into the office.

'Do you need anything?' she asked, and Declan replied by shaking his head.

'We've got houseguests,' he added, his eyes still shut. 'Sutton, Monroe, and probably De'Geer.'

Anjli grinned.

'We'll order some pizza in,' she replied. 'It'll be a slumber party.'

Declan shuddered at the visual image this gave him.

'I have a lead,' Anjli continued. 'The woman who found the body, Stacey whatever, she's around the corner at an event in Cutler's Hall. I was just going to check on her, make sure her story matches what we know, see if she recognises Gary Krohn.'

Declan went to rise, but Anjli tutted loudly.

'Just because you're not being sent home doesn't mean you shouldn't,' she said. 'Besides, I have an easier job for you. Something that involves staying in the building.'

Declan sighed, slumping back in the chair.

'And that is?'

'Ramsey Allen, Ellie Reckless's go-to guy has just turned up,' Anjli smiled. 'He's in reception. Did we invite him?'

Declan opened his eyes and straightened.

'Billy called him before Gary Krohn died, but he might have an insight on why the painting's so important,' he said. 'Let's put him in the briefing room.'

He stopped as his phone rang. Motioning to Anjli that he'd be with her in a second, he answered.

'Walsh.'

'Guv, you need to send someone down here right now,' Sergeant Mastakin, currently on the front desk said down the line, and in the background the sounds of an argument could be heard.

'What's going on?' Declan asked, looking back at Anjli. The phone wasn't on speaker, but she could still hear both sides of the conversation.

'Your Mister Allen arrived a few minutes ago,' Sergeant Mastakin explained. 'Unfortunately, Sam Mansfield has also arrived, and, well, the two of them aren't happy with each other.'

'They don't get on?'

'Not currently, sir.'

'I'll send Anjli down,' Declan quickly disconnected the call and looked back at his Detective Inspector.

'I heard,' she replied, already walking to the door. 'Our "experts" are downstairs, and apparently, they're having a fight.'

'Can you and De'Geer go downstairs and break them up? Get De'Geer to dump them both in the briefing room while you go off and have adventures. But if they can't play nice, get De'Geer to dump them in the interview rooms instead.'

Anjli nodded, leaving the office, and Declan slumped against his chair's back.

He had to be strong now. There was no going home just yet.

And there was a part of him that resisted the idea of returning home, anyway.

Because, with Monroe, De'Geer and Sutton there, there was no way in hell he was going to have a break later that day.

13

PROFESSIONAL RIVALRIES

SAM MANSFIELD WAS GLOWERING ACROSS THE BRIEFING ROOM at Ramsey Allen when Declan finally arrived.

'Are you both comfy?' he asked with a smile, settling back against the desk at the front of the briefing room.

Ramsey took one last icy look at his rival before turning back to Declan.

'Nobody told me this man would be here,' he said, his tone icy. He was in his sixties, still wearing his usual uniform of old school tie, crisp white shirt and navy blazer, whereas Sam was more relaxed in a graphic-design t-shirt and brown leather bomber jacket worn over the top.

Sam, in response to this accusation, gave a lazy wave.

'I wasn't told I was going to be here with this thief,' he replied.

Declan glanced out of the door at De'Geer, who for some reason had refused to enter; apparently while escorting them both upstairs, Ramsey Allen had stolen his wallet and watch. He'd given them both back, but De'Geer now stared through the glass as if Ramsey was some kind of evil wizard.

Which, Declan supposed, he could have been if he wanted.

'If I remember correctly Sam, when I last arrested you, it was because you were also undertaking an act of theft,' he said.

'I think you'll find, DCI Walsh, that when you accidentally arrested me for a crime I didn't commit,' Sam waggled a finger accusingly at Declan, 'what I was actually doing was investigating a forgery ring that was affecting businesses in the City of London.'

Sam returned his hands behind his head, intertwining them as he looked smugly at the DCI in front of him.

Declan fought back the urge to grin, rather than berate him. Sam was indeed correct, but only because the painting he'd forged had, unbeknownst to him, already been stolen and replaced. So, when he arrived to take the painting, placing his own forgery there in its place, he hadn't realised someone else had beaten him to it.

Weirdly, this mistake on his part was one thing that had helped his case a couple of months ago when the Last Chance Saloon had utilised his abilities in taking down their commander, Edward Sinclair. Sam had made a point of playing the part of the vigilante artist, continuing his narrative that evil forgers had been afoot in London ever since.

'So why don't you two like each other?' Declan asked, turning back to Ramsey and Sam. 'I mean, you're both forgers.'

'I'm not a forger,' Ramsey snapped indignantly. 'I don't paint. I'm a thief. A bloody good one.'

'But you were arrested a couple of times, weren't you?' Sam muttered softly, an innocent look on his face. 'Bloody good thieves rarely get arrested.'

'I was arrested by an exceptional detective,' Ramsey sighed. 'One that when I left prison, I immediately started working for, so I think that's a bit of a specific situation, don't you?'

Sam shrugged.

'I'm a thief *and* a forger,' he said to Declan. 'I'll go with that. But this man here stole one of my paintings once.'

'I didn't steal one of your paintings,' Ramsey replied. 'I stole a forgery of a painting, one that you happened to create.'

'How is that different from "you stole one of my paintings?"'

'Your painting wasn't your painting,' Ramsey shook his head. 'Your painting was a terrible copy of a Monet.'

'I do *not* do terrible copies,' Sam grunted, and Declan could see that the argument had started to darken in tone.

'Okay, okay,' he said, holding his hands up. 'You're both pretty princesses, you're both super special, and I love you both. But you're going to need to work together, because Billy needs advice.'

At the mention of Billy, Sam immediately stopped.

'Billy needs our help?' he asked. 'Whatever he needs.'

Declan smiled, watching Sam. If he hadn't thought Billy and Sam had feelings for each other earlier when watching Billy blush, it was pretty much confirmed watching Sam immediately leap into action to help the detective sergeant.

Ramsey, however, had his hand up now, leaning closer with a smile on his face.

'You called me in asking about an artist dying at an event, and as fun as it was nicking your sergeant's things, this isn't about a painting,' he shook his head. 'This is about lost World War Two paintings taken by the Nazis, isn't it?'

'Do you know anything about that?'

Ramsey shook his head.

'It's not really an area I'm an expert in,' he replied and then reluctantly nodded his head towards Sam. 'This guy, however ...'

He let the comment trail off as Sam straightened.

'What have you got?' he asked.

'A dead painter named Lukas Weber, and sadly, that's all we know for now,' De'Geer, edging closer, interjected from the door, still wary of Ramsey Allen. 'We've learned he was murdered, possibly because his grandfather was a member of the German army during World War Two, specifically involved in a unit that confiscated high-end paintings and artwork while in France.'

'Hitler's rainy-day fund,' Sam nodded. 'Although, if you ask the so called "experts," they'll tell you these works were seized from collectors and artists who happened to be Jewish, while others were confiscated and marked for destruction because they didn't conform to Hitler's narrow definition of what "Aryan art" should comprise; that is, classical portraits and landscapes by Old Masters, usually German, as opposed to the often abstract, expressionistic compositions that characterised so many modernist works, which he labelled as "degenerate."'

He sat back in his chair.

'Hitler was a painter,' he said. 'A shit one who couldn't even get admission into the Vienna Academy of Fine Arts with his work. I reckon he did all this out of spite.'

He looked out of the window, at the office outside.

'Einsatzstab Reichsleiter Rosenberg für die Besetzten Gebiete,' he said. 'Translates to "Reichsleiter Rosenberg Task-force," and was a creation of the Nazi Alfred Rosenberg. The

ERR plundered across Europe. Thousands of paintings and sculptures, and millions of priceless books were taken.'

He spat on the floor at the name, and then whitened, looking up in horror.

'Sorry,' he added sheepishly.

Declan waved the issue off; he understood why Sam would be angry. He might be a forger, but he was also an artist.

De'Geer looked at his notes.

'I was just speaking with Miss Li, and someone's been killing people connected to soldiers from the ERR,' he continued. 'Lukas's grandfather was an Ober-Einsatzführer there, which equates to a First Lieutenant in our forces. There were others too, a Professor in Salzburg, who apparently had a Nazi father in the same unit, another in Berlin, and a woman in Paris who was a granddaughter to one.'

'You think this is revenge?' Ramsey asked. 'Nazi hunters gone rogue or something like that?'

'Maybe,' Declan replied. 'Apparently, they all had their moments in front of the war crimes trials, but none of them were big enough to warrant major issues.'

Sam considered this.

'The "Young Artists,"' he whispered. 'The Nazis took from everyone, but many young artists, Jewish ones, were sent to camps and died. After the war, even during the last years of it, there was a groundswell of support against the Nazis for what they did to them.'

He looked at the wall.

'The followers of the "Young Artists" really couldn't show symbols, especially during the war, so they'd kiss each other's necks, leaving a lipstick mark. *This* was their symbol, and if questioned, it was nothing more than a kiss.'

'Lukas Weber had a painting on the side of his neck of a lipstick kiss when he was found dead,' De'Geer added.

'Are you sure it wasn't just a lipstick kiss mark?' Sam questioned. 'They would have been long forgotten by now. This was the late forties—'

'No,' a new voice spoke now as Billy entered the briefing room. 'It might have looked like it was the size of an actual lipstick kiss, but it was painted on with oils – oh, hi, Sam.'

Billy grinned at Sam before sitting down and plugging his laptop into the screen.

'The same painted lipstick kiss was on at least two of the people murdered, and one of them, Lukas Weber, had been initialled with a tattoo,' he explained. 'We think it's another artist, signing their work.'

Ramsey nodded at this.

'There's a ton of families all claiming their paintings were taken,' he said. 'And as the years went on, the paintings became more and more valuable. Some of these are worth millions now, and they're still missing, many abroad in places like America, both north - and south.'

Declan froze at this.

'Sam, are you saying if we had somebody from Colombia, or somewhere around that area, whose family was involved with Germans after the war, there's a strong chance they would know the true history of Lukas Weber's grandfather?'

'Less likely Colombia, but Argentina's in South America,' Sam thinned his lips as he considered this. 'Many Germans went there after the war. People even claim Hitler went there after faking his death.'

'Hitler faked his death?'

'The skull the Russians found? Nothing more than a

female skull,' Sam smiled. 'There's a story there that people are too scared to mention.'

'Of course you'd know this,' Ramsey sneered. 'Stories like this are catnip to forgers and con men. You probably have two fake Hitler skulls ready to go.'

Billy looked up from his laptop.

'Argentina? Are you thinking of Gabriel Bauer?' he asked.

'Bauer's a German name, and he's an Argentine who bought a ton of paintings at the exhibition,' Declan replied.

However, as the name was spoken, Ramsey straightened.

'Bauer,' he said. 'Nobody told me Bauer was involved. That guy's a psycho.'

'You know him?'

'By reputation,' Ramsey Allen shuddered. 'The bastard's been around for decades—'

'How many decades?' Billy looked up. 'We have him in his late fifties.'

'Since his teens, so quite a few,' Sam added. 'Also, he's extremely far right, and he's not afraid to let people know. He's a loose cannon of the highest degree.'

'Is he enough of a loose cannon to kill Gary Krohn?'

At this, Ramsey looked nervously around the room, and then returned his gaze to Declan.

'Yes and no,' he said. 'Yes, he's mad enough to do it, but not mad enough to do it himself, if you understand.'

Declan did. The man he'd chased on a roof had not felt that old, maybe twenties at best. If he'd been outrun by a man almost twenty years older than he was, he wasn't going to be happy.

Billy glanced up at Declan as he checked his laptop.

'He's got a rap sheet, too,' he said. 'Nothing ever proven.'

Declan nodded, understanding what Billy was saying.

Gabriel Bauer was dangerous, but also incredibly clever with it.

'I want to meet this man,' he said. 'Can we arrange something?'

'You really don't,' Sam sighed. 'Seriously. But I can tell you now, he knew Krohn.'

'They worked together?'

'Gary Krohn's worked with practically everyone,' Ramsey answered for Sam. 'But he's had run-ins with Gabriel. Chances are, if Gabriel Bauer learnt he was there he'd pay a visit, and if they were after the same thing, he'd come armed for a fight.'

14

ZERO HOURS

STACEY NICHOLS WAS WORKING AT A PRODUCT LAUNCH AT Cutler's Hall, as Anjli and Cooper arrived, the catering company she worked for providing drinks and canapes to the company holding the event, like the service they offered the day before down the road.

Stacey was in her late teens or early twenties, with long, fine, blonde hair pulled back in a bun, and so blonde it almost looked white. She wore a pale shirt and black trousers, which Anjli assumed were the standard server's gear. On her feet were a pair of black Skechers, probably because she spent so much time on them, and she wore wire-framed glasses and squinted, pushing them up on her nose as she waited for them to walk over. Around her wrist was a silver bracelet, and her watch on the other wrist was silver as well, giving her a slightly colder figure, contrasting with the glasses.

'Stacey Nichols?' Anjli asked. 'I'm Detective Inspector Kapoor, this is PC Cooper. We're here about last night.'

'I guessed,' Stacey replied. 'I was told someone would do a follow up, and the PC here spoke to me yesterday.'

'Good,' Anjli smiled. 'That makes things a little easier. I understand you've already given your statement about last night's horrible circumstances, so I apologise that you have to go through it again.'

'That's fine,' Stacey nodded, looking up at the ceiling while recalling the events. 'I work for Fowler Catering, and they were hired to provide drinks and snacks for the guests in the gallery. We used some of the back rooms to set up as they didn't have a kitchen area.'

'Hot food?' Cooper asked.

'Not really. Some of us would be in the back room placing canapes on the trays, but also some of us would use a couple of portable stoves to heat things up. Most of it was a cold buffet,' Stacey replied, counting things off on her fingers. 'We also poured drinks, arranged trays of champagne, that sort of thing. The glasses weren't being washed, they were just being put aside. We had a pallet of them, and it wasn't big enough of an event to warrant washing and reusing them, and they paid for the glasses in advance. So that was fine.'

'Can you go through the evening's events?' Anjli asked. 'Not in detail, just enough for us to get a flavour?'

Stacey nodded.

'Around seven, we started preparing everything. The event started about half-past, maybe eight o'clock. There'd been a couple of delays.'

'Like?'

'The artist in question hadn't turned up,' Stacey smiled. 'I was serving until just after nine. But just before that, I heard a noise in a room we hadn't been using. I wondered if something was going on in there.'

'What do you mean by something was going on?' Cooper asked.

'We have a lot of young staff,' Stacey said. 'People taking gap years, people at university and working during holidays, nobody does this for a vocation or a career. People were wandering around, looking for quiet rooms to get a little personal, shall we say?'

'Oh,' Anjli replied, understanding now what Stacey was insinuating. Junior staff working temporarily, finding themselves attracted to other members, would sneak off together and find ways to spend their time. She'd done it enough times herself as a teenager, while working for a large hotel restaurant on weekends.

'So you thought someone was shagging in one of those rooms,' she said, more a statement than a question.

'Possibly,' Stacey replied. 'I didn't go in though. It wasn't my job to be the Fun Police, you know. But I had heard a noise, and it stayed on my mind for the next half an hour or so. So when I finished my rotation with the glasses, and as the talk started, I thought I'd make sure everything was okay.'

'Nobody saw you enter the room?'

'I didn't go through the main door,' Stacey said. 'There's a side door at the back. That's where a lot of us were walking through, because the organisers didn't want us seen coming and going through the main door. We would use the back doors and the fire exit to slide through to the front of the rooms, and then work our way back through the gallery.'

Cooper took notes.

'So, you finished your task, went into the back room, placed your tray down, and then?'

'I've said all this before,' Stacey snapped. 'And it was to you.'

'I know, sorry,' Cooper apologised. 'But DI Kapoor wasn't there, so we need to act as if we never spoke, start again from scratch.'

'Okay, so then I went into the middle room,' Stacey sighed, a little too theatrically. 'And that's when I found him.'

'Lukas Weber.'

'He was dead,' Stacey nodded.

'And you were sure of this?' Anjli asked.

'I'm pretty sure he was dead, but I didn't check anything,' Stacey confirmed. 'I just backed out of the room as quickly as I could. I was screaming, and the next thing I know, it was chaos.'

'Did you touch the body?'

'God no, I'm not that stupid,' Stacey replied. 'I literally came out shouting. I think my manager called the police, and then you guys turned up. I hung around, gave my statement, then went home.'

'And you're working today?' Cooper was surprised.

'We're on zero-hours contracts,' Stacey shrugged. 'If I don't work, I don't get paid. I dropped out of college and I'm utterly broke. If I don't work, I don't eat.'

Anjli thought that was a little harsh. To face a dead body one night and being forced to work the following day was not something she expected outside of the police ... or maybe a sales call centre. She didn't really know much about those, but she had her suspicions.

'Why do you do the job?' she asked.

'Sorry?'

'Well, you said it's not a vocation. It's a job that people do while they're waiting to start college or something like that.'

'I've just started a year off,' Stacey, now understanding, explained. 'I'm back at college next year.'

'Doing what?'

'I'm not sure yet,' Stacey smiled. 'I'm waiting to go through clearing, and it could change whether I work in science or train as a lawyer.'

Anjli finished up her notes, closing her book. She nodded to Cooper, who pulled out her phone, showing an image of Gary Krohn.

'Did you see this man at the event?' Cooper asked.

Stacey nodded.

'He was in the back when we were setting up,' she said. 'There were a lot of people in overalls making sure the paintings were positioned correctly. I assumed he was one of them. Is he the killer?'

'We can't talk about an active investigation.'

'But I can?'

'You're a witness,' Anjli replied. 'Did you see him with anything?'

'Not when I saw him,' Stacey shook her head. 'Why, did he steal something?'

'How hard was it to get out from where you were setting up the drinks and food?' Anjli ignored the question.

'I don't know the layout. You'd have to go and look for yourself,' Stacey said. 'Sorry, I can't help there. It was my first time in the gallery. I could ask if anyone else here saw him? Some of them worked the event too, they might know who he is?'

'We know who he is,' Cooper replied, looking back at her. 'Unfortunately, he was murdered earlier today.'

At the news, Stacey paled.

'Another one?' she asked. 'Was it because he was there? Should I be worrying?'

'No, I think you're safe, and besides, you've done enough,'

Anjli smiled reassuringly. 'One last thing, though. We have a witness who says that they overheard an argument in that room, probably around the time that you first heard a noise. Did you hear anything like that?'

'No,' Stacey said. 'I just heard a sound like something fell off the shelf, I think, and crashed onto the floor.'

Anjli considered this; the sound could have been when Lukas Weber slammed his head onto the back of the table.

'Thank you for your time. If there's anything you remember, please let us know.' she said, nodding for Cooper to follow her out. Stacey shrugged and returned to her work, and once outside, Anjli looked at Cooper.

'Thoughts?'

'She seems legit,' Cooper read through her notes as she spoke. 'But something seems off. She didn't have glasses last night.'

'Probably wore contacts,' Anjli looked back at the building. 'Anything else?'

'Actually, yes,' Cooper nodded. 'She said she was utterly broke, but on one wrist was a Tiffany link bracelet, worth somewhere around a grand, and on the other was a silver Cartier watch bracelet, which I kid you not, would gain you somewhere just shy of a couple of grand if sold on the black market.'

'So she comes from money?'

'Or she has it, and this whole "working because I'm broke" thing is bollocks, Guv,' Cooper muttered. 'She needs the money that bad, she's a walking bank. Who knows what her earrings or necklaces cost?'

Anjli stared up at the night sky.

'I think we need to look into Miss Nichols a little more,' she said.

In Cutler's Hall, Stacey Nichols passed a tray to another server and walked through the rear doors, trying to keep her composure until there was nobody else around.

She knew she'd made a mistake wearing the jewellery; she should have been clever and left it at home, but Kyle had been asking questions, and her other watch had broken.

She walked to the end of the corridor, staring out through one of the windows. The DI and the copper were walking off now, deep in thought.

She looked back at the hall, debating whether she should stay or go, and wondering if the others knew the police were looking into Gary Krohn's death.

Gary Krohn's death.

The words punched into her and she doubled over, forcing herself not to throw up a couple of the snaffled canapes she'd eaten when she arrived.

She'd killed Gary Krohn. She knew without a measure of doubt she'd done it.

And she'd been paid well, although she hadn't realised it.

Shaking her head, she grabbed her coat from a hook by the window and left out of the back door before anyone could ask her what the police officers wanted.

She knew she wouldn't be coming back again, zero hours or not.

15

PARLIAMENTARY MATTERS

'WELL, THIS LOOKS COSY,' MONROE GRINNED AS HE ENTERED the small office in Bethnal Green. It was emblazoned with "Johnny Lucas – Fighting for London" banners, probably left over from the election campaign a couple of months earlier. But as the constituency office, or *surgery* rather, of the MP for Bethnal Green and Bow, Monroe knew that today would be the evening that Johnny Lucas would see his adoring public, and in fact, the man himself was there, smiling warmly, standing beside a door, and talking to a couple of older ladies.

Johnny Lucas was a gangster. There was no mistaking that. Monroe had known Johnny for a while, and he'd also known his "twin brother" Jackie, before it came out that Jackie was a part of Johnny's own psyche for many years now.

Came out *publicly*, that was. Because Johnny and Jackie being the same person was one of the worst-kept secrets in London.

In fact, since he'd arrived in London from Glasgow decades earlier, a fresh-faced detective taking his first job away from Scotland, Johnny had been a connection for Alex Monroe. Just under twenty years earlier, Monroe had even worked undercover, pretending to be a corrupt cop and taking money to look the other way when Johnny had performed some of his criminal activities, as part of a terrorist sting that never happened, petering out, while leaving a spoken-word black mark on his record from those who hadn't known the true story.

All of this was water under the bridge now, though, and over the last few years, Monroe had not only saved Johnny's life on a couple of occasions, but Johnny had returned the favour for Monroe, primarily given him places to hide when a killer was trying to take him out a year and a half earlier.

Surprising how things came around in circles, he thought to himself.

Johnny Lucas was in his sixties but looked good for it, his hair combed back into effectively a loose quiff. Greying, but white on top, he wore a pale-white shirt under a navy-blue suit, which still seemed weird because for many years, Johnny and Jackie had differentiated themselves by wearing black and navy-blue shirts under black suits. But pale shirts seemed to be the thing now, and it enhanced his bronzed face.

He was tanned; not bottle tan, but more like "laying on a sun bed for hours" tanned. Monroe knew this was to make him look healthier, but he also knew that Johnny Lucas hadn't bothered visiting Spain for quite a while now. Many of his old friends still lived there today, and many of them still had issues with him.

Johnny had seen Monroe enter and, finishing up his conversation with the two ladies, he said his goodbyes with a smile and a handshake and walked over. Monroe also noticed that as Johnny did this, a tall burly man peeled himself from the wall and started walking towards them as well. Monroe knew Pete the trainer for many years, although now, in this room and currently wearing a black suit, he thought he wasn't going under the term of *trainer* right now; he was probably going more under the term *bodyguard for the MP*. But the fact he was there relaxed Monroe a little. After all, people were trying to kill Monroe, and if someone tried to do it here at least Pete would help him take them out.

Hopefully.

Monroe also noticed that as he'd entered the room, Derek Sutton had kept to the side, keeping slightly out of the way so that Johnny Lucas wouldn't see him. Which seemed strange since Johnny Lucas had known Derek Sutton for just as long as he'd known Monroe, if not longer.

'Detective Superintendent,' Johnny Lucas said, beaming, his hand outstretched for a handshake.

'Right Honourable MP,' Monroe smiled in return, taking the offered hand and shaking it warmly.

Johnny pulled at his lapels as if straightening his jacket.

'How we've risen,' he said. 'Talking of which, Mister Sutton, don't think I can't see you there. Come out. Congratulations on your court case. I understand you're now a man of leisure.'

Sutton reluctantly emerged from the doorway.

'Mister Lucas, sir,' he said.

Monroe almost laughed. He hadn't really seen Derek Sutton speak to Johnny Lucas before and had forgotten the reverence and deferential nature he gave to the man.

Johnny, in return, just smiled and said, 'It's John or Johnny, but just not Jackie anymore.'

'Yes, sir,' Derek replied with a smile.

Johnny looked back at Monroe.

'I'd ask why you're here,' he said. 'But I think I already know. Little birdie told me that Lennie Wright put a hit on you.'

'Wee little scroat tried to take me out today,' Monroe nodded. 'Shot up an area in the City of London. I don't care what happens to me, but this guy was firing wildly. He could have taken anybody else.'

Monroe didn't mention the fact there was nobody else in the area, and the hitman had possibly timed it right. But he also knew that claiming that the hitman was half-assed, or not good at his job, might actually help remove him.

'Problem I have, Alex, is I'm not in that business anymore,' Johnny replied, almost apologetically. 'There's not a lot I can do. I can ask around, but I can't take a hit off you.'

He rubbed at his chin for a moment, pondering the issue.

'You could ask your protégé, Ellie Reckless,' he suggested. 'She's still got some favours owed to her, so she might be able to do something.'

'I'm not looking to have the hit removed,' Monroe said. 'If anything, I want the hit to stay. That hit helps me and the court case against Lennie Wright in a couple of weeks. What I need to know is who's got the job and where they are.'

'You're gonna hunt the hitman?'

Monroe grinned a dark, humourless smile.

'Did you think anything less?'

Johnny leaned back, straightening his shoulders as he bellowed out a laugh.

'Alexander Monroe, you never change,' he said. 'And I hope you never do.'

He looked at Sutton.

'You're part of this idiotic campaign too, right?'

'He got me out of prison, saved my arse a couple of times,' Sutton nodded. 'Saved my daughter, too, which is where the issues with Lennie started. I feel I owe it to him.'

At the news of Sutton having a daughter, Johnny Lucas didn't seem surprised, and Monroe realised again, that he was probably the only person at the time who'd believed Sutton when he'd claimed the kid was Monroe's niece.

'You've always had a strong link to his family, though, haven't you?' Johnny continued, glancing back at Monroe as he continued. 'I remember you going to war for his brother Kenny, so it's only fair that you go to war for Alex as well.'

Monroe shrugged. He didn't really know what to say about this. He hadn't had somebody want to go to war for him - well, at least someone who wasn't part of the Last Chance Saloon - for quite a while.

'I understand you've got a killer as well,' Johnny said, changing the subject. 'Something about paintings?'

'Declan's looking into that,' Monroe replied.

'Yeah, I heard that Gary Krohn took a tumble out of a fourth-floor window or something,' Johnny's face tightened as he spoke. 'Please, if I can help in any way, let me know. I worked with Gary here and there. He was a wonderful artist and an excellent framer.'

Monroe nodded, forcing himself not to smile. He knew Johnny Lucas had worked with Gary Krohn a few times; it had been in the records. But Monroe also knew every single time would be something to do with forgeries, or some kind of illegal activity that was never pinned on Johnny.

'To be honest, we're still trying to work out why he was killed,' he said. 'We know he took a painting from an event where another painter had been murdered. We think the painting had some kind of historical value and somebody wanted the painting from him, throwing him out the window in the process. However, when we looked in the office, the painting was gone.'

'Could the attacker have taken it?'

Monroe shook his head.

'No, Declan chased him across the rooftop.'

At this, Johnny Lucas smiled.

'Of course he did,' he said. 'I would have expected nothing less from the newest DCI of Temple Inn. Let me ask around, see if I can help. Anything else you need from me?'

Monroe wanted to reply in the negative; the fact he was even here was galling enough.

'No,' he replied. 'Just need to work out who the hitman is. I think it's a young Asian lad who worked for Harvey Drake.'

'Harvey Drake?' Johnny Lucas's face darkened. 'Harvey Drake is back in London?'

He looked across at Pete.

'Why didn't you tell me Harvey Drake was in town?'

'Because you're an MP now, boss,' Pete replied. 'And I knew that if anybody—' at this, he glared across at Monroe, '—told you, you would immediately go off, find a gun and destroy your reputation in one shot.'

Johnny Lucas returned his gaze to Monroe, but now it was ice cold and piercing.

'Whatever you need, speak to Pete,' he said. 'Or have a chat with one of the guys in the boxing club. Harvey Drake is a cancer, and I thought I'd got rid of him for good.'

'You have history?'

'Lennie Wright tried to get involved in the London scene once, but we kicked him back up to Scotland years ago. But Harvey bloody Drake seems to hang on like haemorrhoids. You need help getting rid of him, I can do that.'

'I don't need him removed,' Monroe said. 'I just need to know who he's using.'

'If it's an Asian kid, then that I can help you with,' Johnny looked over at Pete. 'I'd suggest you don't listen to this, because it's something that you're going to get annoyed about.'

Pete shook his head, muttering under his breath about "being respectable" and "church and state" while pretending to turn away as Johnny Lucas returned his gaze to both Derek Sutton and Monroe.

'Damian Lim,' he said. 'Young lad, early twenties, currently making a name for himself. He's cheap, which is why Drake likes to use him.'

'Has he killed before?'

'Not that I know of. He's done a lot of simple things though. Breaking legs, spying on people, taking them out on a temporary level, but he's never gone permanent. This is probably his first, maybe second at a pinch.'

Monroe nodded, unsure whether to be relieved or insulted at the revelation his hitman was an unknown amateur trying to take him out.

'Surely Lennie would have wanted an established pro?' Sutton asked.

'Probably knew they'd be easy to connect back to him, while a lone wolf kid starting off might go under the radar when looking for motive.'

Monroe nodded at this, remembering that at Southbank, the man he'd bumped into had been Asian.

'Damian Lim,' he said. 'Thank you. I'll look into him.'

'I want you to do a personal favour for me, Monroe,' Johnny said. 'I want Drake removed.

'You know I can't—'

'I don't mean *click bang*,' Johnny mimed a gun to the head. 'I mean, once you work out that he's involved in a criminal conspiracy to kill a police officer, I'm guessing you can pretty much throw the book at him. I want you to throw the book as hard as you can.'

'I have no problems with that, Johnny,' Monroe nodded. 'I'll look into that for you, and if you hear anything about forgeries, or stolen paintings appearing, I'd appreciate it greatly.'

'I still think you should talk to Reckless,' Johnny said. 'She sorted out her big problem with Nicky Simpson and she's still got a few favours owed to her.'

'I'll have a chat,' Monroe agreed.

This time, Johnny's demeanour returned to a smile, and he nodded, shaking Monroe's hand.

'Good to see you, too, Detective Superintendent,' he said. 'And you, Mister Sutton. Obviously, my Parliamentary surgery hours are short, and I have many people to speak to. So, if you excuse me, I need to—'

'Speak to your adoring fans when we're finished?' Monroe suggested with a smile. 'You go be an MP, Mister Lucas. Make us proud.'

And this said, Monroe nudged Derek Sutton, and the two of them walked out of the surgery office, which was nothing more than a corner shop that had been taken over for the process.

Now, standing outside on Bethnal Green High Street, Monroe looked at Sutton, frowning.

'And what's up with you?' he said. 'Your face looks like thunder.'

'I never thought I'd see him fall so far,' Sutton said, glancing back at the building. 'He's gone respectable.'

'Aye,' Monroe nodded. 'Once he removed Jackie from his psyche and realised he could pin all his crimes on his sister, when she pretended to be the real-life, back-from-the-dead Jackie, Johnny Lucas worked out he had a second chance at life. But I must admit, though, I'm surprised at the direction he went.'

He nudged Sutton.

'Could you imagine Johnny Lucas as our next Prime Minister?'

'From what I understand from your lad Declan, he couldn't make a worse job than the current one.'

As the two of them returned to the pool car Monroe had borrowed from the hallowed halls of Temple Inn, Sutton's phone buzzed.

Looking down at it, his eyebrows narrowed in frustration.

'I'm leaving you at the nearest tube station,' he said.

'Let me guess. Rosanna has a lead and you don't want me there?' Monroe smiled. 'That's fine. I need to write out what we've learnt about the case anyway, and find a spot to hide out tonight.'

'Already done that,' Sutton replied as they climbed into the car. 'We're all staying at Declan's house.'

'We are?' Monroe smiled slightly. 'Does he know?'

'Aye, we talked,' Sutton leant back in the chair as Monroe started the engine. 'You're lucky to have such good friends.'

Monroe paused, looking directly at Sutton as he replied.

'Aye, Derek, I am,' he replied.

Sutton laughed.

'Don't you get soft on me, Ali,' he pointed at the road. 'Just drive me to an underground station.'

I<small>F THEY'D BEEN LESS INTERESTED IN THE CONVERSATION ABOUT</small> that night's sleeping arrangements and more aware of the surroundings, they would have noticed the man at the corner of Ellsworth Street, watching them through a camera lens as they drove off.

Damian Lim pulled out a notebook, noted down the time of the meeting, walked over to his motorbike, a Suzuki Marauder 125 still with its L plates on, placed his helmet onto his head and drove after them, sliding into the London traffic like a ghost.

———

16

CHANGING THE DEAL

It had been a good day for Harvey Drake.

Not only had he gained a new consultancy job with the Seven Sisters, but he was also now discussing another job - a far less legal consultancy type role - for a firm he'd been trying for a while to be involved in.

Since returning to London from Glasgow a couple of weeks back, his days had been quite busy, but now finally he could relax, sitting outside the BFI Bar that was attached to the National Theatre, with Waterloo Bridge stretching over him and to the side as he tried to calm his nerves and enjoy himself.

The problem with being a fixer like Harvey Drake was you were constantly being asked, or even ordered to fix things, and finding himself with even half an hour to forget the world he was inevitably connected to was a welcome break.

However, as he settled back in his chair to enjoy his drink, an enormous figure stood in his way.

'Hello Harvey,' a voice with the intimate Glaswegian accent he knew so well spoke.

Harvey stared up, frowning as he squinted, the sun in his eyes.

'I'm sorry, do I know you?' he asked as the man moved into view, blocking the sun.

Harvey felt his stomach flip-flop as he stared up at the face of Derek Sutton.

It was a face he'd once known well, but he realised had changed quite a bit since the last time they'd spoken, somewhere around thirty years earlier, and there was the slightest hint of familiarity, as if he'd seen him recently but hadn't realised at the time.

Although he couldn't for the life of him remember where from.

'Derek, I heard you were out,' he replied cautiously, still not sure if this was the precis to a pleasant conversation or a brutal attack. 'You look well.'

'Can't complain,' Sutton replied coldly. 'We need to have a wee chat about Damian Lim.'

'What about Damian?' Harvey asked, hoping that by keeping the questions going, he'd have a way of getting out of whatever was going on here.

'Don't play games,' a second voice said, and Harvey turned to see another familiar face.

'Rosanna Marcos? Shit.'

He didn't mean to speak it aloud, but the thought had gone straight to his mouth, bypassing the part of his brain that shouted not to say bloody stupid things. He knew Doctor Rosanna Marcos, and even if he hadn't, her reputation would have preceded her.

In fact, when he had last crossed swords with her, he had actually charged the client double because it had been Rosanna Marcos he'd been forced to deal with.

'Harvey Drake,' she said, sitting down in one of the chairs beside him. 'It's been a while since we saw each other.'

'I had nothing to do with the Tancredi murders,' Harvey said immediately, the words blurting out before he could stop them.

'Yes, you did,' Doctor Marcos smiled, shrugging. 'We both know what happened back then, so there's no point lying.'

'Don't know what you've been told, but it's lies,' Harvey continued his denial.

'I don't need to be told anything,' Doctor Marcos replied, leaning closer. 'I'm a forensic pathologist. I see the signs and clues, and let's just say I see you for everything you are, were, and will be.'

Harvey forced a relaxed smile at this.

'My future?' he said, looking from Marcos to Sutton and back. 'So what, you're a mind reader now?'

'It's not that hard to read your future,' Doctor Marcos leant closer, her voice quietening, forcing Harvey to listen harder. 'I think this part of your life is tragically drawing to a close right now.'

At this ominous statement, Harvey swallowed.

'You can't do anything,' he said, glancing at Sutton for some kind of support here. 'She's a copper. She wouldn't do anything bad.'

'I'm not a copper,' Doctor Marcos replied. 'I'm a divisional surgeon. A consultant at best. If I decide to go rogue and start killing people or finding ways for their bodies to be lost wherever I feel like losing them, that's my choice - and believe me, if I did that, I'd be *really good* at it.'

At this concerning statement, Harvey Drake trembled. It was bad enough knowing that Derek Sutton was an ice-cold killer with an axe to grind, but to know that a woman who was very good at hiding bodies, as well as finding them, was beside him and just as pissed at Harvey Drake as Sutton was a very concerning situation to be in.

'There's witnesses,' he said quickly, waving around. 'You can't kill me here.'

'Who said I was going to kill you here?' Doctor Marcos said, passing his drink across to him from across the table. 'You're not drinking your drink. Looks expensive. Have a sip.'

Harvey stared at the glass, realising that he hadn't been paying attention to it since Doctor Marcos had sat next to him. He also noticed, now on the table beside her, a small glass phial.

It hadn't been there earlier and now it was empty.

'What did you put in it?' he said as he stared back at the glass in front of him. It wasn't smoking or steaming or anything else poison did in the movies, but the lack of knowledge was eating away at him.

'Nothing,' Doctor Marcos replied a little too innocently, tapping the side of the glass as she grinned. 'Go on. Have a sip.'

'I don't know what you want from me,' Harvey said, ignoring the glass and deciding to change the subject. 'But whatever it is, I'm sure we can discuss this like grownups.'

'Then let's discuss it like grownups,' Sutton growled. 'You put a hit out on Alexander Monroe. Damian Lim is the poor sod who's taken the job. We know he's out there, and we know his plan. We would like you to stop him before we do.'

Harvey swallowed.

'Okay,' he said. 'Hypothetically, and I'm only saying hypothetically here, okay? Say I had been involved in some terrible criminal act, such as what you're suggesting—'

'Stop talking like a lawyer,' Doctor Marcos slammed a fist onto the table, the noise halting some of the nearby conversations and spilling the glass as she leant closer, her face a mask of anger. 'We've already said we're not police. I don't care about your legal situation, Harvey. I care about Alex Monroe not being murdered, and currently you're the person who'll stop that. So how about we stop playing games and you tell us how to get this hit taken off?'

'You can't,' Harvey was trembling more as he spoke. 'Damian is a lone wolf. Once you give him the nod, he goes off and does whatever you've told him to do. I can't get a hold of him to tell him to stop.'

'Well, you'd better work out a way to do so,' Sutton said. 'Because if he kills Ali Monroe, you'll be the next body found. In fact, if *anything* happens to Ali Monroe, from *anyone*, you'll be the next body found.'

'That's a threat to my life!' Harvey complained to Doctor Marcos. 'Are you going to let him do that?'

'I already said I'm not a copper,' Doctor Marcos shrugged. 'But I can ask him nicely to leave you breathing. Broken, but breathing. I still haven't worked out how you managed to set up the Tancredi killings, but know I'll make you my personal focus for the next year. Everything you do, everything you see, everybody you speak to? I *will* know, and I'll make sure everyone else knows, too.'

'You're not God.' Harvey hadn't meant to reply so arrogantly, but there was something about the way she'd spoken that irritated him.

However, Doctor Marcos just smiled calmly.

'Did you enjoy your drink today?' she asked. 'In *Doggett's*

Coat And Badge? You were having a friendly chat with a couple of very noticeable people I seem to recall.'

Harvey said nothing, opening and shutting his mouth twice as he realised this wasn't the first time they'd seen him today.

'Now you're wondering just how long we've been following you?' Sutton crouched, so he was eye level with Harvey. 'Let's just say it was long enough to know you were showing Ali Monroe's picture around, and long enough to know you were hired to take the job by Lennie Wright.'

'Long enough to know who else you've been speaking to and what deals you've been making,' Doctor Marcos added. 'And how you're preparing yourself for when Lennie Wright is invariably sentenced to a shit ton of years, and you no longer get to suckle from his teats anymore.'

She leant in closer.

'How do you think Lennie's going to react?' she asked. 'When he learns who you've been talking to? I mean, I'm no politician when it comes to gangland territories, but I'm pretty sure Lennie Wright, being the racist prick he is, isn't a fan of the Seven Sisters, and I know for a fact he hates the Chinese.'

Harvey nodded, understanding the situation.

'I can do what I can,' he said. 'I'll find out what I know—'

'What you know is a way to contact Damian Lim,' Doctor Marcos said.' We would like you to do that.'

Harvey nodded, currently too scared to reply.

'Anyway, good talk,' Doctor Marcos patted him on the back, and he felt a pinprick on his shoulder as she did so. Looking up at her smiling face, he realised she had a ring on with a small push pin held inside it, facing away.

'I'm sorry,' she said. 'Did I catch you with this? I don't

even remember if I put anything bad on it this morning. You're probably okay.'

She leant back over, her breath brushing his cheek as she whispered.

'That's how quick we can get to you,' she breathed. 'A slap on the back with a pin covered in poison, a vial of God knows what dropped into your drink when you're not watching, a slightly careless driver hitting you as you cross the road. I know all the ways to murder someone and get away with it. Do you really want me as your enemy?'

And this said, Doctor Marcos nodded to Derek Sutton, who rose, holding his hand out.

'Good to see you, Harvey,' he said, shaking the confused Harvey Drake's hand now. 'Thanks for all the help you've just given the City of London police. It's very appreciated. We expect you to come back to us very soon.'

He'd spoken loudly, and Harvey hadn't understood why he'd done it so jovially until he realised that the people sitting around had all overheard that last line about helping the police. If this location and this meeting got out to anybody, it would be a rumour passed that Harvey Drake had not only spoken to ex-Glasgow enforcer and enemy of Lennie Wright Derek Sutton, but also the divisional surgeon of a City of London police unit – and it ended with them being thrilled with what he had given them.

'You bastards,' he muttered. 'My reputation's all I've got.'

'And that's a shame,' Doctor Marcos replied. 'Because right now it's worth shit.'

As the two of them walked off, Harvey relaxed back into the chair, puffing out the breath he hadn't realised he'd been holding. Pushing away the glass of whatever it was now, he pulled his phone out and dialled a number.

'It's me,' he said into it. 'We have a serious problem.'
He rubbed the bridge of his nose as he continued.
'I'm going to need more hitmen.'

17

SLUMBER PARTY

DECLAN HAD BEEN DRIVEN HOME BY ANJLI, EVEN THOUGH HE'D pointed out he was perfectly fine. It also didn't help that Monroe and Derek Sutton sat in the back of the Audi, Monroe giving some kind of half back-seat-driver/half comedy routine about being hunted by a half-arsed killer.

Declan wasn't sure if it was the head wound or tiredness, but he simply didn't get it. But watching Monroe out of the corner of his eye, he thought his mentor was filled with an abundance of nervous energy; someone was trying to kill him, and he couldn't settle until it was sorted.

De'Geer was still with Doctor Marcos, working on the body of Gary Krohn.

Margaret Li had been sitting with Billy for most of the afternoon, and not a lot had come out of the meeting, apart from more information on the other murders; every single one of them had been ERR connected; none had been in the unit, but apart from Lukas Weber and Anna Hoffman, who'd both had grandfathers in the unit, the other victims were *sons* of officers in the same unit.

That was too much of a coincidence to avoid.

Billy and Margaret were still working on this as Declan had left, Billy promising they'd be ending soon, but with the desperate look of a man who knew he was held there until his superior, in this case Margaret Li, was bored.

Sutton, meanwhile, was already bored and had complained repeatedly while staring out of the window. He'd been the one to suggest Monroe hide out at Declan's, but he wanted to find the assassin, now named as Damian Lim and take the fight to him. Declan had pointed out this was a bad idea, and Sutton had explained quite patronisingly that this was the head wound talking.

Saviour of his boss or not, Declan was tiring of Derek Sutton.

And the night had been long; there'd been no attacks on them, but then they hadn't expected any. Declan had begged off early, claiming his head wound was distracting him, but in reality he couldn't take another story from "the good ol' days in Glasgae," and watching Monroe's slowly darkening expression, Declan got the feeling his boss was arriving at the same decision.

Jess had called before ten – she'd heard from Billy about the fight and was worried for her dad. Declan explained he was fine, and he'd had worse, in particular when an entire cave had landed on him in the Peak District, and the unconvinced Jess had let him rest, promising to call later in the week.

Declan expected to see her in the office the following day.

De'Geer had arrived before midnight, bringing no new information from the morgue; the painting wasn't in the studio and there was no sign of it being taken. Added to this there seemed to be a confusion on whether Krohn had or hadn't taken the painting, with the witness who found the body claiming she'd seen him leave with one, while the camera from the alley down the road had him empty-handed.

Declan decided to re-visit the gallery in the morning, gave his apologies, and went to bed.

They started singing sailor shanties downstairs at two in the morning.

WHEN DECLAN WOKE, HE FOUND SUTTON, MONROE AND De'Geer all asleep on the floor of the living room, with Anjli curled up on the sofa, his collection of whiskies massively depleted. Even though Monroe had been offered a room, he'd passed out before he'd reached the point of considering it, and Declan took minor delight in being as loud as he could – well, as loud as a man with a vicious head wound and probable concussion could – as he sorted some breakfast. Unsurprisingly, nobody was in the mood for an unhealthy fry up so he conveyor-belted some coffee into all of them before herding them off to the bathroom. Well, one at a time, at least.

At least nobody had puked this time.

De'Geer returned home to shower and change and seemed to be the most sober of all of them, although this could have been because of his late arrival. Either way, within an hour all four inhabitants of the house were showered, caffeinated and on their way back to Temple Inn, with Declan and Anjli changed into new clothes, Monroe promising to change into his spare suit when they arrived, and Sutton unaware he even smelled.

Climbing into the Audi like a family outing, none of them noticed the man on the Suzuki Marauder on the corner of the street, watching them leave.

Damian Lim wasn't on a bike that was motorway legal; 125cc bikes could only use A-roads, and the journey here had been long. But, when he arrived, he knew he couldn't take the old Scot on, not with so many bodies around him. So, he'd watched and waited, noted down what he thought could be weaknesses.

There was a chance the Scot would return here the following night, and he could prepare for that before he left.

Pulling his visor down, Damian Lim rode off.

And, from a second corner, starting his Triumph motorcycle and pulling his own visor down, Morten De'Geer followed him.

———

'Good morning,' Billy tried to make his voice cheerful as he spoke down the phone. 'Am I speaking to the UAL Saint Martin's campus admin department?'

'No, this is front desk,' the female voice on the other end of the line seemed suspicious, as if expecting something bad to be told to her. 'But we haven't opened yet. University enquiries are for after ten.'

'This isn't a university enquiry,' Billy was tapping on his keyboard as he spoke. 'This is Detective Sergeant Billy Fitzwarren of the City of London Police.'

'Oh,' there was a distinct pause down the phone, the woman on the other end probably working out what she'd got herself into by answering the call, so Billy doggedly carried on.

'I spoke to somebody yesterday in relation to a case we're currently working on.'

'Oh, yes,' the woman replied, moving some papers as she spoke, the rustling echoing down the line. 'You spoke to Siobhan, I believe. I'm Maureen. Can I help you?'

'Yes, Maureen. I'm hoping you can,' Billy smiled. He knew Maureen couldn't see it, but he'd been told smiling made your voice sounded warmer, and he'd been doing it ever since. He had no clue if it worked or not. 'I just wanted to check about one of your lecturers, if that's okay?'

'We don't usually give out details, because of data protection—'

'I get that, but it's nothing important, and it's only connected to the case in a loose way,' Billy quickly interrupted. 'So don't take anything from this, but we wanted to know if there's any way that you can tell if a lecturer has been in the building, even when they're not lecturing?'

There was a long pause.

'I'm not sure I know what you mean,' Maureen replied.

'Well, I'm guessing you and other employees of the college have passes,' Billy explained. 'Where you can put the fob against a key scanner, it opens the door, and you can walk around the building freely if you have the right credentials.'

'Yes,' Maureen agreed.

'And guest lecturers?'

'They're on the system, but they're treated like visitors, so when they turn up they're given a lanyard with a piece of paper attached, a printout from when they check in. It also has a picture of them on it.'

'And this is a onetime use?'

'Well, they sometimes use it more than once, but they're not supposed to,' Maureen said, and Billy could hear the irritation in her voice. Not at him, but at these hypothetical lecturers breaking the rules.

'So, if a guest lecturer turns up, I'm guessing they don't get one of these fobs unless they're regular?'

'Well, usually,' Maureen replied. 'But it depends on how often they come in. If they come in more often, then they get one of the fobs.'

There was a pause.

'Look, DS Fitzwarren, I get you can't tell me everything, but I really do have a lot to get through this morning, and rather than going around the houses it would help if you could tell me which lecturer you're asking about.'

'Miles Benson,' Billy replied. It wasn't a secret, and the news of the dead body in his gallery had already hit the papers that morning.

'Ah. He's not really a lecturer, he was only here as part of an event,' Maureen was still rustling through papers as she replied. 'Mister Benson did a week with us as part of an outsourcing event we run every year, and looking at it, he was only given a temporary pass so wouldn't have been able to have come into the college.'

'He couldn't have entered in any way?' Billy frowned. If this was the case, it meant Miles Benson might not have been the one leaving messages on note boards.

'Well, I mean, he probably could have, but he wouldn't have had a pass to look around freely,' Maureen, now in her element, continued. 'Someone would have had to have been with him – a member of the faculty or a student, anyone with a pass, really.'

'Oh?'

'Absolutely. It's the same with guests for the day. Often, we'll get one of the students working with that person to take them to wherever they need to be. So if he came in, it could have been anyone who walked him around.'

'And do your students have fobs?'

'Yes,' Maureen replied. 'Again, they're only with them for as long as they're students. They pay a deposit, and if they lose their fob, then they must buy a new one. But they all have one.'

'Can you track these?'

There was another pause, and Billy knew he was skating on thin ice here.

'Ignore that,' he blurted. 'We wouldn't be able to track him through those, that's all I really needed.'

'Can I ask what this is in connection with?' Maureen asked. 'It's to do with Lukas Weber, the German artist that died, isn't it?'

'Yes, it is,' Billy replied. Again, news travelled fast, especially in the art community.

'Oh, that's such a shame about him dying. He was such a nice man as well.'

At this, Billy frowned, unsure he heard correctly.

'Are you saying you met Lukas Weber?' he asked.

'Well, yes,' Maureen replied. 'When he was here last year.'

'I'm sorry, are we talking about the same artist?' Billy continued, already bringing up another browser window as he spoke. 'Because we've been informed that Lukas Weber never came over to this country before this exhibition.'

'Well, I can't talk about whoever told you that rubbish,' Maureen replied. 'But I can tell you he definitely came over. He was a guest lecturer, a part of the same series of talks that Miles Benson was.'

Billy leant back into his chair as he considered this, his phone still held to his ear.

'So, let me get this right,' he spoke slowly and carefully, determined not to miss anything here. 'On the same week that Miles Benson was at UAL Saint Martin's as a guest lecturer, which I believe was around nine months ago, Lukas Weber was also in the building, lecturing?'

'Well, only once,' Maureen replied. 'This is why I remember the name. It was a very uncomfortable week. He was a lovely man, very soft-spoken, gave the impression of someone who didn't want to cause any kind of fuss. A pacifist, I believe.'

Billy typed this into an open notes folder as she spoke.

'Please, go on,' he encouraged.

'But when he arrived, there were some problems. Some of the younger, more excitable students were unhappy about his familial connections.'

'You mean his grandfather was a Nazi?'

'We don't talk about that,' Maureen chided. 'But there were concerns raised about him talking. After he did his first talk, as we were contractually obligated to pay him for one, even if we cancelled the rest, it was suggested that we cut short his visit.'

'And how did he take that?'

'He understood. He said it wasn't the first time, and that he hadn't spoken to his grandfather for twenty years. But unfortunately, these things happen.'

Billy considered this.

'So, how long was he in the college?'

'A day, maybe two at most.'

'And did he meet anybody else during that time?'

'I couldn't tell you,' Maureen replied. 'He would definitely have met some of the faculty, he had students in his talk and he definitely spoke to a few of those afterwards.'

'Could he have met Miles Benson?' Billy asked.

'Oh, I can guarantee he definitely met Mister Benson,' Maureen almost laughed down the phone. 'It was arranged by one of the students in his talk.'

At this, Billy felt a sliver of ice slide down his spine.

'Do you know the name of that student?' he asked.

'Oh, I can't remember. It was months ago,' Maureen replied. 'Oh, I have it on the tip of my tongue.'

'Was it Cormorant?' Billy asked.

'Lucy? God no, although she was there,' Maureen was rummaging again. 'I'm sure it'll come to me …'

'Do you have a list of the students who attended Lukas Weber's talk?' Billy asked.

'I'm sure I can find it,' Maureen said. 'Would you like me to email it over to you? I believe we did the same with Miles Benson's talk.'

'If you could, it would save me a lot of hassle,' he said.

'Of course, we still have your email. I'll get that done today.'

There was a sudden flurry of action, and Maureen gave a triumphant yelp.

'Got it,' she said. 'Miss Nichols. She introduced Weber.'

Billy froze.

'Stacey Nichols?'

'Oh, did you have it already?'

'Stacey Nichols is a student?'

'Not currently, no, she left at the end of the year,' Maureen replied. 'Not really that much of a loss, to be honest. She's a bit flighty. Didn't turn up to half her talks in the last term. Oh, I can see Lucy Cormorant was also at the talk. If you want, I could ask about?'

'No, you've helped enough,' Billy said. 'We still don't know yet whether there is anything to be discussed here, and I don't want to cause any issues.'

'I completely understand.'

Billy couldn't see it, but he almost felt like Maureen had given a conspiratorial wink. Placing the phone down, Billy leant back in his chair, considering what he'd just learned.

Lukas Weber had been in London, and not only that, but he'd also been at Saint Martin's, the same college where Miles Benson had taught. Lucy Cormorant had watched his talk, as well as Stacey Nichols, the woman who found the body, and who introduced him to Miles.

This was too much of a coincidence.

And, as Billy started preparing for the upcoming briefing, he wondered whether everything they'd been told had already been proven to be a fallacy.

Bloody artists.

18

DE-BRIEFING

MONROE WASN'T STANDING BY THE DOOR THIS TIME AS DECLAN began his briefing. Instead, he sat to the side, nursing his head, mumbling gently to himself.

The rest of the briefing room was busy, with De'Geer, Cooper and Doctor Marcos sitting at the back, Anjli in her normal chair, and Billy at his computer. In Declan's usual position was the German police officer Margaret Li, looking a little confused at what was going on.

De'Geer had arrived ten minutes earlier; he'd followed Damian Lim's slightly battered 2006 Marauder 125cc, which was trying really hard to be a cruiser, but failing in the process to a house in Acton where, after taking the details he'd carried on to Temple Inn and the briefing. Derek Sutton had wanted to go straight there, and De'Geer offered to take him on pillion, but Monroe had calmed him; they needed to see what Drake did first, and it was a simple case to stake someone out to watch the address.

De'Geer had reluctantly agreed, and now glared balefully at everyone from the back.

'I might have something,' Billy was still working on the laptop as everyone settled. 'I'm waiting for a confirmation email though, before I say anything.'

Declan nodded at this.

'Anything on the receipt?' he asked.

'Looking into it later,' Billy replied, but he seemed a little nervous as he spoke. 'I sent it to clearer heads at Lambeth forensics.'

Declan went to reply, to ask why Billy hadn't passed it to Doctor Marcos instead, but stopped as Margaret Li audibly cleared her throat.

'Who is the child?' she asked, pointing at the person sitting next to Billy.

'That's my daughter,' Declan replied. 'Her name's Jess. She heard I was injured and turned up today to make sure I wasn't lying to her when I said I was fine.'

'Does your daughter not trust you?'

'Let's just say she has an investigative style similar to mine, that won't allow her to take no for an answer,' Declan forced a smile. 'And, once she arrived and found we had a juicy murder on our books, she decided she was going to stay for the day.'

Anjli grinned, nodding at Jess who smiled back.

'And you allow this?' Margaret seemed confused. 'Is this like, how you say, "take your daughter to work day?"'

'She's kind of an unofficial mascot,' Bullman, now appearing at the door said, walking over and shaking Margaret's hand. 'It's a pleasure to see you again, Kriminalkommissar. But please don't underestimate the people in this room. Your partner of many years, the one you didn't realise was the son of a serial killer? This "mascot" took his sister down single-handed.'

Margaret looked back at Jess, and Declan resisted the urge to explain that Jess *had* fought Ilse Müller, using a variety of power tools, but had received help from both Billy and Anjli at the end.

Margaret, however, simply nodded at Jess, as if accepting her position in the room.

'Right,' Declan said, looking around. 'Let's talk about what we have.'

'Lukas Weber died of a cardiac arrest caused from a shock-stick blast to his pacemaker,' Doctor Marcos said as she rose. 'It wasn't helped by a fall that he took after he was shocked, that slammed the back of his head against the table. Alone, both shock and blow wouldn't have killed him. Together, however ...'

She trailed off, the statement no longer needing to be continued.

'Someone shocked Lukas Weber,' Declan nodded. 'And then painted a lipstick kiss onto their neck and tattooed it with the initials "J. K." Suspects?'

'Lucy Cormorant is the first option, but she was in the room next door.'

'And she said Gary Krohn could have done it, but he's not really the murdering type, according to our resident criminals,' Anjli replied.

'It could have been an accident,' Monroe suggested now, wincing as he spoke loudly. 'He shocks Weber, and then Weber falls and smacks his skull. Krohn doesn't realise he's dying as he paints onto the neck.'

'Possible,' Declan replied, looking back at Margaret Li. 'Kriminalkommissar, could you please tell us about the painting of the lipstick?'

Margaret straightened in her chair, pulling out a ring

binder from the briefcase on the floor beside her and opening it up, scrolling her finger down the page.

'We first learned of this when Stefan Bierhof was found murdered in his apartment in Berlin a month ago,' she said. 'He was a prominent picture framer and artist in Berlin. We couldn't work out why he had been murdered, or why someone would paint a lipstick kiss on his neck. But when looking into this, we learned from some allies in Austria that there had also been a murder there a couple of weeks earlier, with the same modus operandi, as you say.'

'This would be Borge Pedersen, the professor killed in Salzburg?' Anjli asked, looking back at the German officer.

Margaret nodded.

'Once we had two people with the same lipstick clue, it was very easy to find a third,' she said. 'This was in Paris two weeks ago on Anna Hoffmann.'

'At what point did you realise they were all connected to the ERR?' Declan asked.

'It took a while,' Margaret replied, almost sheepishly. 'We rarely talk about that part of our history, so sometimes checking into it can take a while.'

'So let me get this right,' Monroe said, 'Lukas Weber's grandfather, and the fathers of Stefan Bierhof, Borge Pedersen and Anna Hoffmann were all in the same unit during World War Two?'

'Anna's grandfather was, but the rest is correct,' Margaret replied. 'The Einsatzstab Reichsleiter Rosenberg were stationed across Europe, but their unit was based in Neuschwanstein Castle, which was a repository of stolen artefacts, paintings, books, statues and other such treasures, many taken during the occupation of France.'

She flicked through the ring binder again.

'At the end of the war, it is believed that many of these items were taken when the soldiers in the unit realised the Germans were not going to win.'

'Lining their pockets, I think you'll find,' Monroe muttered to himself.

'We only found the link because we were looking for the pattern,' Margaret continued. 'It is understandable that you did not realise this was part of a series of murders when Lukas Weber was killed. In fact, I believe my department in Berlin was the only place we realised these murders were linked.'

'You might have been the only *police* who worked it out, but you weren't the only people,' Declan said, nodding to Billy, who tapped the laptop, throwing an image up onto the plasma screen behind Declan. It was a shot taken from Declan's phone of Miles Benson's crime wall – well, crime *easel,* anyway.

'Miles Benson had clippings of all three other murders,' Declan said. 'More importantly, Mister Benson believed that his brother Andrew was possibly the cause of these murders, as he had been in all of their locations at the same time.'

Margaret rose and stared closely at the image, even though she'd had time to examine it the previous night.

'Okay. Lukas Weber is part of a series of murders, possibly by Andrew Benson,' Declan continued. 'Although, to be honest, I'm not sure if that's correct. What else do we have?'

'On the night of Lukas Weber's murder, Gary Krohn, known forger and art restorer to the criminal classes was seen trying to steal a painting,' Cooper read from her notes at the back of the room. 'Witnesses stated they'd seen him in over-alls. And when Detective Inspector Kapoor spoke to Andrew on his way back from Romania, Andrew informed her he'd asked for Gary to attend the event, and had sent him a printed pass.'

'But Gary was there purely to steal the painting, not to speak to Lukas Weber,' Anjli added.

'But did he steal the painting?' Declan asked. 'CCTV outside the gallery says no, but a witness says yes.'

There was a ding on Billy's laptop as an email came through, and after quickly scanning it, he punched the air.

'That your "exciting new bit of information," laddie?' Monroe held back a smile at Billy's exuberance.

'Confirmation,' Billy nodded. 'I think our witness is unreliable.'

'Stacey Nichols?'

Billy nodded, pulling up a list of names onto the plasma screen.

'I spoke to UAL Saint Martin's before the briefing,' he started. 'And they informed me of something we weren't aware of beforehand. I've been waiting for the list to arrive before mentioning it.'

'So go on, laddie, mention it!' Monroe bellowed, instantly regretting it.

'Lukas Weber has been to England before,' Billy said, using his mouse pointer on the screen to guide the briefing room to the relevant areas of the list. 'He was here nine months ago as part of the same series of lectures that Miles Benson was on. In fact, I was told by the admin assistant that one of the people who took his course introduced him to Miles Benson... and that person was Stacey Nichols.'

'Nichols was at the college?'

'I checked into her student record, and she was an art student there last year, same year as Lucy Cormorant. Took some of the same classes, in fact, but she dropped out at the end of this year, unhappy with how her life was going, I suppose.'

Declan glanced at Anjli.

'Did she say anything?'

'That she'd met him? She didn't mention that at all,' Anjli replied coldly, her eyes narrowing.

'Okay, then we need to look into Stacey Nichols a little more then,' Declan said, mulling the new information over. 'Lucy Cormorant outed Lukas Weber as a Nazi, claiming that she hadn't known anything about him and had been told on a message board about him.'

'She would have known before that,' Billy said, showing Lucy's name on Weber's lecture list. 'She was there, too, and Lukas Weber only did one lecture; the college decided that thanks to his history, it would be better if he didn't fulfil his scheduled talks.'

'And this would have got out as colleges are terrible for rumour mills,' Jess said, reddening. 'Prisha told me that.'

'Prisha is?' Margaret frowned.

'My girlfriend,' Jess replied, almost argumentatively. But again, Margaret simply nodded.

'But if she knew her lecturer was a Nazi, why make out that she had to research him to see if it was true?' Billy asked.

'You have a point,' Declan replied. 'She shouldn't have needed to, so Lucy Cormorant isn't giving us the full story, either.'

'Could she be involved more than we thought?' Bullman, by the door, asked.

'Cormorant's a popular French name,' Billy suggested. 'And her father's called Marcel, which is French, too. It was changed from *Kormereaux* when they came over here, and we know that many of the paintings taken by the ERR were from Jewish families in France.'

'Perhaps there's something to look into there,' Declan said. 'There was something else that's been on my mind for a while now. Why steal *that* painting? Why do we care about an early Lukas Weber piece?'

There was no answer as he finished, and he realised that everybody in the room was now waiting for his explanation.

'I think,' he said, pacing slightly, doing his best not to look like Monroe when he used to do this, 'I think that Lukas Weber painted over a prior image. I think that the painting he wanted to be left in Austria is something that his grandfather had, a painting that somehow Lukas Weber has camouflaged into his own. A painting that an expert could restore, revealing the original, stolen painting.'

'Lukas Weber apparently hated his grandfather,' Anjli said. 'But maybe he knew the value of the painting?'

'Or he knew the trouble he'd have if he revealed it after all these years,' Monroe added. 'We should see if we can get anything else on that.'

'Okay, moving on,' Declan nodded. 'Tell me about Gabriel Bauer.'

'He's an Argentine Cartel boss, effectively,' Billy said, pulling up a rap sheet.

'Is there even such a thing as an Argentinian Cartel?' Monroe asked.

'Oh yes,' Billy nodded, pulling up a series of images. 'In October 2022, an Italian *'Ndrangheta* mafia leader, Carmine Alfonso Maiorano was captured in Buenos Aires. Argentina's most powerful organised crime group, *los Monos*, or *the Monkeys* is based in Rosario, which is nicknamed "The Argentine Chicago" because of the drugs crime.'

'You know a lot about this,' Margaret was surprised.

'My ex used to work for a Colombian cartel,' Billy replied a little reluctantly. 'I learnt a lot back then.'

He returned to the screen as Margaret stared at him in a mixture of surprise, horror, and awe.

'Bauer's got almost diplomatic levels of immunity. He's pretty much legit on paper, got friends in every level of government, and he's been in England for the last six months working on trade deals with your friend and mine, Charles Baker.'

'Is Bauer a Nazi?' Declan asked, wincing as he realised he had a German in the room, but Margaret didn't seem to be bothered by the terminology.

'Gabriel Bauer is a far-right neo-Nazi,' she said. 'We have heard of him. He has been in Berlin many times, and he has often caused civil unrest there.'

'It seems very strange that we have a far-right neo-Nazi Argentine who's very into art, bidding on a ton of paintings by the grandson of a member of the unit that took other paintings,' Declan said as he looked back to the room. 'Unless he knows something about them.'

'He does, and it isn't strange,' Margaret replied. 'His father, Werner Bauer, was a Einsatzhelfer in the Einsatzstab Reichsleiter Rosenberg für die Besetzten Gebiete. That's like a "Sergeant" to you, and he was stationed at Neuschwanstein Castle.'

'He wasn't involved in the trials,' Billy hunted through some files, the folders appearing on the plasma screen.

'No, because he escaped to Argentina at the end of the war,' Margaret continued. 'It was believed he stole many priceless pieces, taking them with him, using them to finance the empire he eventually gave to his son.'

'Sounds like another screwed-up family dynasty,' Anjli muttered. 'Could he have known Grandpa Weber?'

'Perhaps. The unit was quite large.'

'Maybe that's the plan here?' Monroe leant back in his chair. 'Weber sells his grandfather's paintings under the guise of his own, doing the same as Werner Bauer did? Certain ones, worth ten times what they're sold for, when restored by someone like Krohn? Maybe even items connected to ones Bauer senior had stolen and kept?'

'Maybe, but someone screwed Bauer over, taking the money for paintings,' Anjli looked around the room. 'Anyone else feel sorry for him?'

'Bauer assumes it's Krohn, possibly after seeing Lucy's sketch, sends a man after him, finds no painting, kills him,' Declan nodded. 'We need to speak to Bauer immediately and work out if this seller was another person hired by Andrew Benson.'

'What about the initials J K?' Billy put up an image taken from the crime scene.

At this, however, Margaret Li frowned.

'You mentioned "Young Artists," yesterday,' she said. 'Explain the relevance.'

'Our art experts yesterday told us about the "Young Artists" following during the war,' Billy explained. 'The Nazis took from many young Jewish artists before killing them. People created secret societies, and one was called the "Young Artists." The followers really couldn't show symbols, especially during the war, so they'd kiss each other's necks, leaving a lipstick mark. This was their symbol, and if questioned, it was nothing more than a kiss. But we're talking eighty years ago.'

At the explanation, Margaret Li had a slight smile on her usually expressionless face. It was slightly unnerving.

'Junger Künstler,' she said. 'That is "young artist" in German.'

'J.K,' Declan pursed his lips. 'That's a hell of a coincidence.'

Looking around the room, he took in the faces.

'Okay,' he said. 'Anjli, bring in the Bensons. All of them. I want to know what's going on there. De'Geer? While you wait for more things to examine, go with Detective Superintendent Monroe and Miss Li here and speak to Gabriel Bauer. Billy? Look into Krohn's connections, see how well he knew Bauer. Cooper? Have a chat with Lucy Cormorant again. Don't mention what we know, do it as a follow up.'

'And Stacey Nichols?' Anjli asked.

'She's mine,' Declan growled. 'I'm sick of being used, and I think she knows more than she's letting on.'

19

REMEMBER THE WAR

IF THERE WAS ANYTHING THAT MONROE WANTED TO DO LESS than be hunted by a killer, it was face off against a neo-Nazi industrialist with a God complex, but within thirty seconds of meeting Gabriel Bauer, Monroe knew this was exactly what he was doing right now.

Bauer had an office in St Mary's Axe, in the building better known by Londoners as "the Gherkin," but had agreed only to speak with the City of London police in the circular lobby that surrounded the base of the building. Monroe understood that Bauer probably didn't want police in his office without a warrant, especially if he was as dodgy as Monroe believed, but at the same time it was a hell of a way to make you seem suspicious when you weren't.

De'Geer was amazed by the architectural walls surrounding them, but Margaret Li seemed unimpressed. In fact, she'd been unimpressed since realising she was going out with Monroe rather than Bullman, who she'd apparently built some kind of hero-worshipping basis around.

Monroe understood. Margaret Li saw Bullman as a

success, rising two levels since they last spoke. Monroe, meanwhile, was the man who couldn't speak German when they last met and hadn't rectified that.

He almost started a small-talk conversation with her, starting with something innocuous like "do you have buildings like this in Berlin," but stopped himself. Of course they had buildings like this. If he'd asked, she'd probably lecture him on how their buildings were better.

Gabriel Bauer appeared out of one of the central lifts, flanked by two suited men. They were younger than he was by quite a bit, Bauer looking to be around the same age as their fathers.

Maybe he *was* their father, Monroe wondered. It wasn't the first time someone employed their own children to provide for them. One was slim with a musketeer moustache, the other stockier with a close-cropped hairstyle and a scar across his eye. But what also stood out was that the slimmer of the two had a bandaged right wrist.

The same one Declan had slammed an extendible baton onto.

'Police?' Bauer asked, and Monroe couldn't help but look around; there wasn't anyone else here with a police sergeant in full uniform, and they'd already met before, albeit a blink and you'll miss it moment at the Benson Gallery, so he assumed this was just politeness. Or some kind of weird Argentine power play.

'Aye,' he said, rising. 'We've met before, I'm Detective Superintendent—'

'I would like to raise charges against the Benson Gallery,' Bauer interrupted. 'They stole a quarter of a million pounds of my money and I want them arrested.'

Monroe hadn't expected this and paused as his still-hungover brain shifted to this new line of enquiry.

'You are here about the Gallery?' Bauer quizzed. 'After all, you heard my complaint when you interrupted me yesterday.'

Monroe straightened.

'Yes and no,' he replied. 'Yes, we want to take a statement about what happened, but also no, we'd like a wee chat with you first about your relationship with Gary Krohn.'

Bauer didn't even flicker a change of expression at the name.

'Krohn,' he nodded. 'I know the man. He has restored art for me in the past.'

'Recently?'

'I don't see what that has to do with anything.'

'Gary Krohn was thrown out of a fourth-floor window yesterday,' De'Geer, unable to stop himself growled. 'By a killer who matches the height and build of your man there.'

He punctuated this with a nod at the man with the bandaged wrist.

'How did you damage your wrist?' he asked.

'Do not answer,' Bauer ordered his man before glaring at Monroe. 'Is this how British police act? Accusing innocent men of murder?'

'That depends on the bruise he has on it, doesn't it?' Monroe gave a winning smile in response. 'If he gives us a wee squiz at it, we can end that issue real quick. Either by backing off ... or arresting him.'

The man with the bandaged wrist squared up, but again Bauer barked a command and the man reluctantly backed down.

'It isn't convenient right now, but I will ensure my man provides himself to your divisional surgeon at our earliest opportunity,' he said.

'Aye, you do that,' Monroe smiled coldly, knowing full well the moment they left the man would be on his way to an airport. 'So we're on the same page though, can I have the names of your friends?'

Bauer went to argue, but then shrugged.

'Jorge Aznar and Rafael Kirchner,' he said, with Rafael Kirchner being the name of the murder suspect. 'And your friends are?'

'I was telling you when you interrupted.'

'I was eager to press charges.'

'This is Sergeant De'Geer, and this is Kriminalkommissar Li.'

'German police?' Bauer hadn't expected that, especially with Margaret being Asian. 'This is because of Weber?'

'Among others,' Margaret replied. 'We have met before, Herr Bauer. When you attacked two young men outside a Berlin nightclub.'

'You have me mistaken,' Bauer replied. 'Perhaps you were squinting your narrow eyes too hard—'

'Now, watch your mouth!' Monroe snapped, louder than he intended, and Bauer moved away, chuckling.

Monroe forced himself to calm down and pulled out his notebook.

'Did you know Gary Krohn was at the gallery?' he asked.

'I heard later,' Bauer nodded. 'I didn't see or speak to him. He's an art restorer. I assumed he was restoring.'

'You assumed?' Monroe replied, remembering the words Bauer had used against Benson.

Bauer shrugged.

'I spent little time on him if I am being truthful. He worked for me, but he also double crossed me here and there. Owes me money. I knew if I faced him, I might be removed.'

'Because of the scene you'd make?'

'Because of the blood I'd spill from his many wounds,' Bauer spoke with no fear of reprisal. 'It's a lot of money. But nowhere near what I was robbed of two nights ago.'

'How many paintings had you bought?' De'Geer asked.

'I forget,' Bauer shrugged. 'The one I really wanted wasn't there, so I was keeping myself occupied until they brought it out.'

'"The Kiss,"' Monroe replied, and smiled as Bauer did a double take at the name. 'Aye, we know about that as well. But I was under the assumption it wasn't being sold at the auction?'

'Everything's for sale if you know the price,' Bauer replied.

'Spoken like the kind of man that decides everyone has a price,' Monroe spoke softly, and if Bauer had known him, he would have noticed the tell-tale signs of building anger. 'And if they won't sell it to you, you'll just take it.'

'I'm a businessman, Mister Monroe,' Bauer smiled. 'I don't know what you mean by "take" it. But I am good at convincing people to sell me things I want. I'll give you that.'

'And Lukas Weber was going to sell you a particular painting?'

'Lukas Weber was going to sell me a few paintings I wanted,' Bauer's smile widened. 'And yes, one of them was a piece of his called "The Kiss," something he didn't want to sell ... well, shall we say, he didn't want to sell for the *wrong price*.'

'And you think you found the right price?'

'We will never know now,' Bauer shrugged. 'But I'd been given to believe that there was a way to do this, though. A personal bid, nothing to do with Benson, or his wife ... or his brother.'

The last part was said with such disdain that Monroe wondered whether the problem that Bauer had with Miles Benson was more aimed at Andrew rather than the man himself.

'So, let me get this right,' Monroe asked. 'If you turned up to this event expecting to buy a couple of special paintings, then why spend a quarter of a million on others?'

'Let's just say it was the buy-in,' Gabriel Bauer held his hands up in a resigned gesture. 'You know, when you play high stakes poker, you must turn up and prove you can play with the big boys? Well, this was a similar thing. Weber needed to know I had the money and the intention to stay in.'

He relaxed a little, probably assuming he was in the clear right now.

'There were several paintings I wanted and we'd been discussing it for quite a while,' he said, but Monroe felt that something was off here. Bauer was too calm about this for a man having recently lost so much. It was almost as if he was deliberately lowering his levels of concern to divert the officers interviewing him.

'Tell me more about the painting that you wanted,' he asked.

'I felt it gave a certain naivety to his style,' Bauer explained. 'I was going to buy some, sell them off, keep the ones I wanted and pass them to Gary Krohn, perhaps.'

'Aye, I'm sure he could do his restoring magic on them,' Monroe smiled darkly.

'You act as if the paintings needed to be restored,' Bauer replied calmly. 'Mister Krohn is an exquisite framer.'

He wasn't out of his depth at all, and this concerned Monroe. He hated doing what the suspect expected.

'This isn't the first time you've been buying paintings

though, is it?' Margaret replied, moving into the conversation now, physically as well as verbally, as she stepped closer. 'You were in Berlin a month back.'

'I was in a lot of places a month back,' Bauer gave a smile, a patronising one that sounded more like he was talking down to the police officer than answering her question. 'I visit Berlin often. I have a fascination with the place, and the people that live in it.'

'Like the nightclubs,' Margaret hissed.

'Live or lived?' De'Geer asked, but Monroe held his hand up to wave the Viking sergeant back down.

'So, you assumed this man with the grey hair who took your money at the end of the event was connected to the Benson Gallery?'

If Bauer had been surprised by the change of subject, he took it in his stride.

'There was confusion after the murder – and yes, we knew it was a murder. I was nowhere near it, and neither were my employees, of which there were several there that night.'

'Oh, aye?'

'A man of my stature in business doesn't attend events without security,' Bauer replied. 'I thought, after it happened we would lose the opportunity to buy the paintings, now he was gone. But then a man appeared, claiming to be working on behalf of the gallery. He explained that certain members of the bidding community were being offered a chance to pay there and then for the paintings that they'd ordered. An opportunity to keep them locked at a set price.'

Monroe looked around, contemplating the statement.

'You thought this was connected to Weber's painting, still, didn't you?' he asked. 'You believed that by buying these paintings you'd still get an opportunity to do what you needed to do.'

'By buying the paintings, I had already *done* what I needed to do,' Bauer snapped, now getting irritated by the questioning. But whether this was because he was tiring of it, or because Monroe's questions were striking too close to the mark, Monroe didn't know. 'I had a list of paintings I wanted, and I was willing to spend ten times what I'd bid already. More, even.'

Monroe shook his head.

'You know, you're really making it sound as if there's more to this stolen painting,' he said.

Bauer smiled, shrugging his shoulders.

'I'm sure there is,' he said. 'Paintings hold many secrets. But that is irrelevant. My problem is I gave money in good faith, believing I had purchased the paintings I required, only to find that Miles Benson is reneging on a deal and claiming he never saw a penny of this.'

'Aye,' Monroe smiled now, and it was a genuine one, as he realised this was possibly the only bad thing that seemed to have happened to Gabriel Bauer that week. 'And it's a crying shame someone conned you out of such a large amount of money. But, if you raise a report, we'll get somebody to look into it for you. We'd like a description of the man and—'

'Oh, I can give you more than that,' Bauer said, clicking his fingers. Jorge Aznar, the man on the left that didn't have a broken wrist, pulled out a phone, scrolling through some images and holding one up.

It was a picture taken during the event. A crowd of people were milling around, looking confused.

'This was shortly after the murder had been revealed,'

Bauer explained. 'And taken as the man spoke to a variety of customers.'

Monroe squinted at the photo.

'Aye, I wondered how you knew his hair colour. Do you know who he spoke to?'

'Why? Should I be doing your job, Detective Superintendent?' Bauer snapped. 'No, I don't know who he spoke to, and I don't know who else gave him money. But I know for a fact there were at least two other people in that gallery who were looking to do personal deals with Lukas Weber, and they both knew what was really on offer.'

'And what was that?' Margaret asked, picking up on the misspoken line.

Realising he'd said too much, Bauer gritted his teeth, silently castigating himself.

'This is the man,' he said. 'My associate will send you the photo. I'm sure you can check into who he is. Or I'll be forced to take matters into my own hands.'

'What, bring them to this swanky building?' Monroe smiled. 'Can't see the landlords being happy with that.'

'This is just where my office is,' Bauer replied. 'I have many far quieter warehouses where I wouldn't be disturbed.'

'You do that, and I might be arresting you.'

'You do *that*, and your government would call you off, while I walk free.'

'Well then, as you're such a special case, and loved by the Tories, we'll look into this, laddie,' Monroe said as he pulled his phone out to accept the image.

However, as he did so, he noticed a message that had arrived while they'd been talking.

FROM: ROSANNA MARCOS

Fingerprint match on machete. Argentine
National named Rafael José Kirchner.

Monroe looked up at Gabriel Bauer. The man who had
held the machete was standing beside him, still holding his
injured wrist.

'Maybe you'd like to come to the station?' he suggested.
'Answer some questions there. We could even take a proper
statement.'

'I'm a very busy man,' Bauer shook his head at this offer.

'Aye, then perhaps one of your men could come. Mister
Kirchner, for example? I'm sure he could answer some
questions.'

Gabriel Bauer realised at this point that something new
was happening, and turned to face Monroe, squaring his
shoulders for an argument.

'And I'm telling you that my men enjoy the same diplomatic relationship I have with your government.'

'I'm sure they do,' Monroe didn't back down from this,
instead leaning in closer, his Glaswegian heritage taking over.
'But here's the thing, laddie. Your man there with the busted
wrist? We know he attacked one of my men last night and
carelessly dropped a machete. A machete, by the way, that
has his fingerprints all over the hilt.'

Bauer didn't look at Rafael Kirchner, but his eyes flickered
for a moment, and Monroe wasn't surprised to see there was
no change of expression on his face at this revelation, when
he was likely furious at his man for such a rookie error.

'You really should train your hitmen to be better at
killing, Mister Bauer, because I'm afraid we're going to have
to take him into questioning now.'

Monroe had expected Bauer to stop this, to claim some diplomatic incident or even raise a hand to pause De'Geer as he pulled out a pair of handcuffs. But instead, Bauer nodded, stepped back, and looked at Kirchner.

'I'll send my finest solicitor to you,' he said. 'You know the drill.'

Kirchner nodded and stepped forward, holding one hand up.

'I have a busted wrist,' he said. 'The handcuffs will hurt me. I would rather not wear them.'

'Aye, well you busted it while trying to kill my friend, so I'd rather you *did* wear them,' Monroe said, taking the handcuffs off De'Geer and placing them on both wrists, pushing hard, making sure they were as tight as they could go, hearing a slight outburst of pained breath from Kirchner as he caught his wrist. 'And I don't really give a shite what you think.'

And, with that, Monroe smiled one more time at the still calm Gabriel Bauer, nodded to De'Geer and Margaret to follow, and with Rafael Kirchner in tow they left the lobby of the Gherkin, with Rafael Kirchner already complaining loudly he'd been framed.

One down, one to go, Monroe thought to himself. Gary Krohn's killer was caught; but they were still no closer to finding Lukas Weber's one.

He just hoped the others were having as much fun as he was right now.

20
_____

UNRELIABLE WITNESSES

As Miles Benson squirmed in the interview room chair, wringing his hands together nervously, Anjli stared intently at him, her eyes burrowing into his, trying to decide how best to approach this.

But it was Bullman who spoke first.

'Your brother is next door throwing you under a bus,' she lied, leaning forward and placing her elbows on the desk between them. 'I thought you should know that before we start.'

She reached across and turned on the recording button.

'Do you need your solicitor here?'

'I don't know,' Miles replied nervously. 'Do I?'

'Your brother's calling for his, so you probably want one,' Anjli shrugged. 'But let's start and see how we go. How's that sound?'

Miles nodded, his face expressing someone who wanted to help as much as he could, and Anjli hoped this was genuine, and not an act for the two officers in front of him.

'Interview with Miles Benson,' Bullman said, leaning into

the microphone, 'Ten-thirty am, Detective Inspector Anjli Kapoor and Detective Chief Superintendent Sophie Bullman are in attendance.'

She looked back at Miles.

'Did you hear that?' she asked. 'I'm a Detective Chief Superintendent, and I'm in this room right now talking to you. What does that say about the amount of trouble you're currently in?'

Anjli knew it didn't say *much* about the trouble that Miles was currently in and said more about the fact that Bullman was bored in the office and thought it would be quite nice to attend the investigation. However, Miles wasn't aware of this, and she could already see the sweat appearing at his temples.

'Look,' he said. 'I swear to you, I didn't set up Bauer. I don't know who took his money.'

'And that's your problem,' Anjli said, now relaxing into her chair. 'There are so many things we're here to talk to you about, you don't know why you're actually in that chair, do you?'

She counted off her fingers as she continued.

'It could be because Lukas Weber died in your gallery. It could be because you have a crime board on the back of a painting hidden from everyone, showing other murders across Europe – murders we now know are connected to Lukas Weber's own grandfather. Maybe it's that you've taken money from high rollers at your auction, high rollers including Gabriel Bauer. Or, it could be something else.'

'What else?' Miles frowned, unsure of what she meant.

Anjli shrugged.

'Well,' she replied, smiling darkly. 'It could be the fact that you're an incredibly unreliable witness, and you've been lying to us.'

Miles Benson said nothing, licking his lips nervously and looking around the room.

'How about we start with the truth?' Anjli asked politely. 'How did you meet Lukas Weber?'

Miles contemplated the question and then nodded.

'My brother Andrew,' he said. 'He was looking into unknown artists we could sell in the UK, and a friend of his had mentioned this unknown Austrian painter named Lukas Weber. We were looking for art for the exhibition, nothing more.'

Bullman slammed a fist on the table, the reverberation and noise making Miles jump, yelping.

'For the record, Detective Chief Superintendent Bullman has slammed her fist onto the table, irritated by the suspect's commitment to lying,' Bullman said, looking back at Miles. 'Let's pretend just for the moment Mister Benson, that we're not total idiots and we already know the answer. Please tell us again how you first met Lukas Weber.'

'As I said—' Miles started, but stopped when Anjli raised a hand.

'Let me add a little more to that, before you fall into the massive hole you're digging,' she smiled now, a sardonic, bitter smile with no humour behind it, almost mocking in nature. 'How about we change the question? How did you meet Lukas Weber, *nine months ago at UAL Saint Martin's College?*'

At the question, Miles visibly started looking around the room, as if expecting some secret camera crew to appear out of nowhere and shout "surprise" at him.

'I-I ... d-didn't,' he stammered.

'We know, Mister Benson, that you were introduced to Lukas Weber while lecturing there,' Anjli said. 'We also know that he was introduced to you during the event by a student who watched your talk.'

'I don't remember,' Miles whined. 'Yes, I think maybe I did meet Lukas Weber there, but I hadn't put the two things together until later on when Andrew mentioned the name.'

'So, you hadn't discussed his paintings then?' Bullman inquired.

'No,' Miles replied, a little more secure in his answers.

'But you knew why Lukas Weber had been removed from the event at the college, didn't you?'

'I knew he'd done one talk and then he'd been pulled from the week's lectures,' Miles replied. 'I didn't hear the gossip.'

'You weren't told it was because of certain connections his family had during the war?'

Miles simply shook his head.

'For the record, Mister Benson is shaking his head rather than speaking,' Anjli noted. 'Tell us about the protester at the gallery.'

Miles centred himself a bit, now back on safer ground.

'She appeared out of nowhere, gave some speech about how Lukas was a Nazi. He wasn't, by the way. He was a kind man. His grandfather's problems in the past shouldn't have been something that would get him into trouble.'

'And you'd never met the woman? Lucy Cormorant?' Bullman asked. 'You didn't recognise her from anything?'

'I don't remember,' Miles shook his head, and Anjli realised Miles already knew what the next line of questioning was going to be and was trying to vague his memory a little to get away with it.

'Let's try again,' she said. 'Did you recognise Lucy

Cormorant, who nine months ago had attended your lecture at UAL Saint Martin's?'

'I don't recall seeing her,' Miles replied. 'I had a full lecture hall when I spoke. A lot of people want to learn how to be artists, but more want to learn how to sell their art.'

'So, you didn't recognise Miss Cormorant?' Bullman asked. 'And you'd never spoken to her outside of that course?'

'No,' Miles shook his head vigorously.

'Even when she was involved in introducing you to Lukas Weber?'

'It wasn't Lucy that introduced me,' Miles said. 'It was another student.'

Anjli had been hoping for this.

'Would you recognise the other student if you saw her?'

If Miles Benson realised she'd used a female pronoun in the question, he hadn't reacted.

'Possibly? I don't think so.'

'Good,' Bullman smiled. 'Because we'd hate to think you hadn't recognised the woman who introduced you to Lukas Weber, when she came out of a room at your party telling everyone he was dead.'

At this, Miles trembled.

'He wasn't supposed to die,' he whispered.

'What do you mean?' Anjli asked, leaning closer.

'He wasn't supposed to die,' Miles repeated. 'Look, I'll admit it. Lucy Cormorant came to me. She said she knew how to make some serious money. She said if I outed Weber's Nazi connections during the sale, then people would pay more.'

'And why would she do this?'

'I was working with her on a couple of things.'

'Define working,' Bullman asked, leaning back.

Miles paused, licked his lips nervously, and then nodded.

'I had a debt I wanted to pay to Lucy,' Miles slumped back in his chair, aware now the women in front of him knew everything he'd said was a lie.

'Would this be the debt you owed her father?' Anjli asked.

'Yes.'

'We know you sold paintings for Marcel Cormorant,' Anjli read from her notes now. 'We understand that Lucy even attended a couple of the events when she was younger. Was this how you met?'

Miles nodded and sighed as he tried to work out the words to say.

'I'm quite friendly,' he said. 'Vivacious. Outgoing. You know – a salesman. I attend events and I'm always linking people together. I'm the "fun guy," and I gravitate to younger people. Their energy keeps me going. So, when I'm at an event, you know, I feed off them – not like a vampire – but it inspires me.'

'This is why you did the lecturing?' Bullman asked.

Miles nodded.

'And I didn't know that Lucy was at the college, I swear. She said when she turned up it was quite a surprise – and it was a pleasant one, if I was being honest, as although her father and I had fallen out, Lucy had always been friendly to me, and while there was a little bit of an *Indiana Jones* moment—'

'Okay, you're going to have to explain that one,' Anjli interrupted.

Miles gave her a half smile, almost apologetic.

'In *Raiders of the Lost Ark*, you have this big scene at the start where you see Indiana Jones being all exciting and macho and getting on a plane and flying off, and then the very next moment you see him suited up in a college class, teaching,' he said. 'And there's one part of the scene where he's doing the talk, and one of his students in the classroom closes her eyes and she's written "love you" on them. You see, she's got a crush on her teacher.'

'And you think Indiana Jones returned the favour?'

'Well, there's some concerning plotlines involving how old Marion was when she was with Indiana,' Miles shrugged.

'We're not here to discuss a Spielberg movie,' Bullman said. 'Are you telling us you had a relationship with Lucy Cormorant?'

Miles said nothing for a long moment, as if contemplating the correct reply. Eventually, he looked back up.

'She was legal,' he said. 'And it was after I'd finished my time as a lecturer. She's just turning twenty-one.'

'And that makes it okay?' Anjli asked.

'You think I'm the only man in his fifties to date a woman in her twenties?'

'I think you're the only man I know having a midlife crisis, where he ends up not only having an affair with the student who is also the daughter of one of his clients, and a student at one of his lectures, but then convinces her to speak out against Nazis in the middle of a talk before denying all knowledge—'

'*Of course, I had to deny all knowledge!*' Miles snapped. 'Veronica was in the room with me! How did I explain the woman I'd been sleeping with for the last six months was the one who stood up and denounced Lukas Weber?'

'You could have told us you knew her.'

'And if I told you that, then it would immediately be out that I was having an affair, and my relationship, my marriage, my business would all end!'

'And you don't think they've already ended?' Bullman asked in surprise.

'What, this? All I did was theatre,' Miles replied sullenly. 'Everything I told you is correct, apart from a couple of small things.'

'And those are?'

'That I knew Lukas Weber,' Miles said, and now he straightened in his chair, angry but also desperate to get his story across. 'You want the truth? Fine. Lucy Cormorant was there when I met Lukas Weber at the University. I remember another woman there, but I don't recall who she was. I think she knew Andrew. She was another student, but as I said, I knew Lucy because of my connection to her father. I'd been apologetic about how things had ended with Marcel and said the door was still open for him, if he ever wanted to sell any more artwork. She introduced me to Lukas Weber at the end of the event before he was leaving.'

'This was before the affair started?'

'A good couple of months, yeah. I was in the university cafe at the time with my brother Andrew. We spoke; I had a lecture that I'd promised to watch and I left, while Andrew carried on talking to Lukas. A couple of months later, it was Andrew who suggested we did the exhibition.'

Anjli wrote this down as Miles continued.

'In the meantime, Lucy and I kept in contact, met up twice, purely platonic back then, but we ended up sleeping together for about six months. A couple of weeks back, she came to me and suggested that if I really wanted to help her father, I might give a finder's fee to her for introducing me and Andrew to Lukas in the first place.'

'And you agreed?'

'I was besotted with her, and I said yes, of course,

anything to help,' Miles nodded, now staring at the floor in shame. 'I offered her a couple of percent of anything made. The next thing I know, she's talking about doing something at the event to help with the sales. She was still in contact with Lukas Weber through her friend, and she was looking for ways to increase her percentage, to make more money for her dad. Then at the end of my speech, she stood up and outed the bastard.'

He stopped, staring away, looking at the wall as if reliving that moment.

'I didn't know what she was going to say,' he said. 'I had security ready in case she went over the top, but I hadn't expected her to be so in my face, you know?'

'Have you spoken to her since?' Anjli asked.

Miles shook his head.

'She disappeared after the event,' he replied. 'I tried calling but no answer. I thought she was probably just upset, so I gave her some space.'

'You thought your brother killed the people on that list,' Bullman said, moving the subject on. 'Any particular reason why?'

'Because he was in the same locations at the same time,' Miles shrugged. 'I know because he'd gone there to speak to them.'

'Andrew spoke to Stefan Bierhof, Borge Pedersen and Anna Hoffmann?' Anjli was starting to think Andrew Benson might have been the killer after all.

'Yes, Weber took him.'

'Lukas Weber went with your brother to these countries?' Now it was Bullman's turn to ask.

Miles gave a half shrug.

'I think so,' he said. 'I remember the names. Lukas had

said he had little stock to sell, but then he said these people had been connected to his family, and they all had artwork of his – artwork that if he could regain, he could sell at the exhibition. These were old family friends who had been given early pieces, and the idea was to speak to them, offer a low price – but more than they paid for the paintings – to gain them back, and then sell them for triple the price at the exhibition. We'd make a slight loss on each one at the start, paying them out some money as an advance, but it meant we would have everything he'd ever painted.'

'Why did he care so much about sales?'

'Because he was broke,' Miles sniffed. 'People thought he owned all this land and property in Austria, but his grandfather disowned him twenty years ago, and his father followed the wishes. He had nothing, just what he made from his paintings.'

Anjli leaned back in the chair. Lukas Weber had visited the descendants of his grandfather's wartime colleagues, and all three of them had died shortly after.

Was Lukas the killer? But if so, how was he killed?

'Are you still under the belief that your brother killed them?'

Miles shook his head.

'If he was killing them, I'd be surprised,' he said. 'He's got shaky hands. Always has done. Used to make an absolute farce of painting miniature figures. He couldn't paint a lipstick kiss, even if it was three feet wide. He doesn't have the skill for the detail.'

Anjli nodded, looking back at Bullman.

'We'll need to follow up on these leads,' she said. 'And see if we can find any evidence linking your brother to the murders.'

Or Lukas Weber, she now thought to herself.

Miles sat back in his chair, a mixture of relief and fear washing over him.

'I didn't know Andrew was capable of any of this,' he said, his voice trembling. 'I'm telling you the truth, I really am.'

'We'll see,' Bullman said sternly. 'For now, you'll remain in custody while we investigate further.'

She turned the recorder off after stating the time of the end of the interview and, with Anjli rising beside her, apologised for the quick exit, but that they now needed to confirm this with Andrew Benson, next door.

Walking to the door, and passing through it as if nothing was wrong, Bullman turned to Anjli the moment it closed behind them.

'And where is Andrew bloody Benson?' she asked.

'That, ma'am, is a question I want to know as well,' Anjli replied. 'He wasn't at his house when we arrived, and neither was Veronica. Billy's checking their phones right now.'

'Keep Miles on ice,' Bullman nodded. 'Cooper was going to speak to Cormorant, right? We should contact her. She needs to know this simple chat she was about to have has just turned into an enormous shit-show.'

21

MISSING PERSONS

DECLAN HAD GAINED STACEY NICHOLS' ADDRESS FROM THE company she'd been working for; it was a shared house in Wanstead, a small, well-kept estate at the Snaresbrook end of the High Street.

Pausing a moment before knocking, Declan felt the slight wave of tightness and pain from his head wound, now nothing more than a large plaster across the stitches on his temple, ease back to a dull throb. Once it was bearable again, he rang the doorbell, and a young blond man opened the door, a confused expression on his face as he stared at the stranger on the doorstep.

'We're fine, thanks,' he said, going to close the door, but stopped as Declan held up his wallet card.

'DCI Walsh, City of London police,' he said. 'I'm looking for Stacey Nichols.'

'Aren't we all?' the man said, the door opening slightly again as he relaxed.

'She's missing?'

The man looked back into the house.

'Well, unless she's suddenly learnt the skill to become invisible. She didn't come back last night.'

Declan felt a chill go down his spine.

'Does she always come home?'

'There have been a couple of times she's stayed away, you know, after an event. When she's found a conquest, or she's been one for someone else.'

Declan nodded.

'Is she your roommate, or is she ...' He let the question trail off and fought the urge to smile as the blond man looked horrified.

'Oh God, no,' the man smiled. 'I'm Kyle. We share the house; there's four of us here. I'm doing a BA in Graphic Communication Design at University of the Arts, London Saint Martin's.'

Declan looked around and noticed a couple of curtains twitching.

'Can I come in?' he asked.

'Is it bad?' Kyle asked, and Declan knew what Kyle was *actually* asking was if he had to invite Declan in.

'No, it's fine,' Declan smiled. 'I can carry on talking here. It's just that obviously, having a police officer at your doorstep - you probably don't really want your neighbours to be watching.'

Kyle glanced around, nodded, and let Declan into the house, guiding him straight into the living room to the side. It was a typical "shared house" living room, with a mixture of posters and paintings on the walls, furniture as mishmash as it could be, and a variety of university books and notepads everywhere.

'Student house,' Kyle apologised, clearing a space on the

sofa for Declan to sit. 'It's one reason I didn't want you coming in. We haven't had a maid in quite a while.'

The comment was self-deprecating and made to ease the moment, and Declan appreciated it, sitting down on the sofa – although from Kyle's clipped accent, he wondered if they *had* a maid.

'How long have you known Stacey Nichols?' he asked.

'A year, two years maybe?' Kyle said, thinking back. 'She was a friend of a friend, and last year when we started looking for new digs, she came here. It's quite a journey, as you said, from here to St. Martin's, as it's just off King's Cross. It's all about the rent, unfortunately. But we're right beside the Central Line, so it's easy to get into Liverpool Street from here and catch half a dozen lines there.'

'Surely it'd be cheaper to move to North London?'

'Not really. You're looking at Camden, Clerkenwell, Islington ... all stupidly expensive. We looked at a place on the Caledonian Road; it was peculiar, and the area was super dodgy, and you're right beside Pentonville Prison, so people weren't too happy about it.'

'Stacey left university though, is that correct?'

Kyle nodded, leaning back in his armchair.

'She's taking a gap year,' he said. 'She wasn't happy with what she was doing, and I think she's looking to pivot, change her career, change her everything.'

He shrugged.

'She hasn't been right for a while. Ever since her dad died.'

'Her dad passed away?'

'That's usually what "dad died" means,' Kyle said, and then instantly regretted it. 'Sorry, it's been a long day. I have a painting that just does not want to finish, and I'm on deadline.'

'I thought the college year had finished?'

'It has,' Kyle nodded. 'But we only have the house for a couple more weeks; we have another one for the final year, just down the road, and I need to get it done before I move out.'

'Are you keeping the same people in the house?' Declan asked. 'I know people who shared houses at Uni, and they utterly hated the people they were with.'

'Did you go to Uni?'

'I went the other way, joined the Army,' Declan shook his head. 'Military police.'

Kyle whistled.

'I almost joined the army,' he said. 'But I don't look good in olive green.'

Declan bit back a reply as Kyle continued.

'We're dumping one of the housemates, as we all think she's a narcissist bitch,' he said. 'Stacey said she wanted to stay, and she has a friend who's looking to take Parvita's – that's the narcissist – place.'

'Have you met the friend?'

'Oh, sure, we all had to sign the lease already,' Kyle grinned. 'She's hot, so it's going to be super awkward, especially as she likes dating older men.'

'You don't think you can match up to an older man?' Declan was amused; Kyle did not give the impression of being a shy flower.

'Not when they're twice her age and drive a sports car,' Kyle laughed. 'I'll wait until she realises old men don't have the same stamina – no insult intended – and look for a newer model. We're both third years, so I have a year to make the raven-haired queen mine.'

Declan froze at the description.

'Lucy Cormorant?' he asked.

'Ah, shit,' Kyle's face fell. 'You don't know her boyfriend, do you?'

'No,' Declan replied, forcing a smile to put the younger man at ease. 'We know her from something else. I just didn't know she knew Stacey well enough to move in.'

'Ah, good,' Kyle mock-mimed wiping sweat off his forehead. 'I don't know how well they know each other, all I know is Lucy needed a new place, and Stacey had a spot to fill.'

Declan nodded.

'So, you said her father died, and she hasn't been right,' he carried on. 'Could you explain on that?'

'Sure,' Kyle said. 'Spouted off that her dad died before he could make anything of himself, and she wasn't going to make the same mistake, that she was going to be a millionaire by twenty-five. She started hanging around an older guy of her own. First, I thought she was looking for a replacement father figure, you know? But I think it's a job of some kind. She's been bouncing around Europe, and she has new jewellery, expensive stuff, which she couldn't afford at the start of the year.'

'Have you met the older guy?'

'Which one?' Kyle laughed. 'There's a Brit, a German and some creepy Mexican, I think. No idea what she's doing, but as long as she's happy ...'

He trailed off.

'Hey, you don't think any of them caused her to disappear?'

'I don't know,' Declan rose, offering a card. 'But if you see

Stacey, can you let me know she's around? Or get her to contact me? It's in relation to the event a couple of nights back.'

'Oh? What happened a couple of nights back?'

'It's best you ask Stacey,' Declan gave a tight smile. If she hadn't told Kyle she found a dead body, it either meant she didn't rate him high enough to tell, or, worse still, it hadn't affected her enough to tell anyone.

'Actually, would you mind if I had a quick look at her room?' he asked.

'Sure,' Kyle grinned, more assured now the conversation was ending. 'If you have a warrant.'

He held up his hands quickly in a surrendering motion.

'Couldn't even if I wanted to,' he added. 'We all have locks. No way in, I'm afraid.'

Declan resisted the urge to mention he could probably pick the lock faster than any locksmith could and so nodded, shook Kyle's hand and left the house, with Kyle returning to his painting.

Now alone in the street, Declan considered what he'd learnt.

Lucy Cormorant and Stacey Nichols knew each other better than they realised, and an older German matched Lukas Weber, while the "Mexican" could have been a confused attempt at Gabriel Bauer.

But what that meant for the case, he had no idea.

BILLY WAS STILL WORKING ON THE COMPUTER MONITORS WHEN Anjli and Bullman came into the main office.

'Anything?' Anjli asked, and Billy yelped, looking angrily

at Jess Walsh, who'd not only seen them as they approached, but had deliberately not informed him.

'You told me to sit still and act like I wasn't here,' Jess shrugged. 'So, I did just that.'

Billy grumbled, returning his attention to Anjli.

'Which "anything" are you asking about?' he replied. 'I'm doing half a dozen "anythings" at the moment.'

'Do we have eyes on either Veronica or Andrew Benson?' Anjli added, and Billy pulled up images onto a couple of his screens.

'We've been tracking their phones,' he said. 'And something interesting seems to be happening.'

Billy pointed at the monitors.

'Both Andrew and Veronica are together,' he said. 'The phones are pinging from the same cell tower, and from what we can work out, they're both at St Pancras Station.'

Anjli glanced at Bullman.

'Maybe they're going on holiday,' Bullman suggested, but it was obvious she wasn't serious.

'Unsure,' Billy replied, looking back at Anjli. 'But I'm pretty much sure you told him not to leave town right now.'

Anjli nodded, her lips thinning as Billy returned to the monitors, pointing at one of the screens.

'And it looks to me like they're getting on the Eurostar,' he tapped the map location again.

'Fleeing the scene of the crime?' Jess asked, looking around.

Billy shrugged.

'I've got a payment here by Andrew,' he said. 'It's on a backup card he's barely used over the last few years which is why we didn't pick it up immediately, but it's for two return tickets to Paris.'

'What time are they going?' Bullman was already pulling out her phone.

'From the looks of things? They're waiting for the train right now,' Billy replied. 'Do you want me to hold it?'

Anjli looked at Bullman; now she was higher in rank, she had the authority to do such a thing with no repercussions, but at the same time, this could be nothing. It could even be a feint; they didn't have CCTV showing Veronica and Andrew, just phone pings and a receipt.

'No,' Bullman shook her head. 'If we hold it for no reason, and we get nothing from it, we'll get into trouble down the line. After all, we don't know whether Andrew and Veronica are involved in anything at all, yet.'

'But we can't let them leave,' Anjli wasn't sure where Bullman was going with this.

'Oh, I agree with that,' Bullman smiled. 'Get some uniforms from Kent to stop the train at Ashford International. I'm guessing we'll know their seats from the booking, and we'll be able to pick them up there?'

Billy nodded, already reaching for the phone. Anjli glanced at Jess, who was jiggling on her chair as if she needed the toilet.

'You have thoughts?' she asked.

'One murder was in Paris,' Jess said. 'Maybe they're going back to pick something up? Maybe something that was left there? Or a witness that saw them?'

'But why now?' Anjli asked. Something was going on here and it was annoying her she still couldn't see the full picture.

As the others watched the screen, Anjli glanced back as Miles Benson was walked past them. The cells were on a higher floor, but Doctor Marcos had asked for a new DNA swab, so he was on his way to the forensics lab to do so.

Walking over, she motioned to the officer escorting him to pause and step away as she leant in close.

'Does your wife get on with your brother?' she asked.

'Right now? Not massively, no,' he said. 'It doesn't help that she thinks he's a serial killer.'

'And why would she think that?'

'Because I told her I thought he was a serial killer,' Miles shrugged.

'If that's the case, why would they both be going to Paris right now?'

At this, Miles's expression tightened.

'They wouldn't,' he said. 'You must be mistaken.'

'They're on the next train out from St Pancras as we speak,' Anjli replied, watching Miles carefully, looking for any micro-expressions. 'We're already looking to bring them in.'

'You said he was next door.'

'Well, obviously we were lying,' Anjli smiled. 'We're not lying now, though.'

Miles shook his head.

'If my wife is having an affair, she never told me ...'

'Has your wife been told about *your* affairs yet?'

Miles paused.

'She knows I can't be caged,' he stated like it was a simple matter, and Anjli almost wanted to vomit at the sentence.

'When she comes in, we're going to have a word,' she said. 'Just so you're aware, your affair might be mentioned.'

Miles froze.

'Please,' he said. 'At least let me be the one that tells her.'

Anjli straightened, stepping back as she looked at Miles Benson. He looked helpless, and something tugged at her.

'Fine,' she said, nodding at the officer to return. 'We'll keep you in the loop.'

As Miles was escorted off, Anjli returned to the monitor.

'The train's left, and the phones are definitely on it,' Billy said. 'Ashford police have agreed to pause the train and pick them up.'

'Good,' Anjli said, before glancing around. 'We're going to need more interview rooms.'

ANDREW BENSON SAT BY THE WINDOW OF THE EUROSTAR carriage, staring at the passing Kent landscape, as he tried to work out what to do next.

Veronica, sitting opposite him, was tapping her fingers against the table between them and the staccato sound was getting on his nerves.

'This isn't a good idea,' she said. 'They'll know we've left.'

'I know,' Andrew replied, looking back at her. 'And the moment they see we've run, they'll think we've lied from the start, but we have to get to the apartment. We have to find the proof, clear our names.'

Veronica sat back in the carriage seat, folding her arms.

'You mean yours and Miles.'

'Sure, that's what I meant,' Andrew nodded, a little too eagerly due to his nervousness.

'Tell me more,' Veronica replied.

Andrew sighed, looking around the carriage to make sure they weren't being overheard.

'He was sleeping with her,' he replied softly. 'I'd had a fight with him about it. I didn't realise how bad it was.'

Veronica's lips thinned, but she didn't reply. She'd had

suspicions, Andrew was sure, that Miles had been sleeping with somebody, probably one of the students of his class. But now, knowing it was the same woman who'd outed Lukas Weber as a Nazi ...

Andrew realised he probably changed her entire worldview.

'And you? Were you sleeping with her friend?'

'Christ no,' Andrew replied, almost in horror. 'She was working for Weber. I think he felt better having someone unconnected to the gallery there, and she could speak passable German because of an A Level, whereas the most Miles and I could do was "where is the bus stop" or "I am a rubber tree." Don't ask.'

The train was slowing now; they were coming into Ashford International station. The Eurostar didn't stop at Ebbsfleet at the moment, which meant that as soon as they left St. Pancras there were only one or two stops before they hit the tunnel and France. Once they arrived in Paris, they would catch a cab immediately to the location they needed to get to, and with luck they'd be back that evening, hopefully with proof of their innocence.

And hopefully, with their freedom.

However, as the train pulled into Ashford International, Andrew Benson's heart sank. He could already see the flashing blue lights of the police cars and knew that the police had found them. He'd expected them to eventually work it out, and he'd hoped by using a card he hadn't used for a good year by now that it would be something that they wouldn't pick up until he was in Paris - and again, he was happy to be arrested on returning – it was just leaving that would have caused a problem.

Slowly, he gathered his items.

'We're not going to France,' he said sadly.

Veronica frowned, a full face one, but then her eyes widened as, at the end of the carriage, she saw two police officers enter, walking towards them. She started to rise, but before she could, Andrew grabbed her hand, holding her in place. He was looking the other direction, and had also seen two police officers enter from the other end of the carriage.

'We can't get out of this,' he said. 'It's over.'

They sat in silence until the four police officers arrived, looking down at them. 'Veronica and Andrew Benson?' the first one asked.

'Yes,' Andrew confirmed.

'I'm afraid you need to come with us,' the police officer replied. 'We've been asked to bring you back to London.'

'Of course,' Andrew smiled, rising. 'We were just trying to help.'

'I'm sure you were, sir,' the officer said. 'If you'd just come with us?'

The two officers walked back towards the exit of the carriage, and Andrew and Veronica slowly walked with them. But, as they walked onto the platform, Andrew suddenly darted to the left, sprinting off down the walkway. He didn't know where he was going, or what his plan was, but he knew he couldn't be arrested. If he was arrested, he couldn't prove his innocence.

He needed to show what Lukas Weber had actually been doing.

He needed to find a way of explaining this.

But it was too late. The four police officers at this train weren't the only officers who'd arrived, and as he ran for the stairs heading towards the main exit, he was tackled by two more Kent police officers and brought to the floor, his arms pinned behind him as they placed handcuffs on.

'I didn't do it!' he screamed. 'I'm not the killer. It was Weber! You've got to believe me! It was Weber!'

'The dead artist? Yeah, you can tell that to the City of London police.' The officer that had handcuffed him pulled him to his feet, dragging him towards the exit. 'I'm sure they'd love to know.'

Looking back to Veronica, now also being handcuffed in case she too decided to run, Andrew Benson realised that his attempt to clear his name had completely and utterly failed.

22

BIRD NOISES

IT HAD TAKEN COOPER HALF OF THE MORNING TO EVENTUALLY find Lucy Cormorant, as the address that she'd been given claimed Lucy no longer lived there.

She was provided a forwarding address that turned out to be a friend who had allowed Lucy to sleep on her sofa for a couple of weeks, but then that friend had also moved on. Eventually, after three or four different conversations, Cooper found Lucy Cormorant at her place of work, behind the counter of a coffee shop in Shoreditch.

In fact, the first thing that struck Cooper as she walked in was that the coffee shop was only a couple of minutes' walk from the very building that Gary Krohn had been thrown out of.

Lucy looked up as Cooper walked in, and her face fell.

'I'm at work,' she said before Cooper could even speak. 'Can we do this later?'

There was another woman behind the counter, an older lady, and Cooper assumed that this was the manager, or head barista, or whatever they called themselves in coffee shops.

'Lucy, what's going on?' the woman asked.

Cooper turned and gave her best smile.

'I'm PC Esme Cooper of the City of London Police,' she said. 'And you are?'

'What's this to do with?' The woman, who hadn't named herself asked.

'Lucy is a witness in a crime that happened a couple of days ago,' Cooper replied, keeping her face expressionless, so she couldn't give any clues to why she was truly there. 'We have a couple of follow-up questions.'

'Well, she can do them after her shift,' the older woman replied.

'I'm afraid they're time-sensitive,' Cooper retorted.

'She's not leaving right now, we're too busy,' the older woman stated, and Cooper glanced around the half-empty coffee store.

'I can see that,' she said, half-mockingly, while also wondering if this delaying had been requested by Lucy herself. 'Can I take your name, please?'

'Why?'

'For when I return after not being able to speak to the witness,' Cooper pulled out her notebook. 'I need to inform the DCI running the case the name of the person who interfered with their investigation.'

'I'm not interfering with anything,' the older woman backed away now, her hands up. 'If you want to speak to Lucy, go do it. But she's only got a five-minute break.'

'That's all I need,' Cooper smiled at the older lady, nodding at Lucy. 'If we can find somewhere a little quieter to speak?'

Reluctantly nodding back, Lucy walked Cooper through the rear door, out through a kitchen area, and towards a fire door that led to the back alley outside the rear of the coffee store.

'We have to be fast,' Lucy said, irritated at this interruption to her day. 'What's the problem here?'

'The problem here is that your witness statement was utter bollocks,' Cooper replied. She'd had enough by now. Her entire morning had been wasted playing a treasure hunt, and now she had no time for subtlety or conversational foreplay. 'When did you first meet Miles Benson?'

Lucy paused.

'I think he might have been a lecturer that I saw, but I didn't really put them together at the time,' she said, changing her story but still not by enough to implicate her into anything new.

'So, it wasn't when you stood up in his gallery two nights ago and denounced his artist as a Nazi?'

'I know I said that,' Lucy said, already backpedalling. 'But thinking about it, yeah, I'd like to change my statement on that account. I think I might have met him before, and I don't want it to be weird.'

'What *is* weird,' Cooper said, 'is that wasn't the first time you met him either, was it? Your father had paintings sold by Miles, and you attended his exhibitions.'

She stepped closer.

'And for somebody who's been *sleeping* with him for the last six months? That you couldn't remember his name seems mighty suspicious.'

At this, Lucy's face fell.

'Who told you that?' she asked, her voice only a whisper.

'We have Mister Benson in custody,' Cooper replied. 'We were told quite conclusively that you and he had been having an affair since a couple of months after you bumped into each other at his lecture, and that you introduced him to Lukas Weber, another speaker at your college.'

'No, that's ... that's not true,' Lucy stuttered. 'I didn't ... it was someone else.'

'Was it Stacey Nichols?' Cooper looked up from confirming the name on her phone, where she had received Monroe's text giving her the updated information he'd gathered.

'I don't know,' Lucy replied. 'Stacey Nichols. She sounds familiar ...'

'Let's start again,' Cooper sighed theatrically, turning a page of a notebook as if to symbolise starting afresh. 'We know that you know Stacey Nichols. We know you're going to be sharing a house with her next year. We know you knew her when you both attended the talks at UAL Saint Martin's, and we know she was involved in introducing Miles and Andrew Benson to Lukas Weber, and as her friend, you were there at the same time.'

Lucy looked horrified as the statements were read out, but Cooper hadn't finished.

'We're also aware you sat in a side room for an hour, claiming to see Gary Krohn, a painting in his hand, while Stacey Nichols was working as a server at the same event, and was the person who found Weber's body – and saw no painting when she claimed to see Krohn. Neither did the CCTV.'

Lucy shook her head.

'I was paid to shout—'

'I know you were paid,' Cooper interrupted, now on a roll. 'You told us that already, how you were paid to tell everybody that Lukas Weber was a Nazi. But you weren't performing some kind of civic duty, were you? Miles Benson would make more money from the paintings, and the two of you could run away together, or whatever. So why don't you tell me the truth? Because currently, we have you down as a way more unreliable narrator of this than you should be, and a possible suspect now for the murder of Lukas Weber.'

At the accusation, Lucy shuddered, and her eyes welled up.

'He wasn't supposed to die,' she said.

'Whose idea was it to do what you did?'

'He wasn't supposed to die!' this time, Lucy was more forceful in her statement. 'It was supposed to look like an attack. He wasn't supposed to die.'

'Who attacked him?'

'I don't know. It was part of his plan.' At this, Lucy shook her head.

'Whose plan?'

Lucy sighed, looking up at the sky. She reached into her pocket and took out a packet of cigarettes, pulling one out, placing it in her mouth, lighting it. After a couple of long drags, she relaxed a little and turned to face Esme Cooper.

'Lukas Weber,' she said. 'It was his idea. All of it, from the very start.'

BILLY SAT DOWN IN THE PUB, SMILING AT SAM MANSFIELD.

'I've only got a quick lunch today,' he said. 'Everything's gone to shit in the office.'

Sam smiled, nodding.

'It's okay,' he replied, nodding back to the bar. 'I've already ordered food and drink. I guessed you'd be busy. I've got used to it.'

Billy reddened at this.

'Sorry,' he said. 'But thanks for coming. We had something I wanted you to look at.'

'Oh,' Sam smiled. 'So, this is business today?'

'It's always business,' Billy continued to blush. 'You're a valued connection to the unit.'

Sam didn't reply, simply leaning back on the pub chair smiling, dancing the same steps they'd danced for the last couple of weeks.

'Do you recognise this person?' Billy asked, changing the subject by passing a piece of paper across to Sam. It was a printout of the photo that Gabriel Bauer had given Monroe, of the man who had taken the money from him a couple of nights earlier.

Sam stared down at it, his eyes narrowing.

'Yeah, I recognise that wanker,' he said. 'He's been on the scene for a while. Dropped off a while back, but he was a pain in my arse a good few years ago.'

'Would you have a name?' Billy asked.

At the question, Sam looked up.

'Depends,' he said. 'What's it worth?'

'Well, the unit would—'

'No. What's it worth to you?'

Billy opened and shut his mouth a couple of times.

'What do you want?'

'Dinner,' Sam's smile didn't waver. 'You and me. Not on the clock. Two friends, getting to know each other.'

Billy looked uncomfortably away.

'I was hurt a few months ago,' he said. 'I find it hard to make new friends.'

'Then it's time to start,' Sam said, tossing the page back onto the table as the server walked over with their lunches.

'But I'll give you this for free, anyway. The man in the photo? He's a con artist and an actual artist. Forger, restorer, you name it, he's done it.'

He raised his drink, toasting Billy.

'His name's Marcel Cormorant.'

COOPER HADN'T EXPECTED THE ANSWER, AND IT TOOK HER A couple of seconds to take it in.

'Lukas Weber told you to out him as a Nazi?'

'Yes,' Lucy said. 'We'd kept in touch after he was sent away from the college, and yes, I knew the rumours about his parentage, and then Miles was complaining about the gallery to me. He wasn't making money. Veronica was spending a lot, she seemed to think they were making more money than they were, and the credit card bills were rising. He was looking to get out.'

'And what? He made a plan with you and Lukas?'

'Miles knew about the plan because we came to him and told him,' Lucy said. 'We suggested to him that this'd work.'

'When you say "we," who suggested this?' Cooper asked again.

Lucy thought for a moment, and Cooper wondered if she was trying to work out how to not throw anybody under the bus.

'I will warn you,' Cooper added, 'that if we find that you're talking even more bollocks right now, if something you tell me here turns out to be just as fake as the other things you told us, you're going back in handcuffs.'

Lucy nodded, swallowing nervously.

'It was a brasserie,' she said. 'We'd been invited to Paris—'

'Paris.' Cooper raised an eyebrow. That had to be more than a coincidence.

'Stacey had been talking to Lukas more than I had,' Lucy explained. 'I think she was even working on the side for him and Andrew. There was a business trip that Miles had to go on to Paris with Andrew, and Lukas was going to be there. So, it was decided that maybe we should have the conversation there.'

'And "the" conversation was ...'

'I'm getting to that, I promise. I convinced Miles to take me with him, said it would be a fun weekend together without Veronica. While there, we all met up.'

'All of you being ...'

'Me, Stacey, Miles, Andrew and Lukas. It was a couple of weeks before the event. There hadn't been much interest in it by that point.'

'Tell me more,' Cooper watched Lucy as she continued.

'We suggested to Miles that it would benefit him if we outed Lukas on stage. The plan Weber suggested was I would come out, I'd see Lukas, I'd point to him and shout out he was a Nazi. I'd be dragged away. The bids would go up.'

'How did you know the bids would go up?'

'Gabriel Bauer was going to be there,' Lucy replied. 'I don't know much about him, but I'd seen him at events, but I knew that he had a hard-on for anything Lukas Weber was doing. He'd already put in pre-orders for half the paintings announced, sight unseen. We knew if we could up the interest of the other buyers, that couple of hundred grand that'd be made in fees would turn into a couple of million. The figures we'd have would be enough for Miles to escape Veronica.'

'But what happened?'

'I don't know,' Lucy replied. 'Veronica started acting strange to start with. I think she suspected we were having an affair. Then Miles started acting strange too, started asking me if Stacey had mentioned anything about where she'd been travelling to.'

'Because Stacey was travelling with Andrew?'

'I don't think so. Things were weird with her. Her dad had died, and this seemed to make her focus more on making money than anything else, like she had to beat the clock, you know? Andrew was spending more time with Weber, and Stacey mentioned she'd found a big score. I assumed she meant Andrew, didn't have the heart to tell her he was as broke as Miles,' Lucy shrugged. 'I know Miles was interested in a trip they took to Berlin a couple of weeks before we'd all met in Paris. He was starting to say it was a bad idea to do the exhibition, but I knew we needed to, as it was the only way we'd make the money to escape.'

'You wanted what was best for Miles Benson?' Cooper replied, acknowledging a nod from Lucy before continuing. 'This wasn't you gaining any kind of revenge for your father?'

At this, Lucy froze.

'I don't know what you mean.'

'Your father sold items through the Bensons until around five years ago, right? Why did he stop?'

'I love Miles,' Lucy replied, ignoring the question. 'I would never ...'

'The man who screwed your father over?'

'Sure, when we met back up I knew he'd betrayed Dad, and at the start there was an aspect of working out how to get the money Dad lost, but ... I just fell for him.'

Cooper held her hand up.

'As wonderful as that sounds, let's move on,' she said. 'You went out to do your piece at the exhibition, but when you went to "out" Lukas Weber, he wasn't there?'

'No,' Lucy shook her head. 'We'd been told he'd changed his mind. But he wasn't needed, it would have been the cherry on the cake to point at him but I assumed he'd got cold feet, didn't want to be in any photos as it happened. It was only later I learned he died—'

'In the room next to you.'

Lucy nodded.

'And Krohn?'

'He wasn't part of the plan,' Lucy said. 'Ours, at least. I think he was with Andrew, and by then I'd realised Andrew was making his own plans to screw over Miles. So, when I had a chance to aim you at Gary ... I took it.'

'You *are* aware why everything you've told me now is completely at odds with what you said in your statement?' Cooper asked again.

Lucy nodded once more, now looking a little queasy as she did so.

'And you *are* aware that I now have to bring you in?'

'My manager isn't gonna like that,' Lucy said.

Cooper smiled.

'Good,' she replied. 'I'll arrest her as well.'

23

LEANING CLOSER

DECLAN SLAMMED THE PHOTO OF MARCEL CORMORANT ONTO the table in front of Miles Benson's terrified face.

He understood why Miles looked scared; when Declan arrived at the interview room he had a face of fury, and Miles, having been bounced from interview room to DNA test to interview room must have been wondering what the hell was going on right now.

But right now, Declan really didn't care.

'Who's this?' he asked.

Miles looked down at the image, frowned, and looked back up.

'That's Marcel Cormorant,' he said. 'He's an artist we used to deal with.'

'Yes,' Declan replied. 'But that's not why he's in the picture, is it?'

Miles squinted at the photo in what looked to be confusion.

'Wait,' he asked as his realisation finally took over. 'Is he the one that took the money from Bauer?'

'This was taken by one of Gabriel Bauer's men,' Declan said, sitting down, facing Miles. 'It's looking very dodgy for you, I'm afraid, Miles. The woman that you're having an affair with? Well, it looks like her *dad* took money from a neo-Nazi Argentine for paintings that you'd promised him.'

'I never promised him anything,' Miles shook his head, his eyes wide. 'That was all Andrew.'

'And Andrew will be answering that soon,' Declan said. 'We're having a chat with him next. We picked him up at Ashford International. He's next door and your wife, who seems to already be aware of the fact that you've been having an affair by the way, is in a waiting room. There's quite a queue for meetings today.'

Miles was still shaking his head, as if what Declan had just said was completely wrong.

'Why was he going to Paris?' he asked. 'Your partner didn't know earlier?'

'I don't know either,' Declan's mouth shrugged. 'I was hoping you could tell me.'

Miles just blankly stared back at him.

'Look,' he eventually replied. 'I haven't seen Marcel for years. The last time we spoke, it wasn't a good ending and I hadn't told anybody about Lucy because I didn't want him to know either. You know, for obvious reasons.'

He looked down at the photo.

'Can I ask a question, Detective Chief Inspector?'

'Sure.'

'Lucy,' Miles said. 'Has anyone spoken to her?'

'Funny you should mention that,' Declan smiled. 'She's on her way in too.'

'Could you ask her a question for me?' Miles sat back on the chair, looking up at Declan with the expression of a broken man. 'Can you ask her if she ever loved me, or whether this was all part of some plan?'

He looked back at the paper and the photo of her father.

'Because if her dad was there, there's only one reason he'd be around, and that's to get one over on me.'

Declan felt sorry for Miles, but not enough to give him the benefit of the doubt.

'You'd better firm up your story,' he said. 'Because we're going to have a new conversation very soon.'

Declan rose from the chair, walked to the door to the interview room and once outside, closed it behind him.

Standing in the corridor, he couldn't quite decide what to do next; speak to Andrew, Veronica or Lucy? Sighing, he decided to work it out in the canteen over a coffee, but as he walked down the corridor, he was almost knocked over by both De'Geer and Cooper as they ran past him like the building was on fire.

'What's going on?' he shouted after them.

'Monroe's assassin,' De'Geer shouted back. 'We've got a plan.'

AFTER DE'GEER HAD MOVED ON FROM DAMIAN LIM'S HOUSE that morning, Monroe had called in a favour to an old protégé, and she'd asked Ramsey Allen to help once more, even if it was "off the books." And because of this, on arrival – while Damian walked to a coffee shop nearby – Ramsey had been sent into the house to "have a look around." His mission had been quite specific, but at the same time something he'd done a dozen times before, and within a matter of minutes, he had performed the task asked of him, returning to his car, a battered brown Rover, and was already watching the house once more before Damian Lim, a barista expresso in his hand, wandered back from the High Street.

Ramsey had stayed in the car another couple of hours, listening to the racing on the radio, but eventually, shortly before lunch, Damian Lim had emerged from the house again, this time in black motorcycle gear, a black helmet in his hand. Ramsey had almost laughed out loud at this, considering the "boy racer" there was about to climb onto a knackered looking 125cc Marauder, but there was also the chance this was his work clothing; the leathers and helmet deliberately bland for when he tried to kill Monroe.

He then followed Damian Lim through London in his battered brown Rover, keeping a few cars away at all times, and once he saw him pull his motorcycle into Temple Inn, he also pulled in, aiming at a different area of the car park outside King's Bench Walk, confirming Lim's location and making a call to Monroe's mobile number.

This done, he made a second call, this time to the computer whiz in the building, who was acting as a go-between for Ramsey and that God-awful prick Sam Mansfield and passed another snippet of information. Then, his job now finished, Ramsey Allen drove back off up to Farringdon to see what his *actual* boss would give him for work that day.

DAMIAN LIM WAS STILL LOOKING FOR AN OPPORTUNE MOMENT to take out Monroe.

He knew Harvey Drake had been trying to contact him; his WhatsApp had blown up with messages since the previous night, but that didn't matter to him. Damian Lim had stated from the very beginning that once a contract was on, there was nothing that stopped it. If Harvey was trying to renege on money or trying to change the deal, if Damian hadn't heard anything then he couldn't be the one screwed over.

And Harvey knew very well that if he *did* try to play him, then Damian would just turn the contract on him as well.

Knowing he was getting close to the end, Damian had pulled back into Temple Inn feeling a little bolder this time, on an endorphin rush because of the stress and deadline. The clock was ticking, and Damian knew that the client, Lennie Wright wouldn't want delays.

He pulled into the car park, just outside King's Bench Walk, climbed off his Suzuki Marauder, and wandered over to a tree to the side that had a bench in front of it.

Taking his helmet off, he sat on the bench, watching the target building from a distance. He didn't need to be close; all he needed to do was make out the white-haired figure of Alexander Monroe when he left.

He hadn't seen the battered brown Rover that had been following him, and he didn't notice it pause and then drive off, as if the person inside had made a phone call before leaving.

And five minutes later, he hadn't expected the two police officers to walk over to him.

The first one was a seven-foot Viking of a police sergeant, in full police uniform including a stab vest, as if expecting trouble, and Damian paled a little as he realised he recognised him. He'd seen the Viking at Hurley the previous night, and he had a sudden fear that he'd been followed by the same man in the morning, with visions of a large rider on a motorcycle suddenly coming to mind.

No. You're just overthinking.

The Viking sergeant paused in front of Damian, nodding over at the bike.

'Your vehicle doesn't seem to have any insurance, and we have a report of a 125cc playing at being a real bike, with the same licence plate being registered as stolen,' he said. 'We're running it through our system, but as you're here, can we check your papers, please?'

'My bike is insured,' Damian said, confused. *What was going on? Could it be that they hadn't realised who he was, or why he was there? Or was this harassment because they did?*

'I'm sure it is,' the Sergeant replied, giving a slight smile. 'Basically, we just need to prove that you are insured if you're on Temple Inn property because it's one of the Inns of Court, and if it's not stolen, we need to tick a box to clear it.'

'Oh, of course,' Damian said, reaching into his back pocket to pull out his wallet, currently with his driving licence inside, and realising with a moment of horror that his *gun* was still slipped into the back waistband of his leather biker trousers. 'I've got it here.'

He made a point of struggling, complaining about "tight leather pants" and dropped his helmet onto the floor, letting it roll across the paving stones. As he did so, the large sergeant, not realising this was a deliberate act, turned around and picked up the helmet from where it rolled across the ground, and Damian took this moment to pull out the gun, sliding it down the back of the bench, wedged against the tree trunk behind. It was out of sight, and there'd be no reason for them to expect him to have it now.

The other officer, a young woman, shorter – far shorter, in

fact – than the sergeant hadn't noticed either. But she did pause and point thoughtfully at him, moving closer to Damian and sniffing at his lips.

'Have you been taking any illegal substances?' she asked between sniffs.

Damian shook his head.

'No,' he replied nervously. 'Of course not.'

The officer watched him, checking his eyes as if seeing whether they were dilated.

'Are you sure, sir?' she asked. 'Do you have anything illegal on you?'

Damian felt a sudden sliver of ice slide down his back as he remembered having a crafty puff earlier on. But that was before he got on the bike and surely, he wasn't so stupid to keep the blunt with him. Though, now, he was wondering whether he'd got onto the motorcycle and left it in his pocket – or whether he had thrown it away before riding off. If they were to find a half-finished joint on him, he could probably argue it away. But these guys looked like they were searching for a reason to take him down, and asking if he was smoking drugs, being given the negative and then *finding* them was not a good sign.

'No, but I've got a friend,' he said. 'He smokes. I was talking to him earlier. I might smell a bit because of that.'

'What's your friend's name?' the woman officer asked.

'I don't know,' Damian answered, already regretting what he'd said. 'He's just a guy who lives on the estate.'

'And where is your estate?'

'Acton, West London.'

'You're a bit out of your way for Acton, West London, aren't you?' the Viking sergeant now asked.

'I'm picking something up,' Damian said as casually as he

could now. 'I work as a courier. Deliveroo, UberEATS, anything that pays really.'

'On that thing?' the Viking scoffed. 'You'd be better on a scooter. Just as shit, but smaller, and easier to get through traffic.'

'Could you step over here, please, sir?' the woman police officer asked, waving for Damian to walk away from the bike and the bench, and step over to where she and the sergeant were now standing.

'Is there a problem?' Damian inquired.

'Yes,' the Viking sergeant said as he eventually walked over. 'I think you're lying to me. I don't believe you've not taken drugs, so I'd like to check you, if that's okay.'

'Stop and searches are legal if we have cause,' the other officer added. 'And I think we have cause with you.'

There was a moment when Damian wondered whether this was actually connected to what he was intending to do. *If they knew the DCI, were they looking for the gun? Did they know who he was? Was this just some kind of ruse to bring him out into the open?* Luckily for Damian, he had hidden the gun, and there were no other weapons on him, so he quite happily stepped forward, placing out his arms and allowing the Viking to slowly pat him down, checking for weapons, of which there weren't any, while the woman officer examined the bike. Which was legally bought and paid for and definitely insured.

And fortunately, Damian had thrown his joint away apparently, as that wasn't there either.

After about a minute and a half of vigorous checking, the Viking stepped back, glowering at Damian.

'Your play-bike checks out, and it looks like you're not

carrying,' he said. 'We apologise for wasting your time and thank you for your cooperation.'

'Thank you,' Damian forced a tight smile in return. 'It's good to know the police are doing what we pay our taxes for and keeping the streets safe.'

The Viking looked around as if deciding whether to say something, and then quickly leant close, so his mouth was beside Damian's ear.

'I suggest you leave, find somewhere else to do your couriering, or your food delivering or whatever bollocks you're telling people you're doing,' he said. 'Alex Monroe isn't here, and we'll sure as hell make sure you don't get anywhere near him.'

This said, the Viking stepped back, wished Damian a good day, and then both he and the younger, smaller woman police officer walked off towards Temple Inn's station entrance.

Damian breathed out a sigh of relief. They *had* been checking him; he had wondered, or hadn't dared think he could have been caught. *Who grassed him up? Was it Harvey? Had the wanker got cold feet and decided to get out of it?*

He'd have to have a word with Lennie Wright, speak to the man directly, rather than using the middleman.

Damian walked back to the bench, sitting down casually, reaching back, carefully pulling the gun out from behind it. He slid it into his waistband as he watched around, aware there was every chance someone was watching him through a Temple Inn police window right now. If he was going to do it, he'd have to do it soon. They were already on to him, so he'd have to be clever.

Damian Lim smiled. He'd find the time later that day, when there were too many things happening for them to understand what was going on – and then he'd kill the old man.

With luck, he'd be in and out before it was done.

He looked back at his bike, though. If he did do it, they now knew the registration number. He'd have to change the plates or, rather, steal something else. The Viking had been right when he said scooters were better through traffic.

And now with a new plan for the afternoon, Damian Lim put his helmet on, started his Suzuki Marauder, and left Temple Inn.

24

THE TRUTH

ANJLI WAS WAITING FOR DECLAN OUTSIDE THE DOOR TO Andrew Benson's interview room when he eventually arrived. After De'Geer had run past him, all thoughts for a coffee had disappeared, and he'd decided to crack on with things before the day ran out.

'Anything?' she asked.

'I got the impression he didn't realise that Marcel was there, which means Marcel was there because of somebody else, which leads us to his daughter, or maybe Andrew,' Declan looked back at the door. 'I'll take this one. Would you like to sit in with me?'

Anjli nodded, her eyes narrowing.

'Oh, yes,' she replied. 'That little shit has a lot to answer for.'

Andrew had made the intelligent decision of having a solicitor beside him as Declan and Anjli walked into the room. It was a man Declan had met before, an elderly man, his thinning grey hair neatly parted over a white shirt and striped navy-blue tie, a pair of gold, wire-framed glasses on the end of his nose.

'Mister Willoughby,' he said, nodding. 'How nice to see you again.'

Andrew froze, looking at his solicitor.

'You know them?'

'Oh yes,' Anjli sat down with a smile. 'Mister Willoughby here was the solicitor for a suspect named Laura Snider a few months back. He helped us to capture a killer. Although I don't think he knew at the time he was helping us. You probably should have looked harder for legal counsel.'

'Have you spoken with your client?' Declan asked, sitting down, smiling as Hugh Willoughby glared across the table at him.

'He has spoken to me about what happened, and we would like to discuss this,' Willoughby replied. 'However, we would ask you from the start to not have this on the record.'

Declan raised his eyebrows.

'Anything said that incriminates him wouldn't be on the record, but anything that helps him isn't on it either,' he said.

Willoughby, obviously pained by a request not of his making, nodded.

'I get that,' Andrew said instead. 'It's just that some of the stuff is my own interpretations and, well, I don't know if I'm right.'

Declan nodded.

'Okay, so let's start with what I know,' he said. 'Miles thought you were a killer, did you know that? You were traveling around Europe, and people were dying. I've since learnt you weren't the killer and were, by complete coincidence travelling around Europe with Lukas Weber, who was collecting paintings owed to him by people. Would that be correct?'

Andrew looked uncomfortable at the comment, but then nodded.

'We were in Salzburg, then Berlin, and then Paris,' he said. 'We were building up stock for the event. Lukas was with us. He would then—'

Declan held a hand up.

'Lukas was with *us*,' he said, emphasising the last word. 'Who else was with you? Stacey Nichols?'

'Stacey Nichols,' Andrew confirmed. 'Lukas had taken a shine to her, and she was kind of working as an assistant to him. I think. I'm not too sure, actually. All I know is they met when he did a talk at UAL Saint Martin's, and after that he hired her to work with him.'

'It wasn't romantic?' Anjli asked.

'Oh, Christ, no,' Andrew shook his head. 'Lukas Weber wasn't into anything like that. Stacey, she's attractive, but she's like twelve or something. That's more my brother's line.'

The smile he gave was a little weaker than it was earlier, and Declan saw the true face of Andrew Benson watching him, a face that seemed to regret a lot of recent life choices.

'So, you and Lukas Weber's *assistant* travelled with Lukas to see these people,' he said. 'Stefan Bierhof, Borge Pedersen and Anna Hoffmann?'

'Yes,' Andrew nodded. 'We didn't have that many pieces of artwork, and Lukas had worked out there was a way of getting a payday loan.'

'What kind of payday?'

Andrew didn't answer.

'What kind of payday?' Declan insisted, leaning forward. 'Or we put this on the record.'

'No, please.' Andrew shook his head. 'It's really big, and if it comes out that officially I'm involved in this, it's not just prison that awaits.'

'Then you'd better keep explaining.'

Andrew sighed, and Declan noticed he was trembling slightly as he continued.

'It was Lukas's idea,' he said, waving down Willoughby's attempts to stop him. 'No, I'm ready to explain this.'

Willoughby leant back, rolling his eyes as he nodded at Declan.

'All yours, it seems,' he said.

Andrew straightened in his chair, grabbing the water cup beside him, and taking a sip before continuing.

'Lukas Weber's grandfather was a Nazi, and I'm sure you're aware of that now.'

'I think the entire world is aware of that now,' Anjli said.

'What you might not know is that Lukas Weber's grandfather was part of a unit, a unit that included the grandfather of Anna Hoffmann, and the fathers of Stefan Bierhof and Borge Pedersen.'

'Yeah, we were aware of that, actually,' Anjli muttered. 'ERR, Nazis, all of that, all known. So why don't you tell us something we don't know?'

Andrew glared at Anjli, and for a moment Declan wondered if the "Andrew" who'd been speaking was an act, but he quickly backed down and sighed, sipping more water.

'Lukas had told us he was getting paintings for us,' he explained. 'He said it was paintings he'd done early in his life that'd been passed on to friends of his family. By getting those, we could make more money. He already had a buyer in mind.'

'Gabriel Bauer.'

Andrew nodded.

'Bauer had been after some paintings for a while. I didn't understand why at the time. But I did much later.'

'Because his father was in the same unit?' Declan asked.

'Yeah,' Andrew replied. 'Lukas mentioned Gabriel's daddy had taken some paintings from some big French artist at the end of the war, and Gabriel now wanted the full set for a large pay-out. But all I thought back then he really wanted anything by Lukas.'

'Go on,' Declan glanced at Anjli. She was taking notes down, but her eyes were still narrowed, and her lips were tight, as if she was forcing herself not to speak.

'We visited Professor Pedersen in Salzburg first,' Andrew said. 'Stacey wasn't with us, and Miles was in town as well, but wasn't there either. Lukas went into the meeting on his own, said it was easier if he spoke to them without anybody else there as it was about sensitive matters. I hadn't put two and two together at this point.'

'He was talking to them about their connections, through their grandfathers or fathers, to the Nazis,' Declan said.

'Yes, but there was more,' Andrew nodded weakly. 'He came out from Pedersen's house with two paintings. Land-scapes. They didn't really look like anything Lukas had done before, but he told me they were his, and they were paintings he was going to adjust and restore a little, and then we could sell them with the others in his exhibition.'

'And you agreed?'

'I was looking at the money at this point. If Weber could sell things to Gabriel Bauer, then that was fine by me. He's been one of our biggest purchasers in the past. Then we spent a couple of days in Salzburg. Miles and I had to look at another artist while we were there, but then Weber called –

he said it was very urgent. He said we needed to leave. He had found Stefan Bierhof in Berlin, and we had to go immediately.'

'This would have been around the same time Borge Pedersen was found dead in his car, with a lipstick kiss painted on his neck, right?' Anjli asked.

'I don't know,' Andrew replied honestly. 'I didn't see the newspapers until it was too late.'

There was a long, uncomfortable silence.

'Anyway, Stacey was waiting for us in Berlin. She had arranged the meeting, and Weber went in and spoke to Bierhof.'

'Let me guess,' Declan said. 'The same thing happened.'

'Two paintings,' Andrew nodded. 'Neither of them were anything like Weber's style, or even the landscapes he'd picked up in Salzburg, and at this point, I realised he was gaining other artist's paintings. I asked to see the first two, and he showed me them, and ...'

Andrew licked his lips.

'They weren't the same paintings,' he whispered. 'They were in the same frames, the same size, and they were landscapes, but they'd been changed. Like he used them as a template and painted his own style on top.'

'Why would he do that?'

'I wondered whether he was ashamed of his early styles and had changed this, but now seeing these other two images in Berlin, there was something that threw me.'

'You didn't look for the signature?'

'I did,' Andrew replied. 'But before I could properly look, he took them off me.'

'And then what?' Declan asked. 'Did you question him about this?'

Andrew shook his head.

'Then we went to Paris, and I was already working on how to sell these. By this point, we had four paintings. Lukas had returned to his house in Austria to fix them up—'

'Paint over them.'

'Whatever he was doing, and I went with Stacey to find the third of the people that he wanted to speak to.'

'Anna Hoffmann.'

'Yeah. Again, by this point, I'd had my suspicions, and I was asking around about the people we'd been talking to, and that's when I learned about their connections to the paintings, to the ERR, Gabriel Bauer's father and what their … well, what was done.'

Declan understood Andrew's reaction; this was probably the point he realised he was couriering stolen paintings, taken by Nazis from Jewish artists in World War Two.

And still he continued, Declan considered, and immediately despised the man in front of him even more.

'I spoke about my concerns to Stacey, but she didn't really care. She was tired of what she'd been doing at college, was looking for a "get filthy-rich" scheme, and I think she realised this was a way for her to escape as well. She was being offered a percentage of what she could sell by Lukas, and Lukas wasn't thinking in the same way that we were.'

'What do you mean by that?' Anjli asked.

'We were thinking of these paintings as six new images to add to a collection that we might get five or six grand each on,' Andrew said. 'We hadn't realised that Lucas was looking at six to seven figures per painting.'

Declan leant back in his chair.

'And in Paris?'

'In Paris, I demanded that I went to the meeting as well,'

Andrew replied. 'I wasn't sure what he'd been saying to people, and I wanted to at least witness one of the conversations. Lukas was unhappy about this, but I demanded, and Stacey wasn't there to side with him, so it was me versus him. We went and spoke to Anna, and that's when Lukas was honest. He explained to her we knew she had these two paintings, but rather than inform on her, if she gave us them, we could arrange for these paintings to be sold to a sympathetic buyer in Argentina. She would gain half the profits, and Weber would gain the rest. It was a good deal, as she could never sell them herself, because, well ... because.'

Declan wanted to scream. Actually, what Declan *really* wanted to do was lunge across the table and throttle Andrew Benson.

'Six paintings,' he said, 'taken from French Jewish artists during the war, and held from their family for decades, and you looked at this like a business transaction?'

Andrew placed his head in his hands.

'I know, I know, but at that point, it was too late,' he said. 'I'd seen the news.'

'How do you mean?' Anjli asked, her voice strangely calm and collected.

'I saw in the news that Pedersen and Bierhof were both dead,' Andrew replied. 'I'd realised then that Lukas was going in and gaining the paintings, and then someone – whether it was Lukas, or Stacey, or God knows who – was going in afterwards and killing them. They were placing kisses on their necks to make it look like it was some kind of linked killing, and I think that was probably Lukas's plan from the start, but I couldn't prove it, and God help me, I kept it a secret.'

'"I kept it a secret,"' Declan mocked. 'The road to hell is filled with kept secrets.'

'But there weren't six paintings.' Andrew suddenly looked up. 'There were seven. Lukas had two from Anna Hoffman, but when I picked them up, she said there were three. I managed to leave one there, deliberately hid it so nobody could find it. As far as Lukas was concerned, I was expected to appear with two, and I knew that if there was a problem here, I needed a way to prove my innocence.'

'How does hiding a painting prove your innocence?' Declan asked.

'Because I kept a painting he'd handled there,' Andrew brightened. 'It has his handprints on it. It proves he saw the painting, that he knew it existed and did nothing. If he threatened to throw me under a bus, I could have him done for murder.'

'But Anna wasn't dead at that point,' Declan replied, his face darkening. 'You could have told her to run.'

'I did, but she didn't listen to me,' Andrew muttered. 'I wasn't part of the "family," and I wasn't Weber. She trusted him, his grandfather was her grandfather's superior officer, and that was all it took. Then I had a call about a job lot of cold war statues in Budapest. By the time I finished up, I heard Anna Hoffmann was also dead.'

Andrew sobbed now, tears running down his cheeks.

'I realised at this point that not only was I going to go down for murder, but major art crimes. We're talking about Nuremburg trial levels of art crimes. I wouldn't only be excommunicated from the art community, but I would never see the light of day again.'

'So what was your plan?' Anjli looked up from her note taking.

'There were seven paintings in total that Lukas Weber wanted to sell to Gabriel Bauer,' Andrew explained. 'Six from the others, and one from his own grandfather. I didn't know if these were doctored in any way, or if these were original, Nazi-stolen paintings. All I knew was that Bauer had offered to buy Lukas's work. I thought that if I could get one of them back, and get someone to restore it on video, showing that Lukas Weber had painted over someone else's work, especially classic stolen paintings – then, with the painting that proved he'd been in Paris, perhaps I could prove myself as a whistle-blower. Maybe ...'

'And how did that work out for you?'

'I hired Gary Krohn,' Andrew replied. 'He'd done work for me in the past, and I knew he could help me here. I asked him to help me out. Take the painting, restore it on video, prove my innocence.'

'But he didn't take the painting.'

'No,' Andrew replied. 'I didn't even know if he *had* the painting. I sure as hell didn't know he was working for Bauer and tipped him the nod I was looking to steal it.'

'Krohn told Bauer your plan to steal a painting?'

'It's the only answer I have,' Andrew replied. 'There's no other way Bauer could have known he was involved.'

Declan nodded.

'So, if I got this right, you arranged with Stacey Nichols and Lukas Weber to gain Nazi gained paintings, taken from French Jewish artists during the war, have them painted over in the style of Lukas Weber, and then sell them on at an exhibition to a known Nazi fanatic, whose own father was one of the same unit that stole them. And you didn't think of telling us this until now?'

'I didn't realise what he had done,' Andrew Benson continued to sob. 'Until it was too late.'

'It was never too late,' Anjli snapped, slamming her pen

onto the table. 'The only moment it became too late was when Lukas Weber was found dead in a room.'

At this, Willoughby rose from his chair.

'I won't be representing this client anymore,' he said, the fury in his eyes matching the hatred in his voice.

As Willoughby walked out of the interview room, Declan waited a moment before looking back at Andrew.

'I deserve that,' Andrew nodded.

'You don't get to play the martyr,' Declan hissed. 'Not now, not ever.'

'I knew nothing about Weber's death,' Andrew continued, ignoring Declan's comment. 'I didn't know anything about any kind of plan to do that. I knew Lukas was aware the police would work out he was connected to the murders, by the simple fact it was relatives of the officers under his grandfather. I know he'd discussed with Stacey about possibly doing something where he was found unconscious with a lipstick mark, you know, maybe tried to show that he was attacked but hadn't been killed, something to do with a group of people during the war ...'

'Then the police might look elsewhere,' Anjli rose from her chair, staring down at Andrew. 'You're done. Off the record or not, you're done. When this comes out, no one's going to use you again. No one's going to work with you again. Gary Krohn died because you threw him into the mix. Stefan Bierhof, Borge Pedersen and Anna Hoffmann all died because you took Lukas Weber to their houses and closed your eyes.'

She looked at Declan.

'Do we have everything we need?'

Declan nodded, also rising.

'You really should have gone on the record with this,' he said. 'And you really should have listened to your solicitor.'

Then, walking out of the room, he closed the door behind him – before slamming his fist hard into the plasterboard beside it.

'Sometimes I absolutely hate this job,' he muttered, cradling his now bleeding knuckles. 'Now, where did De'Geer bugger off to?'

25

CATCHING UP

'WHAT THE BLOODY HELL WERE YOU THINKING?' DECLAN stormed into the main office, looking over at De'Geer and Cooper, currently in discussion with Monroe. Both of them looked confused at the question, but Declan hadn't finished; he stopped in front of them, prodding the larger of the two with his finger, now wrapped in toilet paper to stop his grazed knuckles from bleeding anywhere.

'You had the assassin, and you *let him go?*' he asked incredulous.

De'Geer, realising Declan's anger, nodded.

'Yes, sir,' he said. 'The plan was always to let him know we knew, to back him off a little.'

'You could have—'

'He could have done nothing, laddie,' Monroe interrupted, placing a hand on Declan's shoulder. 'Look at it hypothetically. Say we run out, grab Damian Lim, and arrest him for what? Attempted murder? We have no proof. Having a shite-looking motorcycle? Possibly, it wasn't exactly the nicest of models, and even if they had taken him down for something to do with me, do you think that would have ended it? God, no. Lennie Wright would have spoken to Harvey Drake, and there'd be another person on my back within half an hour, another killer to find and take down.'

He shrugged.

'At least with Mr. Lim, we know who it's going to be.'

'Yes, we know it's going to be him, but we don't know when he's going to try,' Declan started again.

'If I get taken out, I get taken out,' Monroe smiled, more relaxed than Declan expected. 'But we have to let him try. Damien Lim needs to kill me, so it can be passed on up the ladder to his boss. In a way, if I *were* to die, it would actually help the case, because we could follow Damian to his keeper.'

'You can't tell me the best option here is your death,' Declan said.

'Oh, I'm not saying that, laddie,' Monroe laughed. 'I intend to be around for a while, and from what we can work out Damian's not taking Harvey's calls, and Rosanna and Derek put the shits up him so much last night he's trying to put a hit on the hitman just to stop him. But I'm just letting you know that everything that was being done there was on my orders. So, I'd appreciate it if you didn't shout at the poor wee bairns for what they did.'

Declan, calming, nodded, turning to De'Geer and Cooper and cocking his head slightly to the side in an apologetic gesture.

'Sorry, guys,' he said.

'What did you do to your hand?' De'Geer asked.

'He punched a wall because he knows what's really going on in the case,' Anjli apologised on Declan's behalf, walking up behind him. 'He's angry at the world because we can't do much about a lot of it.'

'You know the killer?' Margaret Li leant out of Monroe's office, currently being used by Bullman, and Declan almost commented on how *this* gained her attention while a full-on shouting match didn't break her concentration.

'Yeah,' he growled. 'Andrew Benson just basically told us everything, off the record.'

'Off the record?'

'Let's just say I get why he didn't want it on the record,' Declan let out a breath he hadn't realised he'd been holding.

'Should we be having a briefing?' De'Geer asked.

'What we should be doing is arresting the whole damn lot of them,' Declan said, looking around at Cooper. 'Do me a favour. You've brought in Lucy Cormorant, right?'

'Yes, boss.'

'Go and have a chat with her. Not an interview, just friendly conversation while she's waiting to be talked to, to ask if she knows where her father is. Actually, screw that, kick in the door and demand a bloody answer. See if she knows where Nichols is, too.'

'Her father and Nichols?' Cooper frowned, but then simply nodded, not needing the explanation. 'On it.'

Declan thought about this for a minute.

'Actually, once you're done, come back, okay? It might be worth us all having a quick chat in the briefing room.'

Declan turned and walked into the briefing room, not even checking whether he was being followed. He faced the plasma screen to compose himself before turning back to stare at them.

Apart from Doctor Marcos and Derek Sutton, who were currently focusing on Damian Lim's location, everyone was there. Margaret Li sat next to Anjli, Jess next to Billy. De'Geer was with Monroe at the back, and Bullman was in her usual spot at the doorway.

'So, here's the deal,' he said. 'Lukas Weber, from what we've been told, has been accused of being the murderer of Stefan Bierhof, Borge Pedersen and Anna Hoffmann.'

He looked at Margaret Li.

'He visited each one and took paintings from them. Paintings their fathers or grandfathers, in Anna's case, took while working for the Einsatzstab Reichsleiter Rosenberg.'

'You pronounced Einsatzstab wrong,' Margaret Li corrected. 'It has more, how you say, emphasis on the second syllable.'

Declan fought the urge to ask if *this* was the fact she'd gained from the statement, and simply nodded a weak "thanks" back at her.

Margaret Li, in turn, leant back on her chair, considering this.

'We had suspicions,' she said. 'But, when you found Lukas Weber dead, we assumed it was someone else.'

'From what Andrew Benson told us, there were seven paintings,' Declan said. 'All of which were stolen by Nazis. Lukas Weber had decided to sell these to a private buyer at the auction.'

'Gabriel Bauer?' Monroe asked.

Declan nodded.

'I think there was a second level of bidding, but Bauer was the obvious winner,' he said. 'The problem was he went to each place with either Andrew Benson or Stacey Nichols.'

'Nichols?' Billy asked, looking around. 'Where did she enter the story?'

'Apparently, she was working as Lukas Weber's assistant

from the moment they met at UAL, and they met because she was the one who introduced Weber to Miles Benson,' Declan continued. 'So, according to Andrew Benson, they went from Salzburg to Berlin to Paris, and at each point Lukas Weber gained paintings from each of them, promising them equal shares, fifty-fifty, of all profits. However, during this time Andrew Benson started to wonder what was going on, as the paintings weren't Lukas's artwork and only when he demanded to see the first two again, did he realise that Lukas had been painting over the top.'

'He was hiding the stolen paintings ...' Jess muttered to herself and then reddened. 'Sorry, Dad ... I mean, Guv.'

'No, you're right,' Declan replied. 'I believe the term is over-painting.'

'Like the woman who painted over Jesus in Spain?'

'More the Tudors who painted over Richard the Third,' Declan replied knowledgably. 'But your suggestion works, too.'

'So, let me get this right,' Monroe scratched at his beard now. 'Lukas Weber decided to get a payday by taking the paintings ... and then killing the owners?'

'From what I can work out, yes,' Declan said. 'But this is Andrew's testimony. It could have been Andrew, Stacey, or Lukas who killed them, as currently there's no hard evidence.'

'It makes sense, though,' Anjli shrugged. 'Lukas taking the paintings and then killing them meant he didn't have to share the money.'

'And that's when the lipstick kiss was painted on the neck at some point,' Billy added. 'They must have realised this made it feel like some kind of retaliatory murder for war crimes, rather than a random opportunity for greed.'

'But Lukas Weber must have known the police would work out he was involved, either by association with his grandfather or because he'd been at the same places, and at the same times as the murders,' Bullman said from the door.

'Andrew Benson thinks he did,' Declan continued. 'He reckons Weber hatched a plan with Stacey Nichols that he would fake his own attack. He'd be found unconscious, with the same painted kiss on his neck.'

'But, as we already know from Doctor Marcos's autopsy, Lukas Weber was shocked by a stick, fell backward, and smashed his head,' De'Geer spoke up now. 'We still can't work out if it was the heart attack or some kind of cranial injury that killed him. It was probably both.'

'So, Lukas Weber's death was an accident? Really?' Billy asked.

'Really,' De'Geer confirmed. 'Well, it looks to be in as much as Lukas Weber's death was an accident and not a part of his plan.'

Monroe leaned back on his chair, contemplating the new information.

'And that's when Stacey Nichols took the opportunity to make it look like a murder with the lipstick kiss signature,' he finished. 'Aye, she could have done that. She was there.'

'So, Stacey was covering up for Lukas?' Billy asked.

'According to Andrew Benson, exactly,' Declan said. 'She was trying to continue his plan even after his death.'

Monroe sighed. 'At least we have an idea of the truth now. Lukas Weber was responsible for the murders, especially the one in Berlin, and for the stolen paintings. Stacey Nichols tried to cover it up. All we need now is the concrete evidence to confirm this.'

'What about Gabriel Bauer?' Billy asked. 'Was he involved in Weber's death?'

'Maybe not, but there we come to the other issue,' Declan said. 'The murder of Gary Krohn.'

'We have the killer, though,' De'Geer replied from the back. 'He's being held at Bishopsgate.'

'Why there?' Bullman asked, frowning.

'Because the inn here is full,' Monroe replied. 'We have him dead to rights. He can wait a while, and also DCI Walsh here might consider paying him a visit if he's in the cells here.'

'There's also the issue that once we get a confession from him, Gabriel Bauer's in the clear,' Declan said, ignoring Monroe's jibe. 'There's no way Rafael Kirchner's giving up his boss. But until we get that on record, we can still investigate Bauer with no problems from Bauer's extensive legal team.'

At this, Billy's laptop beeped, and he looked down at it.

'Ah, crap,' he said.

'Problems?' Declan asked.

At this, Billy looked up and reddened.

'It's the receipt I sent into Lambeth,' he replied.

Declan frowned and then paused as realisation took hold.

'Do you mean the receipt that my attacker had?' he asked. 'Why did you send it there?'

Billy swallowed.

'Well, funny story,' he said weakly. 'When you gave it to me, I couldn't work out what it said, as it was already faded. It had been in his pocket a while, and it'd, you know, gone.'

'But didn't Davey once show us how to fix that?' Anjli asked now.

'Yeah, when we were up in the Peak District, she showed

us something to do with a hairdryer and heating thermal receipts to bring back the words ...'

'Don't tell me you tried this yourself, ye wee bampot?' Monroe chided. 'You tried to attack the thermal paper with a hairdryer?'

'It's not my finest hour,' Billy looked at the desk, unable to look Monroe in the eye. 'But I had a friend in Lambeth forensics who reckoned he could fix it, but it'd take a day or so. Then I forgot because, well, the big boss found the killer beside Gabriel Bauer, and the fingerprints came through.'

Declan looked back at Monroe, who nodded.

'He's right,' Monroe said. 'I am the big boss. So why are we worried about the receipt right now?'

'Because of something Anjli said to me earlier,' Billy said, placing the recently gained receipt scan onto the plasma screen.

Rising, Anjli walked past Declan and peered closer to the plasma screen, examining the receipt.

'I know why it's connected to us,' she said. 'That's a thermal receipt from the *Cartier* store in Heathrow's Terminal Five.'

'So, Gabriel Bauer has expensive tastes? Maybe Rafael Kirchner was buying something for him, or maybe it was a girlfriend—'

'According to Cooper, when we saw Stacey Nichols last night, she was wearing a silver Cartier watch bracelet,' Anjli pointed at the screen. 'And that there says the receipt was for a silver bracelet Cartier watch, bought three weeks ago for two and a half thousand pounds.'

'Are you saying Stacey Nichols is wearing an expensive two-to-three grand watch, given to her by Gabriel Bauer?' Declan asked.

Anjli smiled.

'Looks like Stacey's got even more secrets,' she said. 'The question is, what did she do to earn it?'

'According to Andrew Benson, Krohn owed Bauer, and gave him the heads up that Andrew Benson had hired him to steal one of the paintings,' Declan added. 'What if it was Stacey that did it instead?'

'I can check her phone records, but it might take a while to get them,' Billy suggested. 'Unless we think she's in mortal danger, there's a ton of hoops to leap through.'

'It'd explain a couple of things, too,' Monroe replied. 'Nichols sees Krohn, then a painting goes missing. We then get a sketch made by Lucy Cormorant, one Bauer recognises as Krohn, Nichols texts him to say Krohn was at the event, and then Bauer sends his men to Krohn's studio to get it back.'

'But he never had it, which means it still has to be in the gallery,' Declan said, but then froze. 'If we have Veronica, Andrew and Miles in custody, who's watching it?'

Before he could answer, though, Cooper returned to the briefing room, with an anxious Lucy Cormorant beside her.

'Are you sure you should be wandering around with suspects?' Monroe asked from the back.

'I think you should hear what she has to say,' Cooper said, looking at Lucy, encouraging her to speak.

'Look, I've been lying and you know that,' Lucy said. 'I was with Miles because I fell for him, but I also wanted a payout for my dad. And, when all hell broke loose, Dad was supposed to "out" Miles as a fraud, and push for damages in court. But instead, when Weber was found dead, he took the money directly from Gabriel Bauer.'

'And why would he do that?'

Lucy looked at the floor.

'Because I told him that's what I was going to do, but then I was held by security. He did it in my place.'

'But why would Bauer give you the money, after seeing you stand up against Miles?' Billy asked.

Lucy looked up at him.

'Because Gabriel Bauer knew we were sleeping together and was holding it over us,' she said. 'Bloody Stacey Nichols gave him the information – she'd been working for him as an informant for months.'

'I thought she worked for Andrew?'

'She worked for everyone,' Lucy said. 'Anyone who paid had her bloody loyalty. Even Gary Krohn, until he turned up at the event without alerting her.'

'Aside from Nichols, tell us more about Bauer,' Monroe's face had darkened.

'I knew Andrew had this plan to make Bauer "buy in," to get a little more cash, so I thought after I did my spot, I'd tell Bauer he'd won and collect the first-round bids. It was a couple of grand, and I'd pass it to Dad. But, when Weber was found, I was classed as a suspect and couldn't get to him. So, Dad did it.'

'Okay, so where's your dad now?' Declan asked.

'That's the issue, guv,' Cooper replied. 'He's not answering his phone, and Stacey Nichols isn't answering hers, either. They were each supposed to meet Lucy today at the coffee shop, but I got to her before they did.'

Declan looked to Billy.

'CCTV, now,' he said. 'See if either of them did—'

'They did,' Cooper interrupted. 'I just spoke to the manager, and she said Stacey walked in, was told Lucy had been arrested and left quickly.'

'And Marcel?'

'He'd been in the coffee shop at the time, but when she said this, he rose, asked the manager to confirm that, and then followed Stacey out.'

'Great, so they're in the wind.'

'Not quite, sir,' Cooper shook her head. 'The manager claims they were stopped by three men in a van and bundled into it. The van drove off before she could get the licence plate.'

'Any descriptions of the men?'

'Yes, but one stood out,' Cooper read from her notes. 'Stocky, South American, short hair and a scar across the eye.'

'Jesus, it's Jorge Aznar,' Monroe rose. 'Bauer's given up playing.'

'Either that, or he's changing the rules,' Declan said, waving for the others to get to their feet. 'Come on – either way, this ends tonight.'

He looked at Billy.

'And good news,' he said. 'Stacey Nichols is now in mortal danger, so you can grab those phone records after all.'

26

ZEROING IN

'When we met him at the Gherkin, Bauer talked about warehouses,' Monroe said. 'He said something like "I have many far quieter warehouses where I won't be disturbed." Which leads me to believe he has multiple.'

'That's what "many" means—' Billy started, but stopped himself at a steely gaze from his superior.

'And if he doesn't want to be disturbed, he won't have them under his name,' Declan looked at Jess, now working on one of the other computers. 'See if you can find a list of London warehouses Bauer, or any of his companies, have rented?'

'Can you pick up phone pings?' Monroe asked Billy, already on his bank of monitors.

'All three phones are turned off or dark,' he said. 'Last time we got either Marcel Cormorant or Stacey Nichols, they were in Shoreditch.'

'This is my fault,' Lucy muttered. 'I should have told him what I was doing from the start. He wouldn't have gone it alone.'

'Could someone please take her back to the cells?' Declan asked. 'Unless you have anything you can help with, there's nothing more you can do here.'

'The paintings,' Lucy said, almost in a whisper. 'They were by different French artists, but the large one, the one Weber didn't want to sell? That was painted by Jacques Kormereaux. The Nazis took about half a dozen of his paintings during the war, and they were never seen again.'

'Didn't your father change your name from Kormereaux to Cormorant when he arrived here?' Anjli asked.

'Jacques was my great-grandfather,' Lucy replied.

'Why Cormorant?'

'Because it symbolised greed, and he'd come here for a fresh chance and an opportunity to make money.'

'Guys, I've got something,' Jess said, looking up from her screen. 'Gabriel Bauer does have warehouses. They're in ...'

She stopped.

'Ah,' she continued. 'He has warehouses in Bermondsey, Harringay, Wapping ... there's another five more ...'

'Needles in haystacks,' Declan muttered, looking at Billy. 'Anything?'

'Just got the records, checking through ... sending Marcel's to you, Anjli,' Billy was scrolling through data. 'Hey, did you know Stacey texted Bauer yesterday morning? She was the one informing on Gary Krohn. It wasn't our sketch.'

'Send it to me,' Declan said, looking at a map of London on Jess's screen. On it were a dozen red dots, each one registering a location Bauer had a warehouse in.

'He has been busy,' he said. 'Any way to narrow it?'

'Working through ANPR,' Billy said. 'The van they were taken in was outside the coffee shop, so we're trying to get a location or direction. That'd narrow some of these down.'

Anjli was now working on her own computer.

'Going through Marcel's locations,' she said. 'Based on his phone records, on the day of the murder, he visited this location an hour before the exhibition. Does it mean anything?'

Before Declan could say anything, Lucy looked at it, her face darkening.

'Mickey Needles,' she said. 'No, I don't know his real name. He's a tattooist.'

'Your dad's into tattoos?'

'No, but he designs them,' Lucy said. 'Makes more money than oils these days doing it. Mickey is old school. Learnt as a teenager in remand centres.'

'You mean with homemade tattoo guns?' Declan asked, spinning around to face Billy. 'Get me his number. Now.'

'Already on it,' Billy said, pointing at a phone that beeped. Declan picked it up, to hear the line already being used, a phone ringing.

'Hello?' A gruff, male voice answered after four rings.

'Mickey Needles?'

'Only mates call me that. I don't recognise you. Who's asking?'

'Detective Chief Inspector Walsh of the City of London police.'

'Oh? In that case, sure,' Mickey's voice relaxed a little. 'I'm Mickey Needles. You want a tattoo?'

'I want to know why Marcel Cormorant came to you a couple of days back,' Declan said, the phone now on speaker.

'Marcel's a guy I use for ink designs, and my clients are—'

'Mickey, it's Lucy, please tell us,' Lucy leant closer, pleading. 'Dad's in trouble.'

'Fine,' Mickey said. 'But if it's anything to do with me, I had no involvement, okay? He borrowed a tattoo gun.'

'A what?' Declan asked. 'Surely that's a massive item?'

'Nah, he borrowed one of the exhibits,' Mickey said. 'I have old prison ones, I'm building a backroom out to show the history all the way back to Sutherland Macdonald, the first professional tattoo artist in Britain.'

'And you didn't ask why he needed it?'

'He said it was for a new work he was doing, promised to cut me in when it was done,' Mickey said. 'It was dusty and on a shelf. Wait, has he used it? That ink's well old inside it. He could get hepatitis or something.'

'Yeah, I don't think we need to worry about hepatitis. We'll speak soon,' Declan said, disconnecting the call. 'So, Marcel had the tattoo gun the night of the murder. Could he have been part of this?'

Lucy, however, shook her head.

'He wasn't,' she replied nervously. 'If he was, he'd have known what we had planned, and we wouldn't be in this mess.'

'Lassie, you're in this mess for way more reasons than just your father,' Monroe said. 'So, what was next in your plans?'

'You can't kill us,' Marcel said as he knelt on the warehouse floor. 'It's murder.'

'Did you care when you murdered Weber?' Gabriel Bauer asked as he walked towards the recently arrived van. 'Did you care when you helped Weber murder others?'

The second line was aimed at Stacey, who stood angrily, facing him.

'I helped you,' she said. 'I gave you information—'

'Information I already had,' Bauer snapped as Jorge,

closing the van door, pulled out a Glock 17, aiming at them while the other two inhabitants of the van climbed back in and drove out of the warehouse, leaving the four of them alone. 'You think I needed you as an informer?'

'What about the gifts?'

'A couple of grand to keep you from alerting either of the Bensons while I went for millions,' Bauer laughed. 'The issue here isn't what I did, but how little you settled for. So much for the bitch who wanted everything by twenty-five.'

He looked from Marcel to Stacey and back.

'One of you took my painting,' he said. 'The others were nice, but the largest one, the painting Weber had brought but wasn't selling? That was his grandfather's one. That was the important one.'

'I didn't do anything,' Stacey whined, but stopped as the muzzle of the Glock rested against her head.

'You'd better hope you did, and that you remember what it was,' Bauer said. 'Or else you both die.'

THEY HADN'T FOUND OUT ANYTHING ELSE OF USE IN THE briefing; Stacey had been working for Bauer, Marcel had a tattoo gun at the event, Lucy had intended to steal the large painting and prove it was her family's work while escaping with Miles, and Bauer had seven active warehouses, spread out across London. With time running out, it was decided to split up and search each one, sending officers from local units there as support.

Declan had gone with Margaret Li to Bermondsey while the others had gone to the others, but they were only a couple of minutes from the destination when Billy called, the voice connected to the Audi's speaker.

'We have the van,' he said. 'But it's not going to any of Bauer's warehouses. It's going to an industrial estate in Rotherhithe, less than a mile away from you in the other direction.'

'How does he know where we are?' Margaret was surprised by this. 'Your cars are tracked?'

'Not officially, but Billy has trust issues,' Declan replied, his lips thin as he spun the Audi at a crossroads, turning a full one-eighty before heading down the other side of the dual carriage-way, heading back to Rotherhithe. 'What's the address?'

'Third turning on your left, head to the Thames, then it's unit six,' Billy said. 'It's a business partner of Bauer, that's why we missed it. Closest help is five minutes away, so hold for backup.'

'Yeah, that's not happening,' Declan said as he discon-nected the call.

'You have weapons?'

'We're the UK,' Declan smiled. 'We have sticks.'

'Wonderful,' Margaret said, and again, Declan wasn't sure if this was real, or mocking, so instead he reached into the glove compartment, pulling out a spare, extendable baton.

'Do you know how to use these?' he asked, passing it across as they climbed out of the car.

Margaret, in response, took the baton, flicking it open, examined down it as if looking for imperfections, then closed it back, sliding it up her sleeve.

'You're not the first person to take me to a gunfight when we have no weapons,' she said.

Declan smiled.

'Don't be so negative,' he said. 'They might not have guns. They might have bigger weapons.'

Before Margaret could reply, however, Declan paused her, holding his hand up. He'd seen a van across the street; a very familiar one.

'There,' he said, pointing towards the side of the unit that Billy had aimed them at. 'That's the van the witness saw outside the coffee shop.'

'There are two people inside it,' Margaret nodded. 'Shall we arrest them?'

'I think we should at least have a conversation,' Declan replied as they walked up either side, with Declan smiling, knocking on the passenger window.

Inside the van were two men. One was European in looks, blond hair cut into a buzz cut, whilst the other one was definitely part of Bauer's Argentine crew.

The European in the passenger seat glowered at Declan as he smiled back through the glass, and the window slowly rolled down as the man eyed him up and down, deciding whether or not this stranger was a threat.

'What?' he asked, with the tone of a man who really didn't want an answer.

'Your brake light's out,' Declan replied. 'We'd like to see your licence.'

The passenger looked at the driver, confused.

'Look, mate. I don't know what you're doing—'

'What I'm doing is arresting you,' Declan said, holding up his warrant card. Detective Chief Inspect—'

At this point and before he could finish his sentence, the European slammed open the door, knocking Declan backwards before he could gather his thoughts, already on him with what looked to be some kind of large Maglite torch being used as a club.

Declan, however, had his baton out already, and could block the first blow, twisting as he did so, using the momentum to send the man past him, doubling over as he tried to keep his balance – until Declan slammed the hilt of the baton into the back of his head, connecting at the junction of skull and spine. It was a stun move, and the European staggered forwards a couple more steps before he crumpled to his knees.

Declan, however, wasn't taking chances, and took the opportunity for a second shot, striking the back of the passenger's head, knocking him to the floor, unconscious.

He spun quickly, looking to help Margaret, but drew himself back up as he realised that not only was Margaret able to sort this out herself, but she'd already taken the Argentine driver, now on his knees, hands behind his head as she pointed the baton at him.

Declan was impressed. He hadn't even heard a blow. Could it be that Margaret Li had taken out the Argentine thug without having a fight?

'All right,' he said, acting as if this had been the plan all along. 'Shall we go inside?'

With the two men now secured, both handcuffed to pipes outside with one still unconscious but not needing any immediate medical attention, Declan and Margaret made their way to a pair of giant roller shutters into the warehouse, a door situated to the right.

Cracking it open, no more than a sliver and glancing through, Declan could see four figures at the other end of the warehouse; two men whose backs were to him and two other people on their knees, one male and one female, both of whom were instantly recognisable as Marcel Cormorant and Stacey Nichols.

'Call Monroe,' he said. 'We need backup here immediately.'

'And how do I do that?' Margaret asked, her voice still emotionless. 'I don't have his number.'

Declan quietly swore to himself.

'Do you have anyone's?'

Margaret's expression brightened.

'I have Detective Chief Superintendent Bullman,' she suggested.

'Great, give her a call,' Declan gave Margaret a reassuring smile. 'Wish me luck.'

He didn't wait for Margaret Li to make some comment about luck not being logical; instead, he adjusted his jacket, placed his extendable baton up his sleeve and entered the warehouse.

'You have ten seconds to give me an answer I like,' Bauer stated, the muzzle of his antique Luger aimed directly between Marcel Cormorant's eyes. 'Because currently, I'm not hearing anything that fills me with joy.'

'I don't know what you want!' Marcel whined. 'You need to give me more information!'

Bauer nodded at a pile of canvasses in black frames, held against the wall of the warehouse.

'This is every single one of Lukas Weber's paintings from the gallery,' he explained. 'Both his own, and the ones he ... shall we say enhanced.'

'The classics he painted over,' Marcel snapped sullenly. 'Let me guess. You don't know which ones are which?'

He laughed at this.

'What, so you don't have the room for all of them on your private jet? Give me a break!'

'I don't have the time to go through each of them!' Bauer shouted, looking at Stacey. 'Show me which ones are his, and which ones are important!'

'Okay, sure,' Stacey held her hands up. 'But what will you do after that?'

'What do you think?' Marcel replied, miming a gun to the side of the head. 'We're only useful while he doesn't know.'

'Not true,' Bauer smiled. 'I do not want to kill you.'

Marcel went to make another jibe, but Bauer beat him to the punchline, swinging down and pistol whipping him across the side of the head, drawing blood from a vicious-looking gash.

'And as you can see, I do not need to kill you.'

Stacey swallowed and was about to speak when there was the sound of a door slamming, and an unfamiliar man walked into the warehouse.

'I told you, don't come in until I tell you so!' Bauer shouted. 'Go and—'

'Sorry, I must have missed that memo,' Declan smiled. 'We haven't met yet. I'm Detective Chief Inspector Walsh, City of London police. I'm the one your man failed to kill.'

'He should have tried harder,' Bauer muttered, shifting his grip on his pistol. 'But it's something I can easily rectify.'

27

VISITING LECTURER

DECLAN SMILED AS HE STOOD ON THE WAREHOUSE FLOOR, HIS hands outstretched in front of him to show he wasn't armed.

'Nazis,' he said with a smile on his face. 'They always ruin everything, don't you know?'

In front of him, still angry at his entrance, Gabriel Bauer faced him, straightening a gun in his hand. Declan could see from where he was that it was a Luger P08, and although it was probably over eighty years old, knowing Bauer it had probably been meticulously cared for, with no fear of a round being jammed in the chamber.

Next to him was Jorge Aznar, also with a gun, although his one was a far more modern, and more readily available, Glock 17.

In front of them, both on their knees, were Marcel Cormorant and Stacey Nichols.

'I have to say,' Declan said, continuing walking into the room, 'this doesn't look good.'

'These two people were breaking into my property,' Bauer replied calmly. 'I was simply protecting my items.'

'With a weapon you probably don't have a licence for.'

Bauer looked surprised as he turned the Luger in his hand.

'This?' he asked. 'This Luger is nothing more than an antique. My bodyguard has a licence for his sidearm, but this is nothing more than a keepsake. I had been showing it when they tried to steal it.'

'Did they now?' Declan raised his eyebrows in mock surprise. 'And you're not angry at them for anything else?'

Bauer watched Declan carefully.

'Oh, I am angry,' he said. 'I'm very angry. This man here stole a quarter of a million pounds from me. I would like that back.'

'And taking them off the street is the way to go?'

'Play me CCTV that shows this, please. My men asked them politely.'

'Yeah, down the barrel of a gun—' Stacey started, but stopped when Jorge aimed the muzzle at her.

'He does that again, I'll make him eat it,' Declan snapped. 'As for the money owed? From what I hear, that was a price for some paintings.'

'I don't want the paintings anymore,' Bauer replied. 'You know what I want?'

'Actually, I do,' Declan said. 'Seven paintings stolen by the Nazis from French artists, in particular one artist named Jacques Kormereaux, during World War Two.'

He pointed at Marcel.

'Who he knows all about.'

'I know nothing about the provenance of these paintings. Just that I wanted them,' Bauer said. 'I have my reasons.'

'Oh, I can believe that,' Declan said. 'After all, your daddy was one of the team that nicked them, wasn't he? When he cut and run from the others, allowing them to stand trial while he hid in Buenos Aires or wherever.'

Bauer didn't reply, and Declan realised that he probably hadn't expected Declan, or any of the department, to realise this little snippet of information.

'You seem to know a lot,' Bauer hissed.

'Actually, you'd be surprised at what I know,' Declan said. 'I know, for a start, that your father was connected to a group of soldiers under the orders of Ober-Einsatzführer Weber, Lukas Weber's grandfather, during the war. I know they stole a lot of French artwork and books and stuff from all over Europe, to be honest, dumping it into Neuschwanstein Castle, and I know that shortly before the end of the war, after Hitler put a bullet into his head, your father ran, taking a ton of looted items with him.'

Gabriel Bauer clapped his hands, still holding the Luger.

'That's a lovely history story,' he said. 'You should do lectures.'

'Oh, I do lecture,' Declan said. 'You're about to hear one right now. It's a very interesting one, to be perfectly honest. You see, most of the unit was captured after they hid the paintings, and these soldiers, they went to trial. They regained their lives, but they knew they were being watched. Because of this, they did nothing with the paintings that they'd stolen. But your father, Werner? Well, he was different, wasn't he? He didn't take the paintings into Europe. He kept them with him as he escaped to Argentina, and then he used his stolen items to build an empire, an empire that you now control.'

'My father was a self-made man,' Gabriel Bauer replied,

his face darkening. 'And anyone who says otherwise will speak to my lawyers.'

'Will they, though?' Declan asked mockingly. 'Or will they speak to some masked and hooded man with a machete, as they try to throw them out of a window?'

'What my bodyguard did in his own time has nothing to do with me,' Gabriel Bauer snapped back. 'He acted alone. He thought he was helping me, but in the end ...'

He let the sentence trail off, shrugging as he did so, the point made.

'So your bodyguards, or whatever these men are, you let them work pretty autonomously?' Declan asked.

'I am a considerate employer,' Bauer smiled.

'Wow, that's great,' Declan said. 'So I can go back to the cells and ask Rafael Kirchner why he had a receipt for a Cartier watch in his pocket? A watch Miss Nichols there was wearing the last time we saw her?'

Gabriel Bauer glanced down at Stacey, clicking his tongue against the top of his mouth in a *ticking* noise as he considered his options.

'Let's just cut to the chase, yeah?' Declan yawned. 'Time's running out, I'm getting bored. Lukas Weber's grandfather worked for the Nazis and also stole paintings. He used a couple of them, and his role as Chief of Police of a small Austrian town to build up a small empire of his own. The Weber's were millionaires; very wealthy. As a child, Lukas Weber probably had everything he wanted. But twenty years ago, Lukas Weber learned of the history of the money. He realised how his family had become so rich, and he cut off all ties with his grandfather.'

'Foolish.'

'Well, that's one way of looking at it,' Declan nodded. 'It

was a problem in one respect because it meant that he was now cut off from any of the lovely money the Weber family had, and he was back to being a penniless artist. But the bigger problem was, he wasn't as penniless as he thought he was, because his history both helped and hindered him. People would buy his artwork not because of his abilities, but because of who his grandfather was, and others would shun his artwork for the same reasons.'

He kept moving closer still.

'And then, over the years, this turned into resentment and anger; maybe he aimed at his grandfather, maybe he aimed it at the world, but either way, Lukas Weber decided he should have a payday.'

Gabriel Bauer shrugged.

'Am I the payday here?'

'We'll get to that,' Declan replied, nodding at Marcel Cormorant. 'Meanwhile, we've got Marcel here. French immigrant, a very good artist, sells his work at the Benson Gallery. Unfortunately, he gets screwed over by the owners, which leaves him with a bad taste in his mouth and with a daughter who wants to find her own form of revenge. However, Marcel here has a connection. You see, Marcel is directly connected to one of the French artists who had his work stolen, Jacques Kormereaux, his surname being changed to "Cormorant" during the seventies, when he moved to the UK, looking to change his life. Maybe at some point he learnt Weber had it. Maybe he followed the conspiracies, I don't know. But Marcel is now here in the story, looking for a way to gain revenge.'

Marcel looked up from his knees.

'It wasn't like that,' he said. 'I didn't care about Weber or the paintings at the start; I wanted to make my money as well. Benson had screwed me out of close to two hundred grand in total over four years. It's why I charged that to Bauer. After all, he was going to grab Grandad's painting for five times that. I was only gaining what I was owed.'

He shifted, not daring to move, though.

'Bauer should get the money from Miles Benson rather than taking it from me.'

'Hold that thought,' Declan said, 'Because now we're coming up to the important part. Nine months ago, Lukas Weber is invited to Saint Martin's where he does a talk. Of course, it's not received well by some people and after one lecture, he's asked to return home. Unfortunately, grandsons of Nazis still cause issues. But, in that talk were two people. Stacey Nichols and her friend Lucy Cormorant. Your daughter.'

Declan walked a little closer.

'Lucy recognised the name because of the family stories,' he continued. 'Stacey Nichols learned about this from Lucy. Miles Benson also spoke at these talks, and again, Lucy recognised the name. She had been to some of the exhibitions and she knew that you'd been screwed over by them. So, Lucy decided she wanted to start some kind of plan to get her dad his owed money; an exhibition perhaps from Lukas Weber, with her in the middle.'

'I know nothing about that,' Stacey said. 'I wasn't brought in at all.'

'I know why you were brought in,' Declan said. 'You realised you didn't want to be a poor artist, and you wanted your own payday. Lukas Weber seemed like an option. You hadn't realised at the time that he was cut off from the family; you thought he was a millionaire, and both of you introduced Weber to Miles Benson while he was having a coffee with his brother, known for his ability to find diamonds in the rough.'

'She fell in love with Miles,' Stacey muttered now. 'It wasn't meant to happen. Lucy was looking for a father figure ...'

She looked over at Marcel.

'You know, with her own being such a let-down.'

She looked back at Declan.

'Lucy was into Miles, but I always felt there was something wrong with the man. I'd also heard the stories of how much of a deadbeat Marcel had been. Andrew decided he wanted to make as much money as possible – he was sick of Miles and Veronica's shit and wanted to leave the gallery, and he saw in me somebody with the same aims. Get money, get out. We were a good partnership.'

'So then what happened?'

'Weber came to us with an idea,' Stacey said. 'He had a couple of paintings that were, shall we say black market and he knew they'd make a fortune. He knew of three other people who had more paintings that had been taken one night from Neuschwanstein Castle.'

'And Gabriel had others from this theft as well, didn't he?' Declan asked.

At this, Bauer shrugged.

'I could not confirm or deny whether I have such paintings,' he said. 'But hypothetically, if I did, I would want the entire set. I do have a bit of a completist streak in me.'

'So you went along with Weber's idea,' Declan ignored Bauer, speaking to Stacey. 'He visited the three people who had these paintings, Stefan Bierhof, Borge Pedersen, and Anna Hoffmann. One by one, they gave him the paintings he then painted over, to make it look like they were his.'

'But then Andrew got cold feet,' Stacey said. 'And I under-

stand why. We started to learn that Lukas didn't like the idea
of paying out.'

'Go on.'

'It was when we were heading towards Paris that we
learned Stefan had been found dead in Berlin,' she continued. 'The dates of his murder matched when we were in
town. We learnt Pedersen was dead as well. Andrew pulled
me aside and expressed his concerns, saying he believed
Weber was a murderer. He was worried, and he decided he
wanted to fix things.'

'And how did he fix things?' Declan asked.

'He told me there was a painting in Paris. One he'd
hidden. Weber had touched it, so it had his fingerprints on it.
If Andrew went down, he could use this as proof it was
Weber, not him, that was killing people. But then Anna Hoffmann was murdered, the painting probably confiscated as
evidence, and he came up with a second idea. He was going
to bring a restorer forger he knew into the event, steal one of
the paintings, and video the painting being restored to its
original background. This way, we could prove Lukas Weber's
paintings were the stolen masterpieces.'

'And how did you feel about that?'

Stacey glowered at Declan.

'I was unhappy,' she said. 'I understood why he wanted to
do it. But we'd lose millions. Bauer wouldn't get his paintings.
Andrew would get his freedom, but I was convinced I'd be
thrown to the wolves. After all, every time Andrew talked
about this, it was always *his* freedom. Not *our* freedom. So I
contacted Bauer and told him about Andrew's plan.'

'Is that when he bought you a Cartier watch?'

'And the Tiffany bracelet,' Stacey nodded. 'He said it was
easier for him to pass these gifts off as trinkets, gifts for girl-

friends, than payments out that could come back to him. If I wanted, I could sell them on, get some money. It was only a few grand, though, and I wanted more. When I saw Gary Krohn at the event and a painting went missing, I confronted him. He told me to basically piss off, and in retaliation ... I texted Bauer.'

'We know,' Declan said, reaching for his notebook slowly, holding it up as he opened it at a page with the corner folded. 'You sent a message saying, "I think Gary Krohn has it."'

He smiled as he looked at Bauer.

'Did you know she has you in her phone book as "Scary Bastard?"' he asked. 'I don't know if I'd be insulted or impressed. But either way, that's why Gary Krohn died, wasn't it? Because you believed he had the painting.'

He looked back at Marcel.

'But he didn't, did he?'

Marcel rose at this point.

'I'd moved it by then.'

'Get back down!' Bauer shouted, raising the gun.

'I wouldn't do that if I were you,' Declan said. 'Killing someone in front of a police officer—'

He didn't finish the sentence as, in an act of desperation, Marcel Cormorant lunged forward, grabbing the Luger, twisting it away from him as he struggled with Bauer.

There was a sharp report – a gunshot echoing through the warehouse – and Bauer staggered back, blood blossoming from his gut, as Marcel stepped backwards, the Luger now in his own hand, waving it at Jorge.

'Put the gun down!' he cried, his eyes wide with adrenaline.

'Marcel, you need to—'

'I need to what?' Marcel cried out triumphantly. '"juge-ment karmique," detective! He got what he deserved!'

Jorge had dropped the Glock and ran to the downed Bauer.

'He needs an ambulance,' he said, looking up at Declan.

'He needs to die,' Marcel said, his face expressionless. 'All of you need to die, if it means I escape.'

28

GUN FRIGHT

DECLAN STARED AT THE GUNMAN, SHAKING HIS HEAD SADLY AS he did so.

'You think we're the only people here?' he asked, looking back at the door. 'I have my entire unit outside, waiting to come in. The moment the bullets were heard, they'll have called SCO19, and you'll be shot down the moment you walk out.'

'You're remarkably calm for a man with a gun aimed at him,' Marcel frowned now.

In response, Declan shrugged.

'Not my first time, and you finished a question I had,' he replied. 'When you said "jugement karmique," you told me exactly what your role was here. I thought the initials J K were for your grandfather's name, but I'm guessing that's French for being judged by Karma?'

Marcel Cormorant's gun wavered.

'I'm not a killer,' he said.

'You're proving yourself to be one right now,' Declan said,

nodding at Bauer but seeing him sitting up now, clutching his side. 'Or maybe not.'

'I'm fine,' Bauer said between gritted teeth. 'Jorge, kill—'

'Jorge, you even go for that gun again and I'll fulfil my promise,' Declan growled. 'Or Marcel here will shoot you too.'

Jorge wisely stood to the side as Bauer glared furiously at him.

'You were at the event to steal your grandfather's painting, weren't you?' Declan asked.

'Not at the start,' Marcel shook his head, gun still trained on Jorge. 'The plan was to rob Miles once he got the money. I'd got into the event, and I was hanging around. Andrew had never been happy about the fact that Miles had screwed me over. Miles and Veronica were their own worst enemies, and Andrew had arranged for Gary Krohn to get in. He also sorted me a pass, thinking I could help Gary. The problem was I couldn't tell my daughter that I was there.'

'Because you thought she'd side with Miles?'

'Oh, she totally would have,' Stacey now added.

'When she saw me, she got angry,' Marcel ignored the comment. 'We had an argument in one of the side rooms where she was waiting to do her speech.'

'Is that when Lukas Weber walked in?'

'I wasn't meant to kill him,' Marcel nodded. 'But he started arguing with me. He knew my heritage. He knew Lucy was my daughter, and he assumed I was there to attack him, that this had been a setup by Miles from the start.'

'What about the shock stick?'

'He walked in with it,' Marcel shrugged. 'I don't know why he did, but we fought and I shocked him. He fell backward, slammed his head on the desk and collapsed to the floor.'

'What did you do then?' Declan asked.

'What do you think?' Marcel snapped back. 'I ran. I dragged Lucy, and we got out of that room as quickly as possible.'

'So you didn't paint the lipstick kiss?'

Marcel shook his head.

'It was already on his neck,' he said, looking at Stacey. 'Go on, tell them.'

'Weber had painted it,' Stacey agreed. 'It had to match the others. I was there with the catering company I did part-time work for, as Andrew had arranged for them to have the contract for the event, and it gave me a reason to be there. I heard a crash; I came in and saw him lying on the floor. I assumed he'd prepared himself for it, but forgot to tell me he was doing it then. He'd been talking about painting the kiss himself, as he knew what the others looked like—'

'Having painted them himself.'

'Yeah, exactly, and he'd talked about shocking himself to make it look more real, so I assumed he'd done this as he laid there, his eyes open. I went to him to ask what he wanted me to do, but then realised he was in real terrible shape, and that the painting was gone.'

'Because you took it when you ran,' Declan looked back at Marcel before returning to Stacey. 'So what happened? Did you call an ambulance?'

'No, I went looking for the painting,' Stacey admitted. 'I saw Gary, and I accused him of stealing it, but he just kicked off back at me, as confused as I was about this. So I ran back to tell Weber, call an ambulance if he was still bad ...'

She looked away, her eyes glistening with tears.

'But when I got back to the room, Weber had a new tattoo on his neck, and he was dead.'

She took a deep breath.

'I could have saved him. If I'd known, I could have called the ambulance then. But I didn't know. I thought it was the plan. So, I did the only thing I could. I knew Miles might recognise me, so I pulled out my reading glasses and threw them on as I alerted everyone.'

Declan turned now to Marcel.

'You went back, didn't you? Before he died?'

Marcel nodded.

'I had to make sure he was dead,' he said. 'But he wasn't. He was wheezing, dying. I saw the lipstick kiss ... I signed it, and watched him die.'

'Why did you have a tattoo gun?' Declan asked, narrowing his eyes. 'This couldn't have been a surprise.'

'I intended to deface the pictures, write things like "Nazi" and draw swastikas,' Marcel shrugged, as if this wasn't a major issue. 'A good restorer can remove paint or ink, but not when it's literally "tattooed" into the canvas. I'd picked up the gun from a friend, but when I learnt of Lucy's plan, I decided not to do it, in case it caused her problems of her own. But then, when I found him, it was too good an opportunity to miss.'

'"Jugement Karmique",' Declan replied. 'Nothing to do with young artists, grandfathers or conspiracies ... just a bitter fight between artists. Then you waited until the chaos started, and walked out, offering to sell the paintings, anyway.'

'You should be nicer to me,' Marcel growled, waving the Luger. 'I have the gun.'

'No, as Bauer said, you have a broken antique,' Declan smiled. 'You think I'd talk like this if I actually thought I was in danger? The Luger was notoriously known to jam after the first shot, let alone the fact the round would breach eight times out of ten. You can see it's jammed at the side—'

Marcel couldn't help himself; he glanced at it, and at that point Declan dived at him, grabbing the gun, aiming it up as it fired a second time. Marcel was desperate, but Declan was trained and fighting for his life. Wrenching the gun from Marcel, he smacked the butt against the artist's head, sending him to the floor.

Jorge had gone for the second gun again, but Stacey got there first, picking it up, training it on Declan.

'I didn't kill him,' she said. 'I didn't kill anyone. I should be allowed to leave!'

'You didn't save him, either,' Declan was cold as he faced her. 'You knew Weber was killing people, and you stood aside, and you told Bauer about Gary Krohn taking his painting when he didn't, causing his death.'

'If anyone here has blood on their hands, it's you,' a fresh voice spoke as Anjli appeared now, entering the door Declan had appeared through, with Cooper, De'Geer and two armed officers following them. 'Put the gun down. You're all under arrest.'

She smiled at Declan as she reached him.

'Sorry we're late, too many warehouses to check, so little time, and you're Billy's favourite,' she said, looking at the Luger. 'Is that a gun in your hand, or are you just happy to see me?'

'Yes and yes,' Declan said, puffing out his cheeks with relief. He really had been bluffing up to their arrival.

'You can't arrest me!' Bauer, still sitting and clutching his side, groaned. 'I have an arrangement—'

'Yeah, that arrangement? It's dead,' Anjli looked back at the fallen Argentine. 'We've been finding a lot of fun stuff in your warehouses. Enough to make sure the Government will want nothing more than to distance themselves from you. Like *really* distance. *Falkland Islands* distance.'

As De'Geer handcuffed Jorge and Cooper did the same to Stacey, having dropped the Glock the moment armed police aimed assault rifles at her, Declan looked over to the side of the warehouse.

'There are millions in stolen Nazi paintings over there,' he said. 'This is about to become a clown show.'

'It already is,' Anjli nodded at the door. 'Monroe's trying to calm the press outside. Seems someone might have let it slip about Weber's paintings being war thefts.'

'Who?' Declan grumbled.

'We don't know,' Anjli started walking with Declan towards the door, after he carefully placed the Luger into a plastic bag offered by De'Geer. 'Apparently whoever it was didn't realise they were talking to a reporter when they mentioned Bauer's name in connection.'

'Great, so we're live in five,' Declan replied irritably as they exited the warehouse, back onto the dockland street.

Monroe, seeing them, gave a wave.

'I understand you gave a wonderful talk about justice,' he said. 'We work out who killed Weber yet?'

'Marcel and Stacey,' Declan looked back at the door as the two were led out, keeping his voice low so the crowd of reporters couldn't hear. 'But it was pretty much by accident, a whole comedy of errors. Marcel was the one who tattooed him as he died.'

'Was it the whole "Young Artist" thing as we thought?' Monroe asked, scratching at his neck, a gesture of nervousness at the cameras now setting up around them.

'No, it was Marcel writing about karma and justice,'

Declan spoke softly. 'Honestly? I get why he did it, but not the method.'

Doctor Marcos walked over, and Declan was surprised to see her; he'd assumed she was still on "hunt the hitman" duty.

'When can my people get in there?' she asked.

'When we've brought out a bleeding Argentine,' Monroe replied. 'And I mean actual bleeding, not an expletive.'

Doctor Marcos looked back at Declan.

'You shooting people again?'

'Not me this time—' Declan stopped. There was a faint roaring noise in the distance, like a speedboat, and Declan turned to see a motorcycle speeding towards the warehouse, the rider in black leathers, his helmet on his head obscuring his identity.

Damian Lim.

'Get back!' Declan pushed Monroe to the side, but the bloody fool returned the favour, throwing Declan behind him as he faced his oncoming killer.

Everything happened at once; the camera crews, realising something was wrong, started to react. The armed police, still securing the warehouse, were only just emerging through the door, and Declan, now barred by Monroe, saw the motorcyclist raise his gun and fire.

The whole thing took less than two seconds before the sounds of three gunshots echoed through the night, and the bike sped off, heading east, with police cars already following.

Declan screamed in anger; Damian knew he'd be arrested for this, but his bloody professional pride had meant he couldn't walk away.

'Anjli, get onto ...' he started, but trailed off as Monroe slumped against him.

Looking down at Monroe's chest, he saw three blossoming patches of blood from the three shots fired.

'Ambulance! Now!' he screamed as he lay Monroe, gasping to the ground. 'You bloody idiot!'

'All ... good,' Monroe wheezed. 'You're ... DCI now. I can leave them ... with ... you ...'

Declan was pulled back as Doctor Marcos knelt over him.

'Don't leave us, you bastard!' she hissed, already waving for the paramedics to come over. 'Alex, don't leave me!'

She started thumping on his chest, and Declan stared blankly at the scene; the crying woman kneeling over the body of Detective Superintendent Alex Monroe while the world's press filmed it.

'Get away!' he screamed, pushing into them. 'Piss off, you ghouls! We need space for the ambulance!'

'Declan,' it was Rosanna Marcos now, looking up at him. 'Declan. Stop. He's gone.'

Declan turned and stared at Monroe, his chest a mass of blood, his eyes closed, and his face at peace.

The case might have been solved, but Lennie Wright had won.

For Detective Superintendent Alexander Monroe was dead.

EPILOGUE

LENNIE WRIGHT WAS IN AN OVERLY GOOD MOOD.

When the guard had told him he had a visitor, he was even happier when he heard it was Derek Sutton. Lennie had been waiting for the visit, or at least some kind of message.

He'd seen, live on the news the previous night, that Alexander Monroe had been murdered, cut down terribly in the middle of the solving of a crime. They hadn't shown the killing itself, but the gunshots were heard as a cameraman tried to turn, and Monroe was then seen on the floor amid the chaos. The idiot PC he'd been with, the tall Viking had run around in the background like a headless chicken, while Lennie had a little singsong at this, even did a little dance.

Alex Monroe was now dead.

One of the major thorns in his side in his upcoming trial was now removed.

Sure, Damian Lim had been arrested, but he'd been paid enough not to grass up his client; Lennie hoped so, anyway. Harvey Drake had been pretty much uncontactable since the attack, and Lennie was more worried about him being arrested than Lim. Harvey was a snake, and Lennie had heard how he was going to lesser gangsters for handouts.

Derek Sutton was another thorn, for he'd been there in Edinburgh as well. But Lennie wasn't that worried about him. Sutton was an ex-criminal, and Lennie's solicitor had already said that they could tear him apart as an unreliable witness, and so, with a spring in his step, Lennie Wright had walked down to the visiting room, where inmates could talk to their visitors under the watchful eye of the prison guards, sitting at metal tables welded to the floor, the seats on either side welded as well.

He sat down at a table and waited. It wasn't really a "chair" he was sitting on as such, and it was bloody uncomfortable, but Lennie didn't mind. He could deal with a minor discomfort on this, the happiest day of his life. He was surprised to see that he was the only person in the room, but then again, it wasn't the normal time for visiting hours, which meant something was off.

The smile faded a little, and now he became a little concerned. *Did Derek know people here?* He might have been in prison for thirty years, but the man knew people, and he had made a lot of money recently. Enough to pay his way to maybe having a private chat of his own, or to pay off a guard as he brought a blade in.

Lennie shook the thought from his head; Derek Sutton was stupid. Muscled and vicious, but stupid, nevertheless. He knew he could take whatever Derek threw at him and laugh it off all the way to freedom.

But Derek hadn't arrived yet, and he had to wait several minutes, growing more impatient by the moment until the door opened and his visitor entered.

'Hello, Lenny,' Alexander Monroe said as he walked in, smiling, sitting down opposite him, a shit-eating grin on his face. 'Bet you weren't expecting to see me.'

'I was expecting to see Derek,' Lennie had paled, as if seeing a ghost.

'Aye, Derek Sutton can't make it.' Monroe smiled. 'He gave me his spot. He thought I ought to have a chat with you.'

He leant closer.

'Your man failed.'

'I don't know what you mean.'

'Harvey Drake? He's on the run, hiding. He knows he's in trouble. Whether it's from you being pissed that he's hanging out with unsavoury types, or whether it's from the unsavoury types themselves, pissed that he was trying to kill a police detective? It doesn't matter. What does matter is we've got everything. We know how you got him to do this. We know how he enabled it with Damian Lim. Who, by the way, is in custody right now and singing like a canary, now he realises he has a deal.'

He stretched his arms out, yawning.

'It's amazing how relaxing being dead for a couple of days can be,' he said. 'I would suggest it to you, but I think most of the people here would prefer it to be a more permanent situation.'

Lennie didn't say anything, staring balefully up at the Scottish detective as he rose, nodding.

'We're done here,' he said. 'I'll see you in court - and don't think about sending anybody else. You're going to be on your own for a very long time. Probably not going to have time to speak to anybody … just how we like it.'

'Wait,' Lennie rose, noting the guards moving in at the

action, holding his hands up. 'How? I saw you on the news. You died.'

'That's the problem with TV, you never know what's real or not,' Monroe shrugged. 'Your man did shoot me, but we got to his gun first. A friend broke into his house and checked the make and model, and then when we pulled him up outside the Temple Inn offices, knowing he'd stash the weapon before talking to us, another ... well, another friend to the department slipped in, took the gun and swapped the bullets for blanks.'

He grinned.

'We knew Damian would try for me quickly, and wouldn't check his sidearm,' he said. 'And if he did? Aye, well, then we'd rely on him being a shite shot. I had a Kevlar vest on lined with squibs, and each time he fired, I set one off. Either way, I would have "died" there, and you would have continued on thinking I was gone.'

He leant closer, the table now between them.

'Think of all the nice wee chats you've already had since you thought I was gone,' he said. 'We have them all. Harvey Drake? We'll soon have him too. All of this is being added to the trial as we speak. You should have just relied on the courts, Lennie. Now, you're definitely going down.'

This decreed, Monroe turned and, ignoring Lennie Wright's shouts as the guards dragged him away, he gave another little smile, a more triumphant one to himself.

It had been a "Hail Mary," and the Kevlar was a last resort, but it'd worked out for the best. Now he owed both Ramsey Allen and Sam Mansfield, who'd both broken into the house and replaced the rounds respectively, some serious thank you gifts.

'I SHOULD HAVE BEEN TOLD,' DECLAN WAS STILL COMPLAINING as they all sat in the briefing room.

'You were concussed, and you're not great with secrets at the best of times,' Anjli said to a glare. 'You can be pissed all you want. I didn't know, and I'm not bitching.'

Monroe was in his office, likely playing up the moment for all he could, and Declan couldn't begrudge him the theatrics. He'd set things up perfectly, faking his death on live TV – at least long enough for Damian Lim to send the kill message before being taken by the armed police waiting for him to do so.

He'd then returned from the dead for everyone at Temple Inn, allowing the original kill message to reach Lennie, each stage being logged and noted, and everyone involved being quietly arrested after they'd played their part.

Even Harvey Drake had helped by aiming hitmen at Damian Lim in some misguided attempt to stop him; this had actually meant Damian came in from the cold and threw a whole load of other people under the bus.

It was quite a good haul in the end.

Declan had been furious at first; there was no way Monroe could have been certain Damian wouldn't have checked his magazine, replaced by the nimble hands of Sam Mansfield earlier that day, but inconceivably he hadn't with Monroe setting off squibs to match the shots.

Damian had been as much a part of the theatrics as anything else, even down to the tracker they'd placed inside his black bike helmet to know where he was, timing the moment – and reusing the very tracker he'd placed on Monroe at the start.

Damian, who now he knew he wasn't going down for murder, and who had now learnt Harvey Drake had sent killers after him, was telling Bullman everything upstairs.

Declan had wondered why Bullman would take the job, but then he'd bumped into Margaret Li, still around as the Weber case was finishing up, and wondered if Bullman was interviewing Damian Lim in a strange roundabout way of hiding from the German detective.

She was quite intense, after all, and Declan was starting to wonder if Bullman was about to wake up one night with Margaret Li at the end of her bed, telling her she "smelt different when she was sleeping."

Bauer hadn't been in custody long; his solicitor had gained him bail, and within an hour he was gone, his private jet flying off in the middle of the night, leaving his men to face the music. Raphael Kirshner had admitted he'd been ordered to kill Gary Krohn by Bauer, and with the Nazi-stolen paintings now in the process of being returned to France, Gabriel Bauer had performed the same role as his father, in running to Argentina before the world caught up with him.

Within minutes of the arrest, the Government had cut all ties as well, and Declan knew at some point he'd have an angry Charles Baker complaining about money lost. But that was a problem for another day.

Of the others, Veronica was the only one released; everyone else was connected in some way or another, and Declan knew the unravelling of this would be a nightmare. Luckily for him, this was the job of the Detective Inspector – usually the headache he used to have.

Now it was Anjli's.

Declan smiled. *Sometimes being the DCI was good.*

'Okay,' Monroe said, finally walking into the room.

'Lennie Wright's screwed, so hooray there. The hit's off, which means Derek can piss off back to Glasgow—'

'Aye, no complaints there,' Sutton smiled.

'—and Harvey Drake won't be bothering us for a while either, which means we've fulfilled a promise to a Member of Parliament.'

'Johnny Lucas?' Billy smiled.

'Allies wherever we can get them, laddie,' Monroe grinned in return. 'Okay. Updates, go.'

He stopped, looked back at Declan.

'Sorry, your show.'

'Look, Guv,' Declan said. 'I know Detective Superintendents stay in the office in a normal police unit, but we're the Last Chance Saloon. We've never been a normal unit. So how about we go back to how it was, just with shiny new ranks?'

'You don't want the office?'

'Oh, I'm starting to like it, but I like being in there *and* out here,' Declan grinned. 'Just like you do.'

Monroe considered this, nodded, and then walked to the front of the briefing room as Declan sat down.

'Gary Krohn?'

'Murderer confessed, claimed it was on Gabriel Bauer's orders,' Anjli said. 'On the condition his family was pulled out of Argentina and given new identities before Bauer got to them.'

'Lukas Weber?'

'Killed by accident after he was shocked with his own shock stick,' Doctor Marcos, loitering at the back of the room, said. 'Heart attack caused by electrical disruption and a blow to the skull immediately after. He would have died shortly afterwards, unable to move.'

'But he wasn't alone,' De'Geer read from his notes. 'Marcel Cormorant admitted tattooing him as he died.'

'Marcel, who also tasered him in self-defence,' Anjli added from the notes.

'Stefan Bierhof, Borge Pedersen and Anna Hoffmann?'

'All believed killed by Weber,' Declan said. 'Stacey Nichols and Andrew Benson both claimed it in their statements, and Paris police found the painting Andrew had hidden, with Weber's fingerprints on.'

'That'll be a fun case for someone else to fix,' Monroe said, smiling at Margaret. 'How's your French?'

'Incredibly fluent,' she replied without a hint of irony. 'I know five languages.'

'Of course you do,' Monroe smiled. 'The money Marcel stole from Bauer?'

'No idea,' Declan shrugged. 'We don't really have anyone demanding it, now Bauer is gone. In a way, Cormorant got away with that.'

'Aye, he can use it on his legal bills, and to hire security for when Bauer's people come looking for *him*,' Monroe muttered. 'Well, this is a fine kettle of wee fishies, as apparently I'm akin to saying, but it'll be someone else's kettle. Anything else?'

Billy nodded.

'I think we should find a way to thank Ramsey Allen and Sam … Mister Mansfield. *Sam* Mansfield. Sam Mansfield the forger,' he stumbled through the words, reddening with each mistake. 'I just thought it'd be nice.'

'Aye, they both helped in more ways than one,' Monroe nodded. 'Get hold of Ellie Reckless, see what her man likes, and get him a bottle of it. As for Sam …'

He winked.

'Why don't you treat him to a nice dinner? On the Unit's expense?' he suggested.

Billy's eyes lightened.

'Yes boss,' he smiled. 'I can do that. I'm seeing him for dinner tonight.'

'Excellent,' Monroe clapped his hands together. 'Let me know the time and place and Rosanna and I will join you. After all, it's a thanks for saving me, so it'd be remiss of me not being there.'

As Billy mournfully nodded, realising he'd been outplayed, Monroe called an end to the briefing and everyone filed out.

Margaret Li, however, motioned for Declan to walk to the side with her. He followed, hoping this wasn't another lecture on how he wasn't good enough, or something similar.

'What can I help you with?' he asked.

'Karl Schnitter,' Margaret Li spoke carefully and quietly, and Declan felt ice slide down his spine. To the world, Karl Schnitter had escaped him, but only a few people knew that not only had Schnitter been taken by MI5 to a black site to stop the CIA claiming him, but that he'd later escaped, and the CIA had wiped his record, giving him a new identity for support he'd previously given them.

'What about him?'

'He's dead,' Margaret continued.

'How do you mean?' Declan frowned at this.

'I have a friend at Berlin CIA Station,' Margaret explained. 'I know he was taken in and given a new life in the USA. A car mechanic in Lombard, near Chicago.'

Declan hadn't known where Karl Schnitter had gone, but he'd suspected similar.

'There was an accident just under a month ago,' Margaret

continued. 'Car crash. Terrible one. His tow truck exploded, and he was burnt to death.'

At the words, Declan paused, his eyes narrowing.

'Definitely him?'

'Apparently so,' Margaret nodded. 'But you know how DNA can be. I wanted you to know that as far as the CIA is concerned, he's a dead asset.'

Declan knew what Margaret Li was saying. The CIA might have classed him as deceased, but she hadn't.

And neither should Declan.

The *Red Reaper* had either been brutally murdered by someone, or was free and somewhere in America.

'Thank you,' he said, and Margaret gave a simple nod, spinning on her heels and walking off.

Anjli, having watched the exchange from a distance, walked over.

'Problems?'

'We need to talk,' Declan said. 'Not now, but tonight. I need to contact Emilia Wintergreen and ask a favour.'

'Asking MI5 for favours never ends well,' Anjli replied.

'I know,' Declan nodded slowly. 'But this one ... it's different.'

As Anjli was called over to Billy's monitor, Declan walked into his office and shut the door.

Standing in the empty room, he released his breath and unclenched his trembling hands.

The last time Declan had spoken to Schnitter, he'd been hunting Francine Pearce, his serial-killer sense of justice at her needing to be fulfilled, before giving himself up to the CIA. There had been a moment of detente – Declan's enemy of his enemy was a reluctant ally.

But if he was in the wind, there was every chance he

could return, and Declan knew without a doubt he would be first on Karl Schnitter's list of people to contact – and possibly kill.

Walking to his desk, he picked up his phone and dialled a number.

'Tom? It's Declan,' he said. 'We need to talk about an old friend.'

DCI Walsh and the team of the *Last Chance Saloon* will return in their next thriller

PRETEND TO BE DEAD

Order Now at Amazon:

www.mybook.to/pretendtobedead

ACKNOWLEDGEMENTS

When you write a series of books, you find that there are a ton of people out there who help you, sometimes without even realising, and so I wanted to say thanks.

There are people I need to thank, and they know who they are, including my brother Chris Lee, Jacqueline Beard MBE, who has copyedited all my books since the very beginning, and editor Sian Phillips, all of whom have made my books way better than they have every right to be.

Also, I couldn't have done this without my growing army of ARC and beta readers, who not only show me where I falter, but also raise awareness of me in the social media world, ensuring that other people learn of my books.

But mainly, I tip my hat and thank you. *The reader.* Who once took a chance on an unknown author in a pile of Kindle books, and thought you'd give them a go, and who has carried on this far with them, as well as the spin off books I now release.

I write Declan Walsh for you. He (and his team) solves crimes for you. And with luck, he'll keep on solving them for a very long time.

Jack Gatland / Tony Lee,
London, August, 2023

ABOUT THE AUTHOR

Jack Gatland is the pen name of #1 *New York Times Bestselling Author* Tony Lee, who has been writing in all media for thirty-five years, including comics, graphic novels, middle grade books, audio drama, TV and film for *DC Comics, Marvel, BBC, ITV, Random House, Penguin USA, Hachette* and a ton of other publishers and broadcasters.

These have included licenses such as *Doctor Who, Spider Man, X-Men, Star Trek, Battlestar Galactica, MacGyver,* BBC's *Doctors, Wallace and Gromit* and *Shrek*, as well as work created with musicians such as *Iron Maiden, Bruce Dickinson, Ozzy Osbourne, Joe Satriani* and *Megadeth.*

As Tony, he's toured the world talking to reluctant readers with his 'Change The Channel' school tours, and lectures on screenwriting and comic scripting for *Raindance* in London.

An introvert West Londoner by heart, he lives with his wife Tracy and dog Fosco, just outside London.

Locations In The Book

The locations and items I use in my books are real, if altered slightly for dramatic intent. However this time, many of the locations are completely fictitious, meaning we can't really look into their history, apart from...

Doggett's Coat and Badge is not only the name of a pub on the Southbank of the Thames, but it's also the prize and name for the oldest continuous rowing race in the world. Up to six apprentice watermen of the River Thames in England compete for this prestigious honour, which has been held every year since 1715. The 4 mile 5 furlongs (7.44 km) race is rowed on the River Thames upstream from London Bridge to Cadogan Pier, Chelsea, passing under a total of eleven bridges.

The winner's prize is a traditional watermen's red coat with a silver badge added, displaying the horse of the House of Hanover and the word "Liberty", in honour of the accession of George I to the throne.

Central Saint Martins College of Art and Design was formed in 1989 from the merger of the Central School of Art and Design, founded in 1896, and Saint Martin's School of Art, founded in 1854.

The pop/alternative rock song *"Common People"* by *Pulp* (named after the movie starring Michael Caine) is based around an art student from Greece whom *Pulp* singer-song-writer Jarvis Cocker met while he was studying at the Central Saint Martins College of Art and Design.

If you're interested in seeing what the *real* locations look like, I post 'behind the scenes' location images on my Instagram feed. This will continue through all the books, after leaving a suitable amount of time to avoid spoilers, and I suggest you follow it.

In fact, feel free to follow me on all my social media by clicking on the links below. Over time these can be places where we can engage, discuss Declan and put the world to rights.

www.jackgatland.com
www.hoodemanmedia.com

Visit Jack's Reader's Group Page
(Mainly for fans to discuss his books):
https://www.facebook.com/groups/jackgatland

Subscribe to Jack's Readers List:
https://bit.ly/jackgatlandVIP

www.facebook.com/jackgatlandbooks
www.twitter.com/jackgatlandbook
ww.instagram.com/jackgatland

Want more books by Jack Gatland? Turn the page...

THE THEFT OF A **PRICELESS** PAINTING...
A GANGSTER WITH A **CRIPPLING DEBT**...
A **BODY COUNT** RISING BY THE HOUR...

AND ELLIE RECKLESS IS CAUGHT IN THE MIDDLE.

JACK GATLAND

PAINT
— THE —
DEAD

A 'COP FOR CRIMINALS' ELLIE RECKLESS NOVEL

A NEW PROCEDURAL CRIME SERIES WITH
A TWIST - FROM THE CREATOR OF THE
BESTSELLING 'DI DECLAN WALSH' SERIES

AVAILABLE ON AMAZON / KINDLE UNLIMITED

THEY TRIED TO KILL HIM...
NOW HE'S OUT FOR **REVENGE.**

NEW YORK TIMES #1 BESTSELLER **TONY LEE** WRITING AS

JACK GATLAND

THE MURDER OF AN **MI5 AGENT**...
A BURNED SPY **ON THE RUN** FROM HIS OWN PEOPLE...
AN ENEMY OUT TO **STOP HIM** AT ANY COST...
AND A **PRESIDENT** ABOUT TO BE **ASSASSINATED**...

SLEEPING SOLDIERS

A **TOM MARLOWE** THRILLER

BOOK 1 IN A NEW SERIES OF THRILLERS IN THE STYLE OF
JASON BOURNE, JOHN MILTON OR **BURN NOTICE,** AND
SPINNING OUT OF THE **DECLAN WALSH** SERIES OF BOOKS

AVAILABLE ON AMAZON / KINDLE UNLIMITED

EIGHT PEOPLE. EIGHT SECRETS.
ONE SNIPER.

THE
B⊕ARD
ROOM

HOW FAR WOULD YOU GO TO GAIN JUSTICE?

NEW YORK TIMES #1 BESTSELLER TONY LEE WRITING AS

JACK GATLAND

A NEW STANDALONE THRILLER WITH
A TWIST - FROM THE CREATOR OF THE
BESTSELLING 'DI DECLAN WALSH' SERIES

AVAILABLE ON AMAZON / KINDLE UNLIMITED

JACK GATLAND

THE LIONHEART CURSE

HUNT THE GREATEST TREASURES
PAY THE GREATEST PRICE

BOOK 1 IN A NEW SERIES OF ADVENTURES
IN THE STYLE OF 'THE DA VINCI CODE'
FROM THE CREATOR OF DECLAN WALSH

AVAILABLE ON AMAZON / KINDLEUNLIMITED

Printed in Great Britain
by Amazon